The Book of
Siavon

Volume 1
The Ruby Child

To Tom,
I hope you
enjoy my book.
Nice meeting
you!

Author's Note

Back in 2011, I published the first of the *Siavon* series with TriGen Publishing Company. The original cover design, though stated as Emily Noyes was actually done by Cassandre Chandler. Due to a publishing error, the wrong name was printed on the inside cover and I apologize to both artists for the mistake. I've decided to re-publish and start over with a brand new cover. The cover design on the 2015 re-release was done by Joe Botzer.

Special thanks to all who have helped me along in this process. Wayne Ruppert Jr., Cassandre Chandler, Cody DiAngelo, Joe Botzer, Karen Franklin, and of course my parents. It has been amazing!

Chapters

Hrotage

The old teakettle toppled from the potbelly stovetop and hit the floor with a clank of rusty metal, spilling its boiling contents into the cracks of the graying wood. Mina hunched to one knee to retrieve it, the weight of her pregnant belly heaving against her willowy frame. She placed the kettle back on the stove and bypassed the mess for just a moment so she could waddle to the dingy window. Outside, Nodens was as she had seen it many times before. Marketers lined the streets with kiosks of edible merchandise baking in the sun while they shouted to the people passing by. Children coming home from class skipped around the mud puddles from a previous rain, giggling and racing their peers down the walk. The thatch-roofed dwellings of townsfolk threw up cobblestone chimneys, through the mouths of which trailed billowing cooking smoke. Inside these dwellings, Mina could imagine housewives just as herself tending to the evening meal for their returning husbands and children. Her own children were already home, outside playing before homework. Mina's husband would arrive home any moment to greet her with a kiss and relay his work day.

Another shock wave rattled each bone in her body in turn and she braced her hands on the window pane for balance. Mina's eyes traveled to the orange horizon. A blurry shape was approaching from the north, gaining recognition as it advanced into the East Village. After the vibrations came a sound like thunder. High pitched screeches whined in her ears ushering forth a shriek of pain from her lips. She let go of the window pane and clasped her hands over her ears as the screeching continued. Outside, Mina heard her two children crying and forced herself to fling the front door open.

Brie and Thomas were standing over their crude chalk drawing of a hopscotch board, covering their ears as they screamed. Mina shouted to them, but her calls were drowned out by the constant screeching that did not seem to waver. A bolt of pain shot through her head as her eardrums burst and a ringing sound whined in tune to the screeching. She hunched over, nearly falling onto her swelled belly. Raising hands to ears again, Mina trudged forward and seized the wailing boy and girl each by the arm and hurried them

4

inside again. She shut the door behind her and corralled them into the small dining room, directing them to hide under the table. Each of them was bleeding from the ears, and when Mina looked at her hands, she saw her own blood staining them. She moaned in pain and revulsion, but managed to hunker down over her children and hold them to her breast.

Then, as abruptly as it began, the screeching ceased. The family was left with a woozy unreality and ringing ears. Thomas held onto his little sister while she wailed into his shirt and looked fearfully to his mother. Mina hugged them close, and leaving them with a strong smile, went to the window again.

The thing that had flown up out of the horizon landed swiftly where the dusty road separated the dwellings and the kiosks. What appeared as the dust settled was not a sight that had ever fallen over the eyes of the East Village or any part of Nodens except in the yellowed pages of long-forgotten religious tomes. A reptilian horror the color of sunlight stood blocking the real thing. Its demonic figure extended enormous veiny wings and a massive head supported by a thick snake's neck loomed from its broad shoulders. Long wispy hair floated forth from its jowls and forelegs and its spiked tail lashed behind it.

Townsfolk hurried out of its path and disappeared into homes, some hiding under kiosks, most stumbling blindly for whatever cover they could find. A horse galloped in a panic down the street, and caught the eye of the grinning golden dragon. In an instant, the poor creature's head was sliding on a slick of crimson from the still galloping body. It separated from the animal's middle and plopped to the ground in front of it in a gory mess, and the mangled legs tripped over it and tumbled onto its back, jerking spastically. Its entire store of blood pooled around it in mere seconds. Uttering a thunderous bawling roar, the dragon reared up and opened its two great golden wings. It began flapping them, creating a gust so great roofs were ripped from their edifices, carts blown onto their backs and swept away, and people became airborne for one horrific moment before splitting open on the ground below.

Shaking, Mina backed away from the window. The screams stayed with her long after they ceased, and she knew they would always be there. Even with the pain of her burst eardrums and the

5

seizing contractions inside her belly, the screams were all that Mina knew.

Brie gave a whimper, which brought Mina back into the dining room. She crouched down beside her children and held them close. Inside of her, the unborn rustled in the womb. She shut her eyes against the pain. Birth was coming early, for her fear had brought it forth. Out there somewhere, her children's father was braving the disaster to get to them. Mina could only pray for his safe return.

The dragon swung its head back and forth on its long glistening neck, eager to meet the arriving resistance. Several cloaked men with bows surrounded it on four sides and aimed high. The order floated over the wind of wings, and simultaneously, ten shots fired long hooked arrows into its neck. In retaliation, the beast swept one of the men from his feet with a massive claw. Two other men were crushed against the swinging tail. The remaining wisely aborted and began running, but with one step the beast had caught up with them, dipped its head down, and snatched a man up in its feathery jaws. The bleeding dragon raised its head high and tossed the body down its throat and with a wet slurp, licked the blood from its jaws and peered down into the crowd for seconds.

The men dispersed, and two or three of them turned around and aimed for the dragon's head. One arrow struck the center of its left eye and spurted forth a frothy liquid. Screeching, the beast bounded into the brigade and pulverized the rest of the men with its bulk. It stumbled over top of a dwelling and knocked it down as if it were a house of cards. The people inside clung to each other helplessly as the woodwork and debris fell down on top of them. The dragon's cold hateful eye leaked sizzling blood down onto the wreckage. With a mighty, pained screech, it spread its wings and leapt into the air, carrying itself high above the destruction, dripping its acidic rain of blood onto the streets.

The door to Mina's house flew open, and in stepped a shape garbed in a long gray shroud, his face shielded by a hood. He stomped with weathered boots over to the family's hiding place. The hood came down with the sweep of a hand, and the brazen handsome face peered down intently at the family. They shrank away from him, the woman holding her children tightly and wincing from her birth pains. A single leather glove reached down to her, but the man spoke not a word. Outside, the screeching began again, blaring and horrible. Mina and the children cringed, but the man did not flinch. He cocked his head, and they could see that he had stuffed his ears with wax. He had prepared for this. Mina placed a shaky untrusting hand into his.

The man ushered the family outside, where a magnificent black mare obediently stood, awaiting the return of its rider. Its ears were also stuffed with wax, and it whinnied affectionately as the man helped the pregnant woman and children onto its back. On the tip of its fleshy nose, a stumpy thick horn grew forth, caked with snot. Long straight horns glistened above the animal's wide blue eyes, like black blades in the orange light. This was a rare horse. Only a few tricorns were known to exist on Aryth, running free in the wild forbidden land of Wendoa. Two of them, however were owned by Vorian Tranore, the reclusive wood hermit thought by many to have been a Siavon Knight, and by some to be riddled with curse induced madness. Mina now found herself wishing she had refused the stranger's hand.

The screeching subsided into low growls as the dragon circled the town. Its very form blocked out the setting sun, completely submerging it in nightfall. The flapping of its wings sent a hurricane of wind down upon the land. It had now circled over Mina's house and was peering down at the magnificent horse which stood its ground despite the swirling winds. The man hiked himself up onto the horse's back with Mina and her children, and with one arm holding them steady in front of him, reached out and twisted the reins around his fingers. He gave a sharp whistle and snapped them hard against the horse's black neck. With an excited neigh, it reared up on powerful hind legs, tossed its head, and took off. The speed was astonishing, and would have knocked Mina and her children from their mount had the man not held them steady. The tricorn stuck its neck out and pointed its long facial horns forward as it dashed onward, faster still. Brie cried out and ducked her head under the arm of her mother, her brother hugging onto her for his own sake. Mina found herself looking upward as the devilish shadow cast over them, and the beast glared downward with one furious golden eye.

The family's dwelling was long in the past now, and they passed many more like it before breaking into the dark forest barriers which held in the town. This was a forest forbidden by mothers everywhere for their children to play in, for no one who entered came back the same. Some went mad, some stumbled out mangled, and others never came out at all. It was said these woods were cursed. It was also where Vorian Tranore was said to live.

The tricorn's sword-like horns cut through the overgrowth of brush like butter as it charged forward into the dark dizzying forest. Mina shut her eyes to steady her gullet as the trees whipped by faster and faster. Behind her, their rescuer held her family fast and did not quiver an inch despite the rough ride. It was as if he were a part of the tricorn itself. His hood fluttered behind him revealing his long mane of hair, as black as his speedy mount.

A crash sounded behind them, and he turned his head slightly to catch the sight of the beast as it burst through the canopy of the trees and landed at last. It folded its wings back and caught up to them in an ambling run. Smoke trailed heavily from flaring nostrils and singed the horse's long black tail. The ground around them was heating up. With another sharp whistle, he pulled the reins sharply to the left and veered the tricorn off course. The dragon thundered past them, bellowing in frustration, turning its enormous head back to watch them gallop away. The tricorn snorted in return and pushed onward, its muscles burning hot under the touch of its rider's hand. The animal was beginning to tire.

The dragon changed its course and continued to chase them, catching up quickly as before. Smoke billowed from its nostrils heavily, clouding its already poor vision. As the horse dashed forward, the dragon stopped in its tracks. It raised itself up on its back legs and began gasping. The wind of its heavy laboring breath shook the trees around it. The tricorn, now a speck in the distance, took the opportunity to slow down. White foam dibbled from its lips and its muscles quivered. The man pulled back on the reins hard, and the animal halted and skidded on hot hooves. The family went lurching forward, to be caught by the man's strong arms. Mina's contractions grew closer and more painful, and she held fast onto her children and cried out in pain. Her water broke out from under her dress and dripped down the sides of the sweating horse. Birth grew dangerously near.

With a grunt, the man dismounted. He watched Mina and her family warily and opened one side of his cloak to reveal a long black sheath hanging from his belt, from which he withdrew a shimmering sword. The finely decorated hilt was cast from sparkling white gold, almost alive with beauty that winked enticingly in the dim dabbled forest light. And embedded in the center, was a flawless red ruby.

"Do not follow me," he spoke for the first time, in a voice low and calming. Mina did not object. Under her, the mare nickered.

They watched the man walk briskly down the path cut clear by the horse's horns. The dragon sucked in air, the smoke now enveloping the forest around it. It watched him with hateful glaring eyes as he made his approach. He stopped a dozen steps away and raised his sword high.

The dragon threw its head back and screamed. The vibrations sent a shock wave across the forest, rustling trees, and stumbling the heavily panting mare. Mina wailed. Her children joined her with their soft sobs. The man remained still and held his beautiful sword high above his head with both hands.

The horse trotted off the path into the brush and hid itself and the family in the security of the woods. They could just barely make out the yellow outline of the beast through the cut of overgrowth that closed them in. Mina muffled a scream. The contractions were rising on top of each other now. Despite the *caveat sen hrotage*, the warning of the savior, she climbed from the mare's back and crouched in the brush, panting heavily. Her children clung to each other high on the animal's back and watched helplessly as their mother prepared to bring their sibling into the world.

The dragon sucked in a final mighty breath and yawned out a great white flame which spun out from its jaws in a thick twisted blaze onto the man below. He braced his legs, but did not try to outrun it. Heavy hands held the sword firm. The base of the hilt pulsed and murmured. Vibrations traveled up the blade and spouted from the tip of it, rippling the oxygen in the air much the same as the fire did. The dragon's flame bounced from an invisible barrier that surrounded the man on all sides, and doubled back into its own face, searing the whiskers from its jowls. The yellow flesh around its eyes and snout shriveled up and turned a scoring crimson, and the stunned creature recoiled. Its head burned and cooked from the heat of its own emissions, and now the golden dragon looked more like a wounded dog, pawing madly at its face, dragging its head in the dirt and catching the ground around it on white fire.

The man had been anchored to the ground like heavy stone, but now he softened. The sword loosened in his hands. The quivering air around him returned to normal. The flames surrounded the beast and entrapped it, but did not spread to any part of the forest. The inferno reflected in the man's calm cerulean eyes while they watched the ground directly circling the dragon become charred beyond recognition.

Mina's birth pains intensified. She fell to her hands and knees and trembled against them. Her daughter called her softly from the back of the horse, but her son was older and knew to keep her close and out of the way. He trusted his mother to know what to do, more so than she did herself. Something was amiss. The pain came, but the child did not.

The white flames licked the convulsing dragon's flesh as it screamed and rose up to the height of the canopy. Its wings opened, doubling its girth, and glowed brilliant yellow from the blazing light behind them. They touched the wall of fire, and instantly, the dragon's body was immersed in it. Cries of agony shook the ground as the creature's flesh bubbled and smoked. Hatred burned in its surviving eye, and its seared chasm of teeth yawned open again. A slick forked tongue slithered forward and caressed the smoldering oxygen around it, and air rocked with its harrowing cries.

He swung the sword and pierced the ground at his feet as the beast enveloped him with a dancing fiery shadow. He released the handle and let the ground become the blade's sheath, then raised both arms into the air as if lifting an invisible weight.

"*Tem n'gard delorach.*" Verses murmured forth from the pit of his throat, over and over as he raised his weaponless hands to the enraged monster. "*Tem n'gard delorach!*"

The blazing dragon sprung forward, claws extended, jaws gaping as it charged at the chanting man over the rise of flames around it.

"*Tem n'gard delorach!*"

In terrific pain, Mina wailed. Her son and daughter dropped from the back of the tricorn and crouched at her side, shaking her, crying helplessly as she drained of blood. The horse whinnied worriedly and cast its doleful blue eyes to its rider in the clearing.

The man pulled the sword from the ground and held it firmly between clenched fists. The dragon was almost on top of him now. Its skin had nearly melted off completely, revealing the charred coiled muscles and slick melting fat underneath. The creature's remaining eye burst, sending gobs of hot optic fluid drizzling down its peeling cheek. It squealed, tormented and angry. The dragon's tattered burning wings flared. Blindly, the dragon propelled itself in one final flying leap. Its outstretched claws shook and twitched as it tucked them under its body and soared forward in a last effort to avenge its own death.

The man uttered the mysterious verse a last time and brought his sword down like an ax. In an instant, a burst of shimmering oxygen plowed forth from his weapon and pulsated through the charging beast in midair. The dragon exploded. There was a horrendous splattering sound as bits and chunks of meat shot out in all directions, littering the tree tops, staining the brush red with ghastly boiling blood. The wings somersaulted in the air and collapsed to the ground like burning firewood. The mangled remaining flesh sizzled and shriveled up into black lumps.

The man promptly opened his cloak and carefully placed the weapon back into concealment. It was over. Save for the woman's noises of agony coming from the brush, the forest was quiet again. He turned, his long black hair hugging his neckline. The woman screams were followed with her children's cries for help.

The man briskly walked in the direction of the ailing mother, and the brush suddenly gained life and bowed down to him, allowing him easy entrance into the family's hiding place. The tricorn reared slightly at the motion and tossed its head in agitation, and the man nodded to it as he knelt down at the foot of the birthing woman.

Her back arched and she cried out again. She had grown sickeningly pale. Blood was soaking the immediate area surrounding her. Her once yellow dress was now a deep red up to the waistband. On either side of her shoulders, her children crouched with blood streaking their hands and clothes. The entire family seamed to glisten with spilled life.

She moaned, seeing her savior approach with the lulling disoriented eyes of one near death. He pulled her skirts up over her bent knees. When he looked up again, his face was dismal.

Both children gaped at him with hopeful and yet hopeless eyes. It was not a natural sight to see so much gloom in the eyes of those so young and innocent, but this was an occasion that called for it. Having no way to save the mother, all he could hope to do was save the unborn.

The man rose to his feet slowly and gazed down at the dying woman and her helpless children. He plucked his hood from his shoulders and pulled it up over his head firmly, enveloping his eyes in shadow. Then he spoke again, tone somber.

"Shyrane, take them."

He was speaking to the mare, which pricked up its ears at the sound of its name and trotted to his side. Blowing air through its nose, it cast its eyes to the children and kneeled on its knobby knees, becoming just the level they needed to climb onto its back.

Brie looked first to the horse, and then to her mother. "Mama?"

Mina understood her forthcoming death and the decision of her savior to spare her children of the moment. She held her anguish and reached out her arms to comfort her son and daughter, then with a swift push, sent them to their ride.

With a gruff neigh, the mare rose to its feet again, carefully, so as not to jar the children clinging to its mane. The man gave the animal a slap to its hindquarters and whistled sharply, and it took off trotting down the previously sliced path. Thomas and Brie, perched safely on its back, turned their heads to gaze upon their mother for the last time. Brie called out for her again, but her brother silenced her.

Now almost completely drained of strength, Mina cast woeful eyes to the man at her feet.

"Please save my child," she pleaded hoarsely. "Please."

"Worry not," he answered her tenderly and crouched down in front of her, hands clasped in prayer. "*Sayo inu*," the chants rose like flowers from soaked earth out of his rumbling voice. "*Sayo, masoon. Sayo masoon.*"

Mina felt her belly warm under his words. The pain that ravaged her became not much more then a dull ache.

"*Inu*," he continued to chant over her in a strained whisper. "*Inu.*"

The warmth engulfed her entire body in caressing little prickles. Goose pimples rose from her flesh, and Mina found she was engrossed in enlightenment. Her fear and pain vanished from her system. In her twenty-one years, she had never felt so unimaginably peaceful. She did not see when the man took forth a steel hunting knife from his cloak. She did not feel when he pressed it into her belly and cut away the flesh. She did not hear the squelched cries of her newborn child when he lifted it from her womb. And she did not feel death when it took her hand and led her to Siavon.

"*Sayo inu*," the man chanted continuously, bloody newborn squirming and crying in his arms. "The chosen one has arrived."

In the distance, Shyrane's brays of distress tingled in his ears. He rose from the body of the mother and took off his cloak with one hand, clasping the tiny infant in the other. With a quick hand, he sliced away the umbilical cord and tied it off. The horse gave another anguished whinny, and he looked toward the sound as he wrapped the child in his cloak and hid it in the brush.

"Be safe," he told the infant. "*Mas an prota.*"

The newborn stopped crying and looked up at him from the bundle of warm fabric surrounding it. It blinked with eyes of deep ruby.

Ahead in the cleared pathway, the mare stood, backside to him as he approached. Its muscled black bulk was quivering on knobby, uneasy legs. Hooves pawed the ground and stirred up the gray dust. The children on its back hid their faces from the sight they beheld. Their whimpers came muffled underneath the horse's mane.

What crouched not but a few yards ahead of them was unlike any creature to normally grace either wood or sky. It seemed the bastard child of both bear and hyena, a twisted mix of two never mated beings infused with a devil's seed. It had high shoulders, flat boxy haunches with short back legs and a stubby curled tail, and was large, larger than even the massive tricorn, all talons and muscle and zigzagged with tan and white stripes. Its wrinkled muzzle jutted into a sharp point of a snout, and when it gaped, the first noticeable feature was its front fangs. They were as long as its mouth was wide, and glistened with yellow drool. A slippery green tongue lashed and licked the edges of its muzzle hungrily. Piercing globes the size of a babe's fists seared with lava stone irises. Above these were black

13

ears that curled devilishly up over its gruesome shaggy head. Around its neck, was a silver chain, dangling forth an amulet in the shape of two crescent moons cradling the full between them.

This new threat stomped its front claws hard on the hoof-beaten ground and roared, a horrendous sound unlike that any normal woodland creature had ever uttered. Shyrane reared and the children tumbled from her back. Had the man not leapt forward and swept them away, they would have been trampled by the terrified mare.

The man shielded the children behind him and withdrew his sword. From the corner of his eye, he could see the woods around him stir. Dozens of eyes appeared in the thickets, sunken into the knurled faces of large black animals that resembled wolves or dogs, or even a mix of both. Each had a heavy head too large and long to belong to a wolf, yet had too thick a bone structure to be that of a feral dog. Their ears were high and tasseled, insides dense with white hair. Their lantern light eyes burned sickly yellow. Greasy, razor fur prickled up all along their backs and necklines like manes of barbed wire. Hideous things were these. Dogs they could have been once, but somewhere, somehow, these beasts had evolved away from their canine cousins to become something much more terrifying. They drooled heavily from the smell of fearful prey in the air. It pooled on the ground at their feet.

The horrendous beast's bellowing was joined by the whiny yowling of these creatures around them. The man knew they were surrounded. On a quick count, he figured out about seventeen separate animals squatting and ready to pounce on them. The girl clung to his arm and whimpered, and he drew her in with one gentle hand while the other held the sword menacingly into the air.

The enormous beast attacked, its claws flexing as it propelled itself. In one springy leap it landed on Shyrane's back, and in another instantaneous moment, the long fangs disappeared deep into the back of the mare's neck. Shyrane's throat was crushed by the shear pressure, and the once magnificent horse sank to the ground, graceful neck nearly severed. Despite her size, strength, and massive cutting horns, the tricorn had been dispatched without settling one injury into her repulsive executioner.

Brie screamed. The high pitched sound pricked the ears of the beast and its surrounding followers in the three people's direction. Around them, the creatures began yipping. Slobber flecked from their muzzles. The giant turned its ugly head toward them, drew back its bloody lips, and growled.

The man held his ground once again, oblivious to the closing circle of monsters growing smaller all the time. The smaller fiends were panting, salivating, snarling, and ready to strike. It seemed that they were awaiting the order of the giant, for they kept swiveling their tasseled ears in its direction at every sound it made. One of them came boldly close to the side of Thomas and snatched a claw out viciously. A scrap of the boy's shirt was torn free, and underneath it, the pale flesh began to ooze blood in three long lines. He cried out and jerked at the pain, and his hands clutched onto his protector's leg.

The man shook the children away from him in a harsh and unexpected gesture and spun his dark form out from the center with a swipe of his sword, and the black fiend gurgled and separated from the chest down. Its entrails oozed forward, and the two closest to it began devouring it greedily. The giant roared again as it started toward them.

Following their leader, the slavering fiends began to close in on the humans; some of them stopped to eat at the eviscerated tricorn and their late comrade, growling menacingly at each other for carcass rights. Most of them, however much they drooled and cast eyes to the fresh meat, crept toward the humans in total unity, the giant striped beast in their lead.

"*Hrotage?*" Thomas uttered simply.

The man looked at him.

"Can you save us?"

For a moment, he just stared at the child. The glaze of fear was upon his eyes, but with that was something else, a spark of unrest, perhaps, or even exhilaration. As the giant neared them and enveloped them in its shadow, Vorian broke gaze from the child and looked into its ghastly red eyes.

"Crocotta!"

The crowd of fiends around them stopped slinking. Their ears pricked forward, inner white hairs providing an odd pattern around

15

them. Even the creatures locked in battle over the carcasses stopped and looked at the humans.

The large beast stopped in its tracks and crouched. A low angry rumble erupted from its throat as it flattened its devilish ears at him. Thick saliva dribbled out of anxious jaws. Its haunches quivered.

"Yes," he continued unabridged, "I know who you are, Crocotta, and I must say this new form of yours befits your winning personality."

The giant rose up from its crouch. The height of its shoulders on four legs reached his own on two. The muscles in its forelimbs bulged against the shaggy tan and white flecked fur. Its anxious growls subsided, and a voice sinister and doggish replaced it.

"Vorrrian," it hissed, green tongue flickering. "Ssso wonnnnderful to sssee you."

The fiends around them tensed at the unfamiliar sounds coming from their leader. They shrank away from it, tails drooping between their legs, ears flattening. Their behavior turned simple, animalistic. The circle broke away from the humans and disappeared into the thicket, leaving quivering brush in their wake.

"I wish I could say the same to you." Vorian replied unassumingly.

Hate flashed in the monster's eyes as it threw its head into the air. A long reverberating roar rustled the birds from their nests and sent them cawing from the trees. Thomas and Brie hugged each other tightly.

"I mmmight have known it wassss you who destrrroyed the great phoenix dragon," the beast said in a voice that was beginning to sound even more human. "Only that God'ssss Breath of yours could make such a ghassstly mess."

A guttural cry uttered from the beast as it rose to its hind legs. It towered over Vorian and lifted its black talons high into the air like they were prepared to catch the sun. Thomas and Brie braced themselves for the attack, but it did not come. Instead, the claws flexed and began to change shape. The entire body of the monster quivered and shook under the skin like an internal river system ran through it, and the creature began shrinking. The large shoulders collapsed and sucked into the neckline, which thinned and shortened. The head, a hideous grinning thing, seemed to liquefy on the neck before a new face dribbled out of it. The nasty black claws softened, shortened, and shrank into round stubs. Its spine made a disgusting cracking sound as the bones contoured and straightened out. Spiny hair shrank back into its thick skin. Afterwards, the skin itself softened and turned pink. Now, the creature had shrunk to just below Vorian's height, and its face had metamorphosed into that of a whole different animal. It let loose with another groan, but this was a far more feminine sound, a human sound.

The woman doubled over as the last of the beast's shape disappeared inside her, and slowly but soundly, rose up again. Her eyes were narrow slits of deep brown. Glossy black hair fell to the small of her lengthy back. Her milky skin covered a beautifully crafted female body. Long luxurious legs rose up from tiny feet. Bony wrists ended with soft hands which lovingly fondled the amulet round her neck. Had she not been seen in her previous form, the woman would have been beheld as a rare beauty.

The children both gaped in shock at what they had seen, but Vorian did not express surprise. His expression told them that he had all along known the real identity of the striped monstrosity.

Crocotta tossed her hair back from her shoulders and plunked her hands on her bare hips. She cast a look to the eviscerated tricorn, proudly laughing at the death she had caused.

"Not much of a fighter was she?" she goaded.

"More fair and brave then you ever were," Vorian replied. "Or, ever will be."

"Oh, Vorian Tranore," she tittered, hand over her heart, "You tease me, so."

Vorian darkened. "Explain yourself."

"My my," Crocotta mused. "So forceful and demanding. Anyone would cower in fear at one such as you, but *I* know the great Vorian Tranore does not raise his sword on the unarmed."

She looked down at her naked body and smiled seductively at him. With a wispy laugh, the woman spun a complete turn without lifting a foot, and when she was facing them again, her nakedness was concealed by a long gray dress with black curled edges of thorns jutting from the shoulders and waistband. Her flowing black hair was now a mass of twisted spidery braids bouncing about as if alive.

"My beautiful, heroic Vorian Tranore," she sighed. She sashayed to him and placed her hands on his broad shoulders,

17

caressing them. "Always there to assist those who need assisting." she peered at the two children and smirked. "I take it their mother did not survive?"

The children slunk to the ground and clutched at Vorian's clothes. He, however, remained still.

"Why have we been troubled with your company?" he rumbled heatedly.

Crocotta appeared taken aback by the question. "My sisters and I have left Siavon," she replied coldly. Her hands left his shoulders. "We have decided to branch out. Spread our wings, so to say. Test the waters. I chose Nodens for its vast geography. You know how I do love nature."

"So it would not be that Garric finally cast you out for your shameful behavior then?"

Crocotta sizzled with anger. She whipped her hands into the air and an invisible force sent Vorian and the children flying back several feet and landing hard on their backsides. She scowled like a pouting child.

"That old fool! He cannot comprehend the mistake he has made. His kingdom will fall to ruin without us!"

Vorian heaved himself to his feet and dusted off his black pants. The children huddled together on the ground.

"It can fall no further then you have dragged it," Vorian said, approaching her once again with a purposeful stride.

Crocotta squinted crossly and waggled a pointy finger in front of him. "You tempt me with your mockery. I could take it upon myself to kill you right now and save the formalities."

Vorian was ready with his quick response. "And I could burst your entrails with God's Breath should you try."

Crocotta outright laughed. The sound echoed dangerously in the forest and shook the leaves of frightened trees. "Always the clever one," she said. "But I will return much stronger next time. Keeping up with a dragon takes a lot out of a simple woman like me. Be flattered, Vorian. I have been honing my skills just for you."

Vorian picked his hood from his shoulders and pulled it up, nodding to her as a gentleman does before royalty. "Until our paths cross again, then."

"Until then," she replied graciously. She slung her arms around his neck and kissed him passionately before hissing into his ear. "Oh, just one more thing. My blachunds have been such good boys today and I have run out of biscuits. It would be in your best interest, and that of those cherubs cowering beneath you, to *run.*"

And in a speck of light, she was gone from his presence. It was now that Vorian saw the ring of hungry yellow eyes surrounding them in the thicket once again, a ring whose side the children were dangerously close to. He spun around, but was too late. Two blachunds lashed out of the brush and seized each child by the throat in its wet jaws. Their squelched cries cut short as the oxygen left them, but their fearful expressions remained unfaltering. Vorian withdrew his sword and leapt forward, and a wall of blachunds sprung forward, blocking his view of the children as their captors carried them into the brush, growls overpowering their squeals.

The blachunds surrounded him, closed him in. They barked frantically at him, teeth bared, black fur spiked at the neckline. Vorian swung his sword and decapitated three of them, and their bodies fell limp under the torrent of their ravenous peers. The remaining began leaping toward him two, three at a time, squealing when his sword took pieces from their bodies. He spun with his sword outstretched and managed to maim two more blachunds, but left his back unprotected. He felt the stinking weight of a large beast as it leapt upon him and sunk long fangs deep into his shoulder. Vorian groaned in agony and sunk to his knees.

The blachunds closed in around him so closely that he could hear their rapidly beating hearts under their reeking mangy fur. The animal on his back let go to drive for another piece of him, but Vorian jumped to his feet again and leapt high above the heads of his attackers. He flipped head over heels in midair, and the blachund fell from his back and landed on the head of another, breaking its neck backwards. When his feet hit the ground again, Vorian's sword pierced through the necks of two gasping beasts. Hot blood spurted forward from the wounds as they fell, gurgling, to the ground. Their bodies were overrun by the feeding frenzy before they had stopped convulsing.

There was now too much blood on the ground for the pack to ignore, and with bristled agitation, they turned from Vorian and tore greedily at their dead. Vorian took off after the children. He could no longer hear their cries, but the wolfish growls in the distance told him they were still in the jaws of the blachunds. He slashed through

19

the overgrowth, panting heavily from his wound. A finite trail of blood showed him the way to a clearing in the forest and stopped. There was neither nary a paw print nor a scrap of cloth to prove that they had been through here. The blachunds had claimed their prize.

The humid ozone in the forest grew distinctly chilly. Vorian's ragged breaths came out in puffs of cloud in front of him. He held his sword firmly and turned in all directions, but there was nothing. Jeering laughter bounced off the trunks of trees and burrowed into his ears like carnivorous worms.

"Crocotta!" he cried out, "*Crocotta!*"

But the laughing had stopped, and the heat crept back inward. All was calm. Slowly, one by one, the birds in the trees began chirping and singing. It was as if nothing had occurred here at all, just the way Crocotta liked it.

When Vorian found his way back, the blachunds were gone, leaving no prints. Their dead too, were gone, the blood dried away. Even Shyrane's broken body had vanished. Vorian sheathed his sword and pressed a palm to his bitten shoulder. The injury warmed under it, and soon, the pain dissipated and the bleeding slowed.

Infantile cries drew him back to the site of the fallen mother. She too, had disappeared. Vorian searched for the baby wrapped up in his cloak and found it exactly where he had left it, unharmed. The infant's unusual eyes glistened trustingly at him from its cool dirt cradle. Vorian bent down and carefully lifted it from its bloody bundle of cloak. In his hands, he held the last fleeting chance on Aryth. The chosen one had arrived in the realm of one of the Danaan sisters.

Vorian observed with awe how wee and delicate it was. Its pink skin was warm and wriggling with innocent life. *Hrotage* it may become one day, but for now, it was helpless, vulnerable, and dependent. With a curious coo, the infant placed a chubby hand on the end of his large nose and squeezed. Vorian's heart melted.

"Worry not, young one," he comforted. "I care for you, now."

Tulley's Warning

Nodens' East Village bustled with market activity in the high hour of dawn, when the sun had just barely peeked over the horizon like a child over a high table. Cool air kissed away the dregs of humidity to draw the diurnal creatures from their holes. This was a particularly crowded day at the market. The circus was in town, so inhabitants from many rolling counts across the land were drawn in to see the exotic shows and animals. A circus wagon latched to a pair of donkeys was resting patiently by the supply store. The driver had gone inside to get directions from the merchant while an awestruck crowd collected around his wagon outside. The sloppily painted words 'BARRA'S WONDERS' marked both sides of the wagon in curly yellow writing. A large barred cage made of solid steel nestled comfortably on the back of it, and inside this cage was a cockatrice.

Now the astonishing thing about the cockatrice was not its bizarre looks or its large size, but its origin. The most common theory of how the creature came to be was that when a rooster reached a ripened age, his very last task would be to lay an egg and die. The egg would be taken from the barn by a snake and tended to by it until the offspring, a cockatrice, emerged. There was no proof of this, but many farmers would take it upon themselves to behead old roosters that were showing signs of slowing up. No farmer wanted a cockatrice terrorizing his land. Quick, aggressive, and agile (though with the intelligence of a chicken), cockatrice were seen strutting in the tall grass rooting up insects and berries but once in a lifetime. Their homes were being dug up for farm ground, and the cockatrice was becoming scarcer with every growing season. People were fascinated by this particular creature for a reason. It was a rarity to see one in captivity, for they were fast as a steer and twice as mean. Whoever had caught this magnificent creature had to have the wits of a hundred wizards.

Even with a leather muzzle sheathing its deadly beak, the cockatrice was a strange and intimidating looker. It was an odd mix of both rooster and serpent. The lean body, the same size as an ostrich, was covered in dark brown feathers from its head to its thighs. On its head, a red cock's crest grew. The curved elongated

21

beak was filled with a forked snake's tongue. Long black horns jutted evilly from just above its bulgy eyes. It had no arms, but leathery black wings folded behind it, awaiting a flight that would never happen for the heavy beast. The long reptilian tail, dotted with luminous green scales, came lined with a rounded red sail on each side somewhat resembling hardened feathers. The cockatrice was an odd sight to behold!

The animal in the cage was quite obviously enraged. It strutted about and raised its wings, protesting angrily with a muffled voice, and its head butting the bars of the cage. The people around it backed up and laughed uneasily at its feeble escape attempts. They had no fear, for its sharp beak was bound. The most useful weapon of the once terrifying creature had been immobilized. Now all it could do was stumble around in its cage and crow at its onlookers.

The brown dirt road that separated two sides of the street was crowded mostly with human women and waddling wateroggs, wee bipedal, fish-headed creatures that gurgled and slurped their language rather than spoke it. Their blue bodies, despite being pitted on land, always glistened with slime, which kept them hydrated while they scuttled about in the hot sun. They populated the streets alongside their human counterparts, hoping to snag fruit out from under the eyes of the vendors. Sweet fruits were a rarity, for they lived outside of the town in muddy holes along the river. A fresh strawberry or peach was an absolute delicacy to a waterogg, which fed mostly on grasses and algae.

In less abundant numbers, catfolk dotted the streets carrying baskets. These were creatures barely three feet tall, cats, simply enough, similar to the domestic house pets that farmers used to catch mice, but different in their genealogy.

It was said that eons ago, the original catfolk, a male and a female, were born from the womb of a human princess who mated with her prince husband on the night of their wedding and became pregnant. It was only after the children were born that the prince revealed who he truly was, Dynes, the simple mouser of the castle stables.

Dynes had fallen deeply in love with the princess while watching her visit her unicorns, and begged the stable inhabitants to help him win her hand. The unicorns obliged happily, for he rid their homes of pests and was kind to them. They transformed him into a handsome prince, and he wooed the princess and married her. On their wedding night, the spell was broken, for the only condition of his transformation was that Dynes could never mate with his human wife. The unicorns feared the children would be born as catfolk, and they did not wish to undermine Garric, the world's creator, by unleashing a new species upon Aryth against his will. Nevertheless, catfolk came to be. They proved to be a fine addition to the world, for they were aptly skilled at medicine and crafts and were wise teachers of ancient techniques. Some were even known to possess strong magical abilities. Because of this, Garric forgave the unicorns.

The catfolk lived in small numbers, mostly located in the North and South villages of Nodens, further beyond even the waterogg breeding grounds. This was not because they were banished, unlike their slimy neighbors, but because they chose to avoid the perversion of humankind. The fast paced, noisy town commotion distressed them, for catfolk liked things quiet. They built their thatch huts far apart from their neighbors and lived in close family groups. Once a week or so, catfolk could be seen in the markets stocking up on supplies. They moved about quietly and unnoticed, and were regarded with respect by many.

A particularly plump waterogg, which stood no higher than a man's knee waddled in next to a kiosk of freestanding pomegranate fruit and reached a webbed hand toward it curiously. Before it could grasp the luscious red fruit, a thwack from a rounded rod sent it blubbering from sight. The lean, fiery haired owner of the kiosk shook the rod after the retreating waterogg and cursed it.

"Damn you, oily bandit!" he shouted. "Keep away from here!"

"Grada, a fine morning to you."

Instantly, his conduct softened and he turned direction to the fat man on the other side of the kiosk. He seemed entirely absorbed in examining a pomegranate.

"Likewise, Alasdair," Grada greeted him. "Fresh pomegranate today?"

Reluctantly, Alasdair placed the fruit back with its companions and rubbed his jiggling stomach in reply. "Nay, but my girth expands greatly from them. My wife would be displeased." He

23

broke a chuckle and reached again for the pomegranate, lips moistening. "Then again, my wife is elsewhere."

"That's the way, Alasdair," cheered the vendor with much enthusiasm. He reached under the stand and pulled up a cloth bag as he blathered away. "They remain in season for such a short time. Indulge while they're on hand. Go ahead," he encouraged. "Taste one."

Alasdair did not hesitate. With one yawning bite, half the fruit was gone. Alasdair wrinkled his face and chewed thoughtfully. He swallowed the juicy pulp and licked the dribble from his lips. "Seedless I see."

"Made possible by my daughter's deseeding spell," Grada said proudly. "A bag of them, then?"

Alasdiar held up two fingers. "Twi. My wife dismisses my ingestion of sweet fruits, but when there is enough for us both, she is silent as the grave."

"She has no choice when her maw is stuffed full of them." Grada joked as he began filling the cloth bag.

They shared a spur of laughter which was interrupted by the shouts and scolding coming from across the road. At the circus cart, the crowd murmured with apprehension as a young boy ventured ever closer to the bars of the enraged cockatrice's cage.

"Kavandor! Keep away from there!" His mother shouted from a safe distance. "That thing will snip your head from your neck!"

"No he won't, Mother," the boy muttered over his shoulder. "He's caged up."

"Kavandor!"

Kavandor found his footing carefully as he approached the side of the cart, plainly aware of the crowd of onlookers eyeing his every move. One hand reached between the steel bars and brushed the toenail of the cockatrice's right foot. Startled, the bird squawked and drove its bound beak down upon him, missing his hand by a fraction as he drew it back in surprise. The boy stumbled backward and landed hard on his backside, and his mother hiked him to his feet and scolded him.

The onlookers chuckled at the display, and did not take notice of the angry cockatrice's whipping plated tail. As the bird dipped its head to butt the bars again, the end of the tail snaked through the bars and snapped the backside of one of the donkeys. A loud bray of alarm preceded the kick to the back of the cart, which rattled the cage and enraged the cockatrice even more. It spun around and dove for the donkey, squawking angrily, but blocked by its prison. Even so, the attack startled the already spooked animal as well as its mate, and the cage creaked and groaned as the back of the wagon endured stronger kicks from both animals. Chaos ensued in the crowd before the cage tipped over and burst apart. The crowd scattered as would tiny skipping fish as a sportsman plunges his spear into the center of a pond. The mother of the daring Kavandor now scooped up her terrified son and took cover in the supply store, bumping into the owner of the cart just as he was exiting. He came in time to witness the prized circus property rise up from the broken cage and leer into the crowd. It spread its enormous wings and shrieked. Even with its beak bound, the idea of obtaining freedom could be seen in its attitude.

The cockatrice rushed at the terrified crowd. A waterogg, with its webbed claws filled with peaches, gurgled and grunted, waddling at full speed (which wasn't very fast at all) from the mania. The cockatrice turned its angry sights to the creature and rushed at it, wings extended, head lowered. It butted the retreating waterogg out of its way with such little effort it was almost humorous. The rogg went flying head over flippers, peaches tumbling from its arms, and smacked into the side of the pomegranate stand. In no time, it was on its feet, gathering up its dropped load.

The wagon driver was the picture of panic. Pale and shaking, he pulled from his belt a rope lasso and spun it high above his head as he ran toward the rampaging cockatrice. With a yell, he tossed the loop of the rope over the animal's neck.

The cockatrice looked up in surprise and turned to glare at him. Snorting, it cut the ground with one of its deadly talons and rushed him. Someone in the frantic crowd screamed as the cockatrice leapt upon its keeper and slashed him from hip to knee, spilling blood like rain. He let go of the rope to do the wise thing and run for cover. The cockatrice raised its crest of feathers, spread its frightening wings, and crowed menacingly at the fleeing crowd.

Satisfied that it would no longer be bothered, the cockatrice wandered off to the very pomegranate stand where the two men stood in awe at the crazed events unfolding before them. Terror overran Grada who, forgetting his sale, dropped his customer's bag of fruit and darted off down the road to disappear in the panicked crowd. Alasdair stood agape, pomegranate half way to his open mouth as the bird terrorized the stand, pecking at the fruit with its bound beak in desperation, swinging its massive tail and clearing the entire shelf of the next door apple stand. He groaned in dismay as he watched luscious fruit after fruit become a pulpy mess from the sharp end of the beak. Desperately, he waved his hands at the animal and tried to shoo it away.

"Be gone!" he shrieked, clapping his hands. "Shoo!"

The cockatrice raised its crest and glared at him. Its chest heaved as it rose to its full height and stomped its feet.

Alasdair began to back away, hands protectively in front of him, stumbling over spilled fruit.

"Now, now," he muttered fearfully. He scuttled like a crab as fast as he could away from the creature. "No need for that."

The cockatrice squawked and rushed him, one talon raised to eviscerate. Alasdair held up his arms and drew his body inward to protect his soft guts. The crowd cried out loudly around him at the ruckus. Alasdair awaited the final blow, but the talon did not come down upon him. When he looked up, the rope around the creature's neck had tightened, and it was being dragged backwards, flapping and squawking in anger. Behind it, on a magnificent black tricorn, a figure, shrouded in a cloak, clutched the end of the rope in black gloved fists.

The tricorn was already backing up with its rider who held fast to the cockatrice's rope. It reared and neighed as the beast swung its shiny green tail and missed its front legs just barely. The cloaked warrior shouted something which went unheard under the enraged crows of the cockatrice and the whinnies of the horse. With no effort at all, he braced his weight against the pulling beast and shouted a command to his mount. The tricorn began to back up faster, pointing its head forward as the warrior pulled in the slack of the cockatrice's rope to drag the animal into the lethal horns. The bird shrieked, as if knowing what he was about to do, and dipped its head underneath the loop of rope and ran off.

The gathering of people at the fronts of the stands and buildings murmured as tricorn and rider galloped after the escaping cockatrice. Now, the warrior unsheathed a long shinning sword from a sheath lying at the side of his belt. The intricately carved handle glistened with white gold and a ruby, red as blood, winked in the butt of the hilt like an evil eye. Those closest enough to see knew that this was God's Breath, the sword of the Man of the Blade.

With sword held high, the rider galloped his steed after the escaping cockatrice, cloak riding the wind behind him as he leaned forward on the saddle. The hilt of God's Breath sparkled sharply underneath his leather fist. The cockatrice weaved to throw him off, but he had anticipated this and was prepared to yank the reins to the left and right, gaining fast on its swaying tail.

Folk were quick to leap out of the way as the bird and its pursuer cut through the village; however, one waddling waterogg and her two wee nits were not so quick. Whistling in fear, they ran, as fast as wateroggs could run, on stubby webbed feet as their impending doom rushed upon them. The cockatrice would have had no qualms about trampling the creatures, but the rider thought differently. An opportunity had presented itself almost as though he had called it to him.

The rider leaned in close to the ear of the tricorn and whispered something to it. As he expected, the bird weaved once again, and instead of veering off after him, the tricorn claimed speed as its ally and shot forward on a straight path like a finely aimed arrow. The horse gained ground quickly, and soon was leading the chase, with the cockatrice flagging behind.

The mother waterogg stopped running and hovered, gurgling over her children. The tricorn ran straight for them, and just when it seemed as though its heavy hooves would make porridge of the family, it made a tremendous leap over them. The cockatrice veered off course again, missing the wateroggs entirely.

Rider and steed swerved in dangerously close to the kiosks, sending citizens running, preparing for the crash. With God's Breath raised high, the rider bid his steed to dip underneath the awning of a rather large fruit stand that smartly had its merchandise suspended in fishing net from the wood bracers on the awning, out of the reach of children and wateroggs alike. The sharp broadsword sliced through the netting with ease, and littered the ground with rolling red and yellow apples. At that time, the cockatrice was back on course and bolted, shrieking, into the mess. Its talons stumbled over the spilled

27

fruit, and the creature flew, useless wings fluttering, hit the ground, and rolled over thrice.

The tricorn slowed up and trotted back to where the bird had fallen and its rider jumped from its back and sheathed the magnificent God's Breath at his side. He pulled forth his lead of rope and knelt at the bird's deadly claws, then tied and knotted the feet together and stepped back.

The bird crowed angrily and lifted its head. Its body wriggled desperately in an attempt to hike to its feet but the ropes held fast, and the exhausted animal finally gave a screech of defeat and lay down, gasping heavily.

The warrior brushed off his hands and turned at the sound of the cheering crowd that closed in around them. Among the front few was Alasdair. He bowed humbly to his *hrotage* and took his hand.

"A thousand merits to you, my lord," he said, looking down upon the hand he clasped as if it were made of gold. "I surely would have been slain, if not for you."

The leather glove rose to pull down the hood. Underneath, tan skin glowed under the sunlight, and ruby red eyes glittered. A wave of shoulder length hair, coppery brown in color, flowed away from a young freckled face. She smiled and inclined her head courteously.

"You are welcome, good sir."

Alasdair teetered back on his haunches and disturbed the dust falling into it. The look of surprise overwhelmed his chubby face. "Mine eyes deceive me!" he gasped, "A girl!"

The crowd began to murmur and talk amongst itself. Someone whispered in not too low a voice, "That is Tranore's apprentice girl; the one he's attempting to mold into some sort of wild huntress."

A smarmy laugh issued from another. "Waste of his time. She could be put to better uses." The owner of the contemptuous voice made himself known at the front of the crowd. It was the wagon-driver, leg caked with blood, face pallid. He looked the girl with the ruby eyes up and down and asked her, "Why aren't you back in the forest panning for gold flecks with your sire?"

The girl reddened noticeably at the insult but remained stoic as she flipped her hair from her shoulders. "Seems I was needed here today. And shall I be needed again, I will prevail."

28

Laughter rumbled from the crowd, silent and cautiously at first but soon spreading around her like a bad rash as those less brave took the opportunity to fit in theirs.

The driver snuffed a breathy note and nodded at the incapacitated animal at the hooves of the tricorn. "You act as though you've committed some noble deed today, lass. Whipsaw is a trained show bird, accustomed to interacting with humans. He was merely spooked." He looked to Alasdair as the fat man climbed to his feet and retreated to the crowd's edge. "He would not have done this man any serious harm."

"*Could* not have done harm," Alasdair was quick to say. He pointed a still shaking finger at the bird's leather muzzle. "His beak is still bound."

The crowd murmured again, more laughs seeped through, accompanied by jeering looks in the girl's direction.

She referred her hand to the gaping wound on the wagon-driver's leg. "Do you require medical assistance, sir?"

He looked down at it as if noticing it for a first time. "For a scratch? Nonsense."

Humming thoughtfully, the girl nodded to him and blinked. She picked up her hood and shrouded her head once again as she turned to her horse. The tricorn pawed at the ground impatiently and waited for her to climb on, then reared as she pulled back on the reins and peered down at the wagon-driver with her ruby glare.

"I would take it upon myself to keep a closer watch on that animal if I were in your position," she warned. "Next time, it may be more then a mere *scratch*."

Laughter this time came directed at the wagon-driver. His face reddened and he sneered hatefully as the teenager raised a hand and kicked the sides of her mount.

"Yah, Annick!" she shouted, and the tricorn neighed in response and galloped from the scene of the crowd, its rider's cloak floating like a wing behind them.

***

The rider left behind her the jeers of the town on the back trail of the traveling cockatrice cart. Once the dwellings and stands were but a wink in the distance, she slowed her steed to a gait. The

29

road cut through the middle of the valley of tall golden grass, dotted with bits of yellow and blue flowers. Their heavy perfume made her feel lazy. The swirling feelings of rejection and embarrassment soon left her as she allowed the scents to absorb into her lungs. It always delighted her to trot Annick through the Ardor Flower Valley and allow the sweetness to melt away the troubles of the day. And these days, it seemed like trouble plagued her at every opportune moment.

A count or so down the road, the tiniest dot of brown rose against the endless golden field. The florals in the air mixed in gracefully with the aroma of cooking smoke and acrid scientific concoctions, and then the rider knew she was close to her destination. She kicked her heels into the sleek black sides of the steed and galloped him toward the rising speck in the distance.

It took no more than a minute or two for the speck in the distance to materialize into a clearing dominated by a small thatch hut. To one side, a healthy vegetable garden tempted the tricorn's gasping nostrils with exotic smells. To the other, an old stone well stood lonely against the horizon. Dozily grazing in the grass was an old donkey who lifted his head only momentarily at the appearance of the larger equine approaching his territory. Inside the hut itself, the town's resident potion master could be heard busying himself in his tiny kitchen. The young rider dismounted and approached the moldy door, not bothering to tether her ride. The tricorn nickered and shook his head, as if to assure his mistress that he could be trusted to stay put. His watery blue eyes watched her let herself into the dwelling.

He was bustling himself about a brick pit fire, over top of which a black pot hung by the straps of a metal cradle, its contents boiling. Glass clinked and clamored in response to a stubby finger's agitated probing into the shelves. In the crook of his arm, he held a bundle of differently colored bottles. Being barely able to carry all of them, the old potion master dared to snatch one more from a low lying shelf and added it to his store; then with a grunt of effort, hiked all of them into a more manageable position and lugged them to the foot of the fire. He set them down carefully in a row, picked out a small yellow vial, popped off the cork, and sniffed the contents thoughtfully with a ruddy button nose. He did not notice his young visitor watching him at his front door, but continued about his work with the utmost concentration.

"Lembordok seed oil. Ah, very good," he prattled to himself, his voice a mixture of age and wisdom. Daintily, the old master tipped the vial over the pot until the desired amount dribbled into the concoction. Then, he quickly replaced the yellow vial with a larger, green one, and so on, adding ingredients from colored bottles one by one and stating them to himself as if for an invisible record.

"Bumblefish venom, iris petal paste, a touch of unicorn spit and—" The master slowed his pace for this particular addition and peered at it with green goblet eyes, allowing only a tiny drop to enter the boiling liquid. "Careful, *careful*." The thick mucasy globule hit the bubbling liquid with a harsh hiss, and at once the pot's contents changed from blue to black.

"Wonderful!" he said joyfully. "Just the right touch."

At this final crucial point, the girl at the door spoke up tentatively. "Tulley?"

But her caution made no difference. His concentration unhinged, the master leapt into the air and spun around, his long misshapen tail sweeping most of his opened potions to the ground around him. Instantly, the weathered wooden floorboards became a sea of swirling colors.

"Brasser's bloody diddies!" he cried, more in surprise than anger. His attention swept from the girl to the mess about him and the last teetering vial at his feet. He snatched up the vial and corked it, saving its contents from certain ruin. Turning again to the intruder at the door, the old catman's head nodded in relief.

"Fair universe, child," he scolded, though his tone was that of lightheartedness. Never sneak about so like a ghost in a cat's home! You're liable to get scratched."

The girl bowed slightly. "Sorry, Tulley."

Tulley shook his head and cocked back his pointed ears in a manner very much like his common ancestor, despite his upright and eerily human frame. "Come now, hand me that vial," he beseeched his visitor, pointing at a shelf higher than his three foot self. "The blue one there."

She did so, lowering her hood in respect while kneeling down to present it to him. Tulley plucked it from her palm, and he walked very carefully with it to the edge of the pot. The girl followed, and had to stay on her knees to see comfortably at his level.

"Yes, yes, bogle's blood." Tulley licked his flat muzzle eagerly, peering through gold rimmed glasses that balanced, armless, on the tip of his nose. "Very rare to come by, my dear. It is the key ingredient in this particular potion." He held it out for her to see. The light from the single window next to the door winked in the shine of the blue bottle, and the contents sparkled.

"What potion is that?" Asked the child, ruby eyes enlarged with interest.

"You'll see, you'll see." The catman pulled the bottle away teasingly, and waggled a clawed finger at her. "But *only* if you're patient."

He began to shake the potion while he spoke, his broken tail swishing in anticipation. "I heard about your adventures in the market today."

The girl frowned. "So soon?"

Tulley gave a soft huffing chuckle. "Word travels fast in these parts. A fact you should have considered before taking on your sire's sword and armor and mounting his steed, an ill-advised decision, even for you, Keavy."

The one the old catman called Keavy took instant offense. "What does that mean? I defeated the cockatrice without blundering once! I saved a man's life today!"

Tulley answered her retort calmly. "You were lucky."

To which she boldly replied, "I am in top form to face Crocotta."

Concentration once again broken, the master let the vial slip from his claws. The winking light cried out as it was shattered into a dozen or so misshapen shards at the catman's feet. With an almost comical movement, Tulley jumped back just before the bluish goo reached them.

"Damn!"

Keavy was the example of remorse as she clasped her hands together and bowed to him. "Oh, forgive me!" she fretted, and reached for the mess instinctively. With surprising speed for such an old creature, Tulley grasped her arm and stopped her.

"No!"

Keavy followed his wise gaze to the blue goo, and gasped in a combination of horror and amazement as the soiled part of the floorboards began sizzling. The mess disappeared into the wood, dissolving every bit it touched and leaving a smoldering, stinking hole where it had made contact with the ground. Keavy found herself gulping back a shudder at the image of her own hand touching that highly acidic material.

"In top form for Crocotta, ha!" Tulley's bent whiskers twitched jeeringly at her. "You have much more to learn before you'll be ready to tree *that* possum. For starters, the bogle's blood has the potency twice that of sulfuric acid, but only in seniors of the species, those aged over forty years. And as you know, bogles are very devilish and clever little beasts." The tinge of contempt in Tulley's sodden rumblings led Keavy to believe he had first hand experience to back up his opinion.

"I have yet to see one with my own eyes," he admitted, "And yet I know they live very close to me, perhaps under these very floorboards."

Both Tulley and Keavy allowed their focus to wander to the smoking hole again, dark as a dead man's pupil.

"This is why obtaining perfectly aged blood is so difficult…and expensive."

"I am very sorry for destroying your potion, Tulley."

Tulley licked his palm and ran it across his whiskers. "Ah, the past giggles at us." He hunkered down beside the mess on the floor and plucked up a single shard of what was once the bottom of the vial. Once he held it into the light, Keavy caught glance of the smallest amount of winking blue goo still clinging to the glass. Tulley's jagged tailed swished happily. "In truth, I only needed one drop."

He gingerly held the shard over the boiling pot, and with a flick of his wrist, the goo sizzled into the mixture, turning it an ill purple. The catman then reached for a silver ladle hanging tarnished on a hook on the wall (located three feet above ground, just Tulley's level) and dipped it into the mix. In another set of quick and plainly routine motions, he had deposited a single ladleful of hot purple fluid into an empty vial and corked it.

Another coughing laugh, and the old catman held up his project with a grin. "It's finished."

Keavy sat back on her heels and keenly observed the potion master as he, with modest refinement, found a place for this vial amongst many others on his low set shelves. He was an aged creature, which to those of the catfolk race was quite a feat in itself, seeing as how most catfolk met an untimely end in the early years due to their genetic faults. His personality fit the description of the modern catman flawlessly; solitary, aloof, and, although at times a little graceless owing to his mix of human and animal heredity, exceptionally swift. However, Tulley was a special breed all his own. He was a celebrated scientist, well known for his inventions and cures, even written of in science books for his breakthrough Walite bite cure. He was in fact somewhat famous, though his extreme solitude kept him from accumulating too many visitors. His hut was further out of town than any other of the catfolk variety, much closer, you could say, to the waterogg breeding grounds than most citizens of Nodens would dare to venture. Tulley would state that he enjoyed living so close to the grounds because the useful medicinal plants that grew there were more accessible to one as old as he. Only those who knew Tulley best might assume that the real reason he lived out by the banks was because he rather liked and felt sorry for the roggs.

As far as appearances went, Tulley tended to stand out, even amongst his fellow catfolk. First of all, he was an orange striped, coloration found mainly in the catfolk race's quadruped cousins. Most catfolk ran their colors dark: black, gray, brown, and sometimes flecking all three colors, but almost certainly never orange. For this reason, Tulley was unusually shy amongst his own kind, and when he sought company at all, sought humans and other boorish breeds, something unheard of in his proud community. Even his coat itself was different than most, for it was longer in the facial and tail areas. Most catfolk had very short almost bristly fur.

A second noticeable trait of Tulley was his physical condition. His bushy orange tail had been broken and healed many times over, resulting in a shape resembling a crumpled scarf. His high erect ears came marked with the battles of youth. The right was missing a jagged crescent moon of flesh, while the left was pierced with two identical gold hoops which jingled together at every move of his wispy head. Large feral eyes shown bright green upon his short muzzle, the left glazed over with cataract, and the dregs of white age fell like falls on either side of his face, forming a shaggy mane of sorts.

Third and last, Tulley dressed plainly, choosing to wear only a white cotton tunic and slacks made of soft burlap. Like all catfolk, he wore no shoes, relying on his padded feet to guide his way. His clothing carried the scent of dust and age with him wherever he went. Everything he wore, he sewed himself.

Keavy mined through her knowledge of the master before her with adoration until he turned around and clasped his stubby fingers with their curved white claws together, a gesture of excitement for upcoming tasks.

"Help me clean up and we shall begin our history lesson for today."

***

A sun's short journey later, Keavy found herself sitting cross-legged in front of the fire pit, the cradle and pot now removed. Tulley sat on the other side of the flames in a similar position. He brushed back his wispy mane and gestured to the flames, which rose to his own height at the movement. "Bedivere, Nodens, Elgeron, and Murias," his old voice murmured. "Tell me what you know of them."

Keavy spouted her memorized lesson with clarity and confidence. "They are the four realms haunted by the Danaan sisters, Sephora, Sorka, Vetala, and Crocotta."

A nod from the old catman. "And how did these sisters come to power?"

"Garric, the ruler of Siavon fathered them and raised them to do his white magic, but they turned against him and came to Aryth." Keavy's ruby eyes could not hide their quest for praise when they met the green goblets of her teacher's.

Tulley's muzzle spilt to reveal a sharp approving smile. "You have been paying attention, Keavy. I am pleased. Today, we will finish the story."

A spark of adrenalin lit up the young girl's pretty freckled face. An entire season had passed since Tulley had first begun recounting the tale of the Danaan sisters, but never once had he ventured past this point in the lesson. It was impetuous to think so, but Keavy was sure this meant her training would finally begin.

A creak interrupted both the concentration of the catman and the inward musings of the girl, and both turned their attention to the small hut's entrance. In the frame a tiny creature struggled to push open the heavy mold covered door. It was a difficult task, for this creature was no bigger than a waterogg, smaller in fact, but far less rude to the eyes. The legs looked like they belonged to a deer, but the creature stood upright, and the deer's qualities ended at the waist and gave way to a more human physic, apart from the reddish agouti fur covering the entire body of the creature. Short arms ended in hairless honey colored three-fingered hands that in hard black nails rather than hooves, and the neck braced a head that was human-like in shape. In the face occurred the qualities of a young girl save for the twitching rabbit's nose and wide dark deer's eyes. Long pointed ears sprung forth from thin locks of soft wispy hair that she brushed out of her face now as she finally made her way past the door and stumbled to Keavy's side. Her hooves made a clicking sound on the wooden floor.

"You're late." Tulley said, without much enthusiasm.

"Most repentant, Master Tulley!" The appropriately classified wood faun puffed in a high pitched and still gasping voice. "Innes fashioned a snare outside of me burrow and snagged me by me hooves! It was most embarrassing, but luckily I was able to swing to a tree and untie me ropes, I was."

"Nessa Mool."

Nessa peered up hopefully, black eyes quivering in their sockets. "Yes, Master?"

"What have I told you about lying?"

The faun took in a breath and puffed out the line as if she expected it on a test. "Liars begin in the mouths of swine and end at the tails."

"Precisely," The catman finally met her glance with a sly smile. "At which end are you, Nessa?"

Nessa blushed. Her fleshy nose wiggled and she looked to the much larger creature smirking beside her. Her nostrils flared excitedly and her liquidy eyes bulged and shook in their sockets. "Hello, Keavy! Heard all about your daring cockatrice chase in the

East Village, I did. I reckon you showed those blinkered circus folk a thing or two!"

Nessa began to wag her tiny puff of a tail in eagerness, something she wished to break herself of. If there was anything a wood faun disliked, it was being compared to a dog.

Keavy opened her mouth to answer, but Tulley interrupted with a harsh grunt.

"Your fathers do not pay me ten nuggets a week to listen to gossip," he said curtly. "Now if you'll take your seat, Nessa. I was just about to finish the Danaan story."

Nessa leapt from hoof to hoof and twiddled her fingers happily, tail fluttering. "Oh, the one about the four sister witches who wish to destroy Siavon and rule eternity and time itself?"

Tulley lowered his gaze and cleared his raspy old throat. An orange paw gestured at the ground below the prancing faun. "Precisely. But I shall tell the story *my* way."

Keavy reached her hand over and flicked her friend softly on the rump to distract her from her agitating bounce. It wasn't entirely the faun's fault she had such strong desire to move about. Wood fauns were well known to have a taste for sweet forest berries and other sugary foods.

Once Nessa had settled, the old cat hunkered down and reached to his left side, where he had set an old sheepskin purse half the size he was. He reached inside and came forth with a handful of silver powder. His one clear green eye sparkling as he did so, Tulley cast the powder into the fire and watched the flames dance about, roaring, until the oxygen turned it blue, and a garbled blackened image appeared before them. It looked vaguely like a castle, but with the shimmering firelight, it was hard to tell exactly. But as soon as Tulley began to speak, the image became clearer, gained color and life, and a story unfolded before their very eyes.

"This occurred in a time long before your births and mine, before Nodens was more than a wooded wilderness, before Elgeron was immersed in total night, when Murias and the Tail was a vast sparkling paradise, and Bedivere was a land richer in folktale than gold."

Tulley tossed another bit of powder into the fire, and the castle's image grew stronger. Keavy and Nessa could make out bluish shimmering bricks, slime upon the walls, even light from within the stained glass windows.

"Enter Siavon," Tulley continued. "The city of souls, home to the greatest warriors our great world has ever known. Among them was Garric, the Painter of Life." The images of living creatures danced about the flames as Tulley spoke of them, almost as if they had been waiting for their cue.

"He created many wondrous creatures from his own blood and sweat, the mighty dragon, the regal gryphon, and yes, even the majestic unicorn who as you know, birthed forth Annick's ancestors."

Outside, the donkey brayed, as if in wish to be included.

"Ah yes," Tulley chuckled. "Yours too, Igor."

The donkey brayed again and Annick nickered after. Nessa and Keavy smiled at each other.

"Garric loved his wondrous creations, but he longed for companionship, and that is when he created the eleven porters of Aryth. These were gods charged to manage the world he created. Alesta Velhund, the goddess of the moon and stars, became his wife." Another handful of silver dust revealed a lovely woman with hair the color of night and skin as white as winter's eye.

"She was a magnificent beauty, beheld by all as the truest and most perfect of all women. Garric loved her so, and sired four daughters with her who were equally as beautiful but, as he later found out, not nearly as true."

The image of the four babes that had materialized burst apart so violently that Nessa leapt to her feet and braced herself to run. Keavy reached over and placed a calming hand on her head, and the faun settled down again. Tulley continued on without much notice of this. He was deeply absorbed in his tale.

"At each of their births, he placed around their necks enchanted amulets to seal in their powers. Being the children of gods, they did not have the ability to retain magic for extended periods of time outside of the holy land. These amulets, blessed by the Knights of Siavon, would prolong their powers. As evil became known to them, the sisters gradually grew to envy it, for Siavon was a place of righteousness and convention, and the world below it was its every opposite. It was a temptation their weak wills could not fight, and soon they began to bring evil into Siavon. The porter gods of Aryth forced Garric to cast them out of the holy grounds, and upon hearing of this decision, the sisters conspired and killed his dear Alesta out of revenge. Gods and goddesses cannot die obviously, but they can be expelled from Siavon, and that is what happened to Alesta. Forever she is trapped within her nightly realm among the stars, never to be with her husband again, controlling the phases of the moon. Enraged, Garric cursed his daughters, sent them to Aryth, and attached each of them to a realm from which they could not leave. One of these was Nodens."

Keavy could not help but hiss the name. "Crocotta."

Tulley's voice darkened harshly. "Yes, Crocotta, the Empress of the Wilderness."   The next scattering of dust gave birth to someone whom Keavy would recognize had her memory gone back to infancy. A beautiful black haired woman with many of the same characteristics as her mother, morphed wickedly into a horrid bear-like monster. Nessa cowered behind Keavy at this part. She was all too familiar with the fiends that lurked about her forest home.

"She was cursed to the form of a hellish hound and forced to live out her life in the wilds." Tulley grunted uneasily. "There, she learned how to manipulate her power over wild animals to her advantage, hence blachunds became her army, owls became her eyes. She still lurks in our forest, the part of it that wasn't destroyed for farmland, that is. And she will reemerge from time to time to snatch away unruly children who disobey their parents, as she did hers."

"What of the phoenix dragon that attacked upon my birth?" Keavy blurted, aware that this would annoy her master, but unmindful. She was too curious.

"We will get to that," he said sharply. "Let us examine the rest of Garric's happy little family." Another handful, another woman, this one much darker in appearance, heavy black hair, pointy jaw, lips as red as blood, skin as pale as the dead.

"Vetala, perhaps the most troublesome of the four, the Empress of the Darkness. She rained down her gloom upon the city of Elgeron, and thus coaxed forth the forces of the dead to join her in constant celebration. She was always the carefree one in her family, you see, and had no desire to dabble in real work of any kind. As she grew older, and more voluptuous, she saw an advantage in lonely

39

teenagers, who proved easy to hypnotize into vicious killers. And when the spell wore off—"

The cloud of images showed the fanged beauty biting into the neck of a hapless lad and sucking him dry of blood before it too, shattered.

"Oh, I can't watch this any longer," Nessa fretted, stubby fingers covering her eyes. Had it been long enough, the faun's tail would have hidden between her legs. "It puts me frightful, it does."

"Murias." The image Tulley conjured up now was filled with blue, the sea. Inside this blue, was another maid, this one with hair colored like tanned animal hide, and the tail of a fish where there should have been legs. "You see, Sorka, the second born sister, settled here amongst Murias and its sister islands."

The mermaid darted about in the water like a dolphin, a look of genuine joy on her face. Her shiny tail flicked her forward gracefully into the murky gloom of the ocean, and she disappeared into it, only to race forward again, chasing a school of tiny red fish. She plucked one from the group and popped it whole into her mouth. Her smile lit up the image, and the fire grew hotter.

"Sorka had no true evil in her heart at first," Tulley finally said. "She was very gullible and easily manipulated by her sisters, and simply fell into the plan to kill her mother. When she was cast out, she disappeared into the Talla Muro, the Tail of Murias, wanting nothing more than to live her life. Unfortunately, her weather-controlling powers, while modest in Siavon, are amplified from her watery home according to her mood. Sorka is a very, very angry creature."

The mermaid flicked her tail and was gone again. In the flames, the image melted into that of a shoreline brimming with fishermen. Sorka's head peeked above the surface of the water, her expression changed into that of pure fury. The flames grew hotter still, and Keavy actually had to slide back from it a little.

"Her empathetic mind can pick up on all of the heartache, all of the sinful wicked plans of man, and Sorka hates negativity. All she ever wanted was to fall in love." Tulley sighed wistfully, as if projecting the maid's own sorrows as she disappeared back into the deep. "She is quite a romantic soul. Sad about her, really."

"Sadder for the people of the Talla Muro." Nessa sighed back.

"Ah yes, you're right." The catman replied. "Because of Sorka's moodiness, the Tail realm has fallen into famine, as the weather conditions make the sea extremely dangerous for fishermen."

Keavy began to feel a bit impatient. The best part of the story was slow to come. "Let's hear of the oldest sister."

Tulley glared at her in warning, and threw a last handful of dust into the flames. The image of the sulking mermaid hissed and sputtered away, revealing underneath the worst image of all. A woman, or what was supposed to be one, for she was deformed, scrawny, and harboring the characteristics of a bird in the vilest ways.

"Sephora," Tulley said the name in the deepest heat of hatred. All over his body, his fur stood up, and the claws on his hands extended and contracted into his fists. "The name of her prickles my fur. The Empress of the Elements, she is the oldest, wisest, meanest, and ugliest of the sisters. It was her idea to kill Alesta, and her influence that drew her sisters to evil. Even now, as she rules the golden land of Bedivere, her sisters look to her for guidance. She has the power to harness the elements and use them through dragons and other great beasts. She wishes to take control of magic in hopes that she and her sisters will one day break the barrier between Aryth and Siavon and conquer. Fourteen years ago, she sent a dragon to Nodens to search for the ruby child."

The phoenix dragon morphed out from the ugly picture of the harpy and began stalking about Bedivere. Flames roared from its mouth straight at the vision's onlookers. Both Keavy and Nessa shivered.

Tulley was not finished, though the images had now rapidly started fading and the fire began to fizzle down to its original state. "However, once outside the barriers of Bedivere, Sephora's influence on the creature dwindled enough for it to regain its own will, and it began to mindlessly trash the villages, which angered Crocotta. She alerted Vorian of the whereabouts of the ruby child through a dream, and he set out to find it. This is how Vorian came by you, Keavy. You are the ruby child."

The image diminished completely in a cloud of smoke, and all was normal once more. Tulley coughed and waved the smoke away.

"Ever since I was young," Keavy said dreamily, for her mind was still venturing in the flames. "Vorian has been training me to one day fulfill my destiny. I must travel to the four Danaan realms and remove from the witches the amulet Garric gave them all at birth, the source of their powers."

"Well, at least you have a head start," Tulley added knowingly. "Crocotta lives on the edge of Nodens." He then lowered his voice to a mere grumble. "In a place called End of the Path."

"Sounds dreadful, it does!" Nessa whimpered.

"She is aware of your every move, Keavy," the catman was quick to say. "That is why you have not seen her yet. She knows you are in training, and let me tell you that she is eager for the day you are ready to face her. Listen well to yon sire, Keavy."

Keavy closed her eyes and bowed her head. "I shall."

***

Annick's silhouette was but a dark shadow against the orange and red sky. Keavy stepped out of the master's home and shaded her eyes against the final battle between the sun and moon. Behind her, the two smaller beings were shielding theirs. The air picked up a breeze and tossed it at the trio, tickling hair and fur into a delicate dance.

Annick's ears flickered in the direction of Keavy's sharp whistled note. He pulled his long head up from his graze, shook his head, and trotted obediently to her side.

A light tug on her pants leg distracted Keavy. Below her, Nessa was clasping her hands together and looking somewhat embarrassed. "Could you spare room for a humble faun? I don't likes walking home in the dark, I don't."

"Happily."

Keavy grasped her furry friend around the waist and hiked her onto the steed's back first before climbing on herself. Tulley gave the horse a firm pat on the front leg as high as he could reach, which was barely beyond the animal's knee. Annick lowered his nose to Tulley's eye level for the old creature to stroke him. The catman opened his strangely split feline lips to say goodbye and instead issued forth a series of gurgly coughs. Both Keavy and Nessa frowned down at him, but he was quick to regain himself and smile at them the way only catfolk could.

"Old age is quite a burden to bear," he said as-a-matter-of-factly, a curled claw against his heaving chest. "Conjuring up elapsed images does not come as easy to me as it once did."

The claw spanned the sky in a short arc above Tulley's head. At the end of his wavering finger, a point of blue white light hung in nothingness; a frozen drop of rain on a vast empty plain.

"Look at the sky," he bid them. "Siavon hails high above us, but it is sick with corruption." Below this bright, almost blinding pinpoint of light, a large golden moon was arising, an omen that Tulley read well.

"Alesta's Wheat Moon rises, and Crocotta's minions will be awakening soon. Best to return home beforehand." He stumbled as Annick nosed him a bit too roughly and caught himself before an embarrassing fall could occur. Tulley patted the tricorn again to appease him and then tentatively stepped back from the range of his horned snout. "Give my best to your father, Nessa. And Keavy?"

Keavy looked at him.

"Imprudence is the blight of adolescence."

Keavy inclined her head. Reins in hands, she gave her mount a kick and cantered him back down the path she traveled four days a week. Tulley waved at them, his orange fur floating around his face in the breeze. Even with her back turned to him, he knew she was glaring.

"Imprudence is the blight of adolescence." Keavy mocked the old master's grumbling voice once she was sure they were out of range of his sensitive ears. "Good riddance to that! I saved that man's life today. I may have saved a good deal more lives from that cockatrice, and I am chastised for it!"

Behind her, Nessa was clasping tightly to Keavy's clothing, trying not to allow Annick's bumping muscles to throw her. "He is just looking out for you, he is. He knows how capable you is."

"They treat me like a child, all of them," Keavy snorted. Her mood was gloomy, despite the perfume of the appeasing flowers in

43

the valley they now passed. "Well no more. Soon, I am going after Crocotta."

Nessa gasped. "Me stoles and minks, Keavy!" She scrambled for hold as Keavy pulled the horse to a stop for the passing of a rabbit across the road. "Don't joke like that! Words like those could send me into shivers, they could!"

The rabbit made a dash into the covering of the tall grass, and Keavy again nudged Annick forward. "I am not joking."

Nessa's little puff tail twitched. "You can't defeat Crocotta! Not by yon selfies, no!"

"Oh, but I can," Keavy said proudly. Her right hand slid from the reins to the sheathed sword hanging from her belt. "I have God's Breath."

Nessa trembled. "I don't like it. No, I don't like it at all."

They had reached the end of the road, which split into two. The right one led to the now sleeping streets of the East Village from where Keavy had come. The left led down a bumpier, rockier path to the forest that skirted the West. Annick automatically pulled his head toward town, for he knew his way home even without the encouragement of a human on his back. However, Keavy gave his reins a pull in an unfamiliar direction. Snorting in disagreement, the horse tentatively slowed his pace and began clopping down the rockier of the two.

"What are you doing, Keavy?" Nessa cried. "It's getting dark, it is!"

"We're safe with Annick."

"But we're not supposed to take the woodland path! Vorian said so!"

"Vorian says a lot of things."

Nessa's little mouth pursed shut. For she knew that there was no further arguing with Keavy once she had made up her mind. The faun pricked up her ears and listened intensely to the crickets and the owls, hoping that the telltale sound of silence in the woods would not signal the presence of a predator. These types of trees made her nervous at night, for they had rough black scales instead of bark and looked very much like dragons looming in the shadows.

It was only as the scaly trees began to reach their moss encrusted arms down at the riders, and the moon had finally won the battle for the night, that the talk began once more.

"We should have left earlier," Nessa's wee voice tremored.

"It is always like this when we leave Tulley's," said Keavy smoothly. "Why does the dark frighten you so?"

"The *dark* doesn't frighten me," the faun retorted, a bit insulted. "It's what lingers within."

Keavy scoffed with a little more patronization than she meant to convey. "Stop being such a timid little thing! There is nothing to be afraid of."

"Tell me papa that," Nessa said quietly, voice barely audible against the cricket symphony. The deer's ears upon her silky head were flickering in irritation.

Embarrassed by her own words, Keavy said no more on the subject. Gnal Mool, Nessa's father, had been nearly torn to pieces once by a predator of which he had still yet to remember the identity. The faun had been brutally scarred by the experience, both physically and mentally. It was rare that even an ally of the forest such as Keavy herself got a glance at him. She had only met him by mere accident during a hunting trip, when she had nearly run him through with an arrow thinking he was in fact a true deer. After the proper apologies, Gnal had introduced her to the Mool clan, and suggested that Nessa, who was the closest of his children in age to Keavy, join the ruby child in attending Tulley's lectures. The young wood faun and the human girl became fast friends after.

The scaly trees were now hugging the rocky path on which the tricorn and his riders traveled. The only light came forth from the speck of light that was the City of Souls winking at a great distance behind the Wheat Moon peeking up over the canopy of the forest. It was just light enough, however to bare the path ahead of them, but not enough for Keavy to see much past a tree or two into the forest. At the horse's feet, the brambles reached forward and threatened to snag and trip him, but the animal had an amazing sense of touch and was able to elude them even in the low visibility. Upon his back, Nessa's dark eyes glowed silver. She had excellent night vision, and to her, even the darkest part of the forest seemed like dawn. This did not save her from her apprehension. Predators were known for their excellent eyes too, and many a young wood faun had fallen victim to their own recklessness.

"Keavy," Nessa spoke up. "Stop. I hear something, I do."

Knowing better than to take Nessa's warnings for granted, Keavy grasped Annick's reins and pulled them tight against his muzzle.

"Halt, Annick."

The mount stopped immediately. Long horns dug impatiently at the dirt, and Annick grunted, obviously in a hurry to be off again. Nessa leapt down from his back as agilely as her four legged cousin, got down on her furry haunches, and froze. Her silver coated eyes gleamed in the moonlight. Her nostrils were flaring madly. With one hand on the ground and the other held to her chest, the faun stared straight into the forest without a movement save for her long rotating ears. It was a position of alertness.

Keavy climbed down from Annick's back and hunkered down next to Nessa, waiting. A minute passed, perhaps two, before she ultimately asked the faun what she was listening for.

Nessa's ears swung in Keavy's direction, but no other part of her flinched. "Something's not right," she said. "Listen."

Keavy listened intensely and heard nothing.

"I don't hear any—"

"*Listen!*" Nessa hissed.

Keavy sighed and strained her ears again, and again she heard nothing. Absolutely nothing. And that was when she became aware that cricket symphony had come to an abrupt end in the middle of an encore. Keavy could had kicked herself for not noticing it earlier. There was a disturbance in the woods, the only reason the crickets would have fallen silent. Something was out there. Keavy withdrew God's Breath and rose to her feet, eyes dancing back and forth between the trees, scanning a dark scene for even a hint of movement, but seeing nothing. It was up to Nessa to spot the trouble.

"What do you see, Ness?" Keavy whispered. She tried to keep the quiver from her voice and failed.

Nessa smelled the air. Her ears were ever turning as she slunk forward on four limbs, hands now becoming fists to better synchronize with her back hooves. Suddenly, her ears and tail stood straight up, and her head turned to the right. Her body froze once more.

"Fur against flora," a small voice quavered, "Mitt against loam." The wood faun rose to her hooves and backed up slowly, bunched muscles fighting the urge to flee from the scene. She found her comfort behind her human companion and clutched onto her calf with shaking hands. "Keavy, we are being stalked."

Keavy drew the sword into a fighting position and faced the direction of the sound she had not heard. "By what?"

"I-I don't know," stammered the fearful creature at her heel. "A beast of no smell. The noise has stopped, but it is close." She tugged at Keavy's pant leg. "We should run."

Keavy shook her head. "If we run, we'll only provoke it to chase."

Nessa opened her mouth to protest, and instead ushered a squeak of terror. A branch had snapped no more than ten or fifteen feet away from behind them. A second stalker had arrived completely undetected, even by Nessa. They were faced with a threat on either side. Annick let out a whinny and reared suddenly. Distracted, Keavy let the heavy sword fall and scrambled to grab the horse's reins to steady him. God's Breath hit the dirt with a clinking thud. The ruby in its hilt sparkled against the moonlight. And in front of them, the first beast roared.

It was an awful sound, grating and terrible, unlike anything they had ever heard before. Annick whinnied louder and backed away from Keavy's attempt to steady him. He reared again and took off galloping down the path, leaving his riders to themselves. Nessa clung, shrieking, to Keavy's leg, and although Keavy tried to shake her off, no amount of strength would have pried her fearful grip loose. Nessa's eyes bulged and shook, ears erect to their tallest. Keavy gave up on shaking her loose and dove for the sword lying in the dirt, very aware that she was putting herself in great danger by moving so quickly and possibly attracting more attention from whatever was behind them. But she had to feel the cold grip of the sword's hilt in her hands. She needed a weapon or they were surely easy prey.

More branches and bushes crackled in front of them as the roaring thing charged. Behind them, a rustle of brush as the second beast came forward. Regardless of her position, Keavy would be turning her back to a predator. So, reluctantly, she chose to face forward and readied her stance. She would take at least one of these things down with her if she could.

Another roar, closer, rattled the skulls in their heads. More broken foliage alerted them to its position. It was coming right for them, and Keavy could now make out a pair of red eyes upon a looming dark shape.

"Nessa, what is it?" she cried, but Nessa was frozen, and she did not answer. She would be no help now that fear had overcome her. Keavy was on her own. Hot rivers of sweat poured from her temples. The sword began to slip from her sweaty grasp. The world around her began to dwindle.

The beast ahead bellowed a third time, and then, there was an answering snarl behind them. The second creature did not sound the same. Its voice was familiar and domestic, more like that of a dog's.

Or a blachund's.

It appeared on the path first, though Keavy did not see it burst forth from the foliage because she could not take her eyes from the red globes now just at the edge of the woods. Its black shape charged forwards, a streak in the night. Right past the human it flew, startling her to the end of her consciousness.

Nessa snapped out of her trance and unlatched herself from the leg just in time to jump out of the way. Keavy went down heavy, God's Breath once more falling to the ground and bringing up a cloud of dust around it. It was Nessa who could later recall seeing the blachund lunge at the looming red eyed shape before them, foaming and snarling madly. The enormous beast growled angrily and, although she wasn't quite sure her mind hadn't been tricking her, Nessa heard a faint hiss of humanity within the creature's monstrous voice. A garbled hiss that sounded very much like a real word.

Child.

***

Keavy awoke in the jaws of the shadowy beast. Its hot drool slathered over her entire body. She could feel the heat from its monstrous belly and the stink of its earthy breath as it swallowed her whole. Screaming, she bolted upright and smacked her head on something cool and hard. The dimly lit world around her clouded, and before she knew it she was on her back again, fighting for her consciousness. She could not pass out a second time, not before she tore a bleeding hole in the monster's hateful gut.

Something clawed at her arm and she swung at it, knocking whatever it was free. From somewhere to her left, a heavy thud was followed by a squeal and the noise of scampering hooves. There were high pitched cries to her right, followed by more scuttling, and then a splash of freezing water gushed into her face. If the fauns had not held her down the second time, Keavy would have bolted upright and hit her head on the roof of the burrow again.

"Hush, youngling," a gentle voice called to her in the dimness. "You are safe."

Keavy tried to sit up again, but a barrage of tiny hands prevented her from doing so. She fought the urge to thrash again.

"Where am I?" Her own voice sounded garbled and unfamiliar to her, clotted and hoarse.

"Don't try to move. You're under ground, in shelter," the voice continued. "It was a little bit of a tight squeeze, but we managed to get you inside and out of the dark. I am afraid this is the largest space we had for you."

Keavy at last recognized the voice as that of Senga, Nessa's mother and the resident healer of the Mool clan. She was practiced in many sorts of remedial cures, and Keavy knew her well from her bumps and bruises days of youth.

It was now that Keavy realized the beast that had her in its jaws was actually the faun clan trying to revive her, and the saliva dripping from her body was actually her own sweat. Keavy moaned in realization.

"Nessa? Where is she?"

"I'm here, Keavy," Nessa reassured her in the darkness. A small hand grasped her own. "You belted me a good one, you did. Thought I'd spatter like a lizard on the rocks!"

"Forgive me, little friend."

"Me body will live another day," Nessa said with a titter, patting Keavy's shaking hand to stillness. "It's you we worried about. You suffered quite a sock on the top, you did!"

"What happened?"

Nessa recounted the events proceeding Keavy's fainting spell as if it were ancient history. It was a useful trick of the faun to be able to get over trauma quickly. Useful, considering how easily spooked the species was as a whole.

"The blachund was sudsing at the jaws," Nessa told her. "Me thinks it was mad, me does. No sane animal would attack such a monstrous thing! Luck be ours when the two beasts chased each other into the woods and forgot us. I went for help after, and me brothers pulled you down here, they did."

Down here. Once the initial panic of awakening in a strange place had subsided, and the shock of her attack dulled, an entirely new fear awoke deep in Keavy's gut. She was under the ground, deep in a faun burrow that was barely wide enough for the fauns to walk around her, and not high enough for her to even sit up. A crawl at best would be all Keavy could accomplish in such a tight spot. But even to crawl back up the burrow would be a task in itself. The fauns had dragged her inside headfirst, and turning around would be impossible. Keavy was essentially pinned headfirst in an underground trap, and the confinement sent her into a panic.

"I have to get out," she breathed labouredly "Now!"

Tiny hands of at least half a dozen fauns found their way to her arms, legs, and shoulders. Nessa continued to hold her hand and squeezed it gently while Senga stood at Keavy's head and stroked her hair.

"Get me *out*!" Keavy cried. She ripped out of her friend's grasp and began clawing at the ceiling, knocking dirt loose down onto her own face, which sent her coughing. "I can't *breathe*!"

Senga continued to calmly pet her. "Keavy, you must be still, dear one."

Keavy's increasingly ragged breathing alerted the fauns. They began letting go of her and scooting out of the way of her dangerous thrashing limbs. But Senga bent down to whisper to her. "Struggle, and you will frighten yourself to death," she told her. "Find your calm and I will help you turn around."

"Breathe in, Keavy," came Nessa's voice in the dully lit burrow.

Keavy turned her head to the voice and matched it with a pair of silver eyes. Beside Nessa, a smaller faun, Innes, lit up an oil lamp and filled the earthy room with warm light. Around her, the fauns began blinking their night adjusted eyes and twitching their noses like a colony of rabbits. Keavy felt a little better with the added light and mustered up enough strength to roll onto her belly and crouch on her hands and knees. Her back pressed against the cold dirt roof, and a swell of panic nearly overcame her again, but now she could see Senga in front of her, smiling warmly. She was a dainty creature, with ashy hair falling around her round little face. Dark almond eyes shone with wisdom. Around her, Nessa's two sisters and three brothers crouched with curious expressions and comically erect ears. One of them, Nessa's older brother, Masiko, who had just begun budding his horns, was holding a clay jug which had previously contained the water now soaking Keavy's clothes. Nessa stood off to the side, crouched on her haunches. Their eyes met and she smiled.

"Are you calm, Keavy?" Senga asked, not a touch of irritation present in her tone at all, despite all the commotion the invading human had caused.

Keavy felt her cheeks flush despite herself. She nodded and sniffled against the cloud of dirt in the air. "Yes."

"Good. Now, begin backing up," The healer instructed. "Do not rush. You are not far from the surface."

Keavy did as she was told with no more interference, and in a matter of minutes, she felt a cool blast of night strike her on the behind, and relief set in. She rose up out of the burrow and immediately stood, a bad move. Her head was still reeling and her muscles were sore from being cramped up inside the burrow. She would have suffered another fall had not a familiar nudge in the small of her back stopped it. It was Annick. He had followed her scent and waited for her outside the burrow. Instead of scolding him for fleeing in the first place, Keavy instead hugged his large long head tightly, being careful to avoid his horns. He accepted it without complaint, almost as if he felt guilty for running away and abandoning her.

From the glowing light inside the meager hole in the ground which marked the entrance of the clan's home, Senga and Nessa appeared, looking very much like large two-legged rabbits in the dark. Between them, they gripped the hilt of God's Breath and held it out to her. Keavy took it with a deep bow, wondering briefly where they had been hiding it as she carefully replaced it at her side. Its weight was wonderfully comforting.

"Thanks to you for your help," she said severely. The cut in her ego was bleeding and visible now. "I must go now. Vorian will worry."

Her own words brought realization, and a fresh chill haggled her wet body, along with a new breed of panic. She swallowed hard enough for the fauns to hear it. Nessa smirked at her, tail fluttering. Before Keavy could glower, her mother did the job for her. The adult faun's ears curved back in a manner that read *I will deal with you later* in vivid apparentness. Nessa's tail drooped, and the smirk shattered. She nodded her head solemnly.

"Goodbye, Keavy. See you at lessons."

Keavy nodded her return. "Thank you, Senga."

"Pleasure, youngling," Senga answered with an elegant bow. "Ride safe."

It was only after she left the company of the fauns and mounted Annick, that Keavy realized just how late it was getting. A series of piercing yips chilled the night air, but there was nothing to fear. Though it was blachunds for sure, they were counts away and probably on a kill. By the height of the moon in the sky, and Siavon's light at its brightest, it had to be closing in on midnight, and this was their time to roam. Even so, the scare she had suffered refused to be taken lightly in her mind, and she kicked the sides of her steed and galloped him the rest of the way home, worried more so about meeting Vorian's disappointed gaze than the jaws of any dark fiend.

She was not far from home. Once she had ridden over a small hill, the clearing became visible, as well as the house that occupied it. Deep in the forest, away from the hustle of the town, Vorian had built a bungalow from scratch out of smoothed over river stones and the strange plated bark of scaly trees. As a result, it looked like a green and gray lump with a roof of dark thatch reeds. It would be considered ugly to anyone who didn't live there. A stone chimney billowed strong smelling smoke during the cold days, but now it was sleeping. Inside the two front windows, a pleasant yellow light would have welcomed her home had she arrived earlier. All Keavy saw tonight were two dark eyeless sockets as she rode over the small hill and followed the pebble paved path.

Leading away from the path nearby to the bungalow, there was a smaller edifice made of plain wood that had at one point been painted white; it was now faded, splintered, and overgrown with ivy. It was the barn in which Annick lived, and Keavy did not waste time in leading him inside and removing his reins. He blew with relief and took no coaxing to go into his stable. The horse bobbed his head and turned around to nuzzle Keavy's hand as if to say *Good luck tonight.* Keavy stroked one long deadly horn and planted a kiss on the side of his soft muzzle. Then, once her mount had been settled, Keavy left the barn to finally enter the home where her almost surely cross sire would be waiting

The place was fast asleep when Keavy crept inside. There was no oil lamps lit to guide her, so she had to pick her way across the room to avoid making noise. On the hollow floor, her leather boots seemed to clomp like ox hooves.

Had there been light, Keavy would've been looking in on the small common room. Its polished stone walls were decorated here and there with hanging pottery and bits of dried flowers. Draped over the handcrafted rocking chair by the fireplace was a bundle of fox skins under which a young Keavy had once dozed warm and safe after a day of play. A shaky end table sat in front of a bench draped in red wool. On it, a clay cup sat still partially filled with Vorian's musket tea, cold and tasteless by now.

Keavy could only make out the outline of these objects in the dark, but it was not the rocking chair or the fox skins she was looking for anyway. Above the fireplace, was an iron rack made for a sword, a rack which now stood empty. Keavy reluctantly removed the magnificent God's Breath from her belt and replaced it as gently as a mother with her child. There would be no denying her theft of the sword in the morn, but Keavy would own up to her mistake and accept her punishment when it came to it. Right now, she wanted nothing more than to go to her room and change out of her wet clothes. Her room was newer and had a less settled feel to it. Vorian had built it onto the bungalow for her when she was old enough to leave the crib. It housed not much more than her cot, mirror, and chest of clothes, but it was hers, and she did not feel entirely safe until she had entered it.

As soon as a single foot stepped inside, a whooshing sound heralded a blue spark and a sudden dull light rendered the contents of the room visible. There was Vorian, sitting on the edge of the cot, an oil lamp in his right hand, but no match in his left. He had created the flame from a mere thought.

She was not at all surprised that Vorian was awake and waiting for her. Regardless of the rising apprehension in her stomach, Keavy was very glad to see him. Nevertheless, she gasped in alarm.

Vorian stood. He placed the lamp down at the cot's foot. A tall man, Vorian's aura was ethereal and shimmering with the wisdom of his years. His gray swathes seemed to be growing on his body rather than concealing it, for they flowed perfectly cued with his movements like blood through veins. The long black hair that fell well beyond his shoulders was tied back at the present moment, save for a few stray strands, some of which were silver. Cerulean eyes, lined and sundamaged, became filled with the concern of a father. Over the years, Vorian Tranore had aged very little, but his true life's span shone through like dying stars in his pale eyes. And at the moment, he looked at Keavy with every year of his life doubled.

Keavy took an instinctive step backwards, mouth unwillingly falling open. "Vorian," she began fearfully. "I can explain."

"Are you injured?" Vorian asked firmly.

Keavy's flesh burned. She shook her head rapidly. Once again, hot tears began to fill her vision and, at last, she tore gaze away from his and looked at the floor, blinking as fast as she could to hide them.

"Come here, please."

Keavy stepped forward, her chest hitching, and her heart breaking with every remorseful beat. Vorian placed a large hand on her shoulder. The blood inside it warmed Keavy's wet and wretchedly cold skin.

"God's Breath is the sword of Idris Rotonzael." His intonation, ripe with poise, spoke deeper than his words. "Its origin is unknown, but it is thought that Idris obtained the sword from Garric himself. Its power is inconceivable to the greatest of swordsmen, even to me. Harnessed improperly, God's Breath can unleash a torrent of suffering upon the user, even death. You were fortunate today, but further misuse of this sword can and will cost you not only your own life, but the lives of those you wish to protect.

You cannot allow yourself to fall to temptation like this again. Am I understood?"

Keavy nodded, unable to say a word. The tears finally began to drop from her eyes, and it was all she could do not to begin sobbing audibly.

"You must not take unwarranted risks for the sake of pride," Vorian warned darkly. "I took it upon myself to raise you safely to adulthood so you may meet your destiny. You are the chosen one, Keavy. You must think before you allow youthful impetuousness to put you in harm's way." He lifted his hand from her shoulder and brought her chin up so he could penetrate her eyes with his own. "I will not lose you to Crocotta's scabby slavering mongrels."

"Yes, my sire."

Vorian picked up the lamp at the foot of her cot. "You are not ready for Crocotta, young one," he said. "As strong and willing as you are, it is not yet your time." He turned suddenly, and Keavy started. "However, I can tell by your daring actions in the course of this day that you are ready to heighten your training."

"Do you mean it, Vorian?" Keavy wondered aloud, lighting up despite her attempt to stay meek. "Soon?"

"Tomorrow," Vorian said, and a crack of a smile broke in the corner of his mouth. "For now, sleep well. You will need your energy."

And with that, Vorian's shape disappeared from the doorframe.

***

As Keavy undressed herself from her wet clothes and slipped into a crisp white nightgown, safe within her sire's bungalow, one particular being on the other side of the forest was at unrest. There was a place where the storm clouds took refuge and hung angrily even on the brightest of summer days. The land was not flat but lay burdened with trip holes in which one could break an ankle, and was not carpeted in grass but with sharp gray stone that would cut any woodland animal's padded feet that dared to walk over it. No trees grew here, just a light spattering of snake shrubs with their black sticky tendrils leeching out across the ground eagerly awaiting the landing of an unsuspecting bird. It was a place at the conclusion of the forest known as End of the Path. It was also where the Empress of the Wilderness resided.

Crocotta was pent up deep inside a sulfur-stinking cave carved into the world like an old pock mark, alone but for a strange creature crouching in the corner. With beady eyes too small for his head, the creature watched Crocotta, roaring, her monstrous claws ripping down moss covered shelf upon shelf of priceless spell books and artifacts seethed in her bestial form like a rabid madness had overcome her. She swung her massive head at the sound the cowering creature released, a sound similar to that made by a rattler's shivering tail. Yellow drool flew in huge gooey clots from her jowls and hit the walls with a sickening *shlop*! She rose to her haunches and roared hideously. The thing in the corner rattled again, and then produced a meek garbled whine, black eyes batting fearfully, bushy tail held low.

Crocotta's snarls subsided, and she began her horrifying morph back to her human form, chuckling softly through the crackling and sucking sounds coming from her changing vocal chords. The shadow of this nightmare danced on the wall behind a pit flame.

"Ratah, Rut."

The beast's thick neck craned upward at the call of his now human mistress, and without reluctance, he rose to all fours and obediently came to her. Now that she was human, he was quite large in comparison to her, around the size of a pony, his unsightly face almost eye level with her now quite lovely one.

"Forgive me, my darling," Crocotta purred, a long fingered white hand reaching out to stroke the wooly muzzle of the thing she called Rut.

His neck craned out even further to receive her affection and he rattled again, the sound made when he shook the two hard pairs of pincers similar to an insect's mandibles anchored to each side of his jaw.

"I am incensed at this sudden turn of events," Crocotta told him, and touched the silver amulet between her breasts. "But I shall slaughter that worthless cur in time. For now, a new plan has hatched within me, a plan that will not fail." She took Rut's heavy head in her hands and sunk her fingernails into his flesh as she gazed at him. "That is, if you recall your training, my darling."

Rut's jaw opened to reveal a two sets of menacingly huge fangs. A fleshy tongue lashed out and lapped at her collarbone. With a gust of stinking air, Rut rattled again and moaned woefully.

Crocotta smiled a wicked smile. "You know what to do." She stroked the beast under the chin, then with frightful suddenness, pulled back and swatted him with a hand which had turned back into a hideous black claw. A roar of pain, and Rut spun round and ran for the cave's opening, his bushy brown tail swaying.

"Go!" Crocotta screamed after him, a manic laugh swelling in her throat. The claw covered in Rut's blood lifted above her head in triumph. "Do what you were made to do!"

Rut burst from the cave opening and landed on the stony ground. Two large curved talons on each foot scraped at the steep jagged rocks for purchase, hurtling the animal with great speed across the perilous landscape without damaging him. Upon his furry muzzle, the deep gouge from his mistress's claws had already nearly healed. He clacked and rattled as he loped over the rocky terrain that was End of the Path, focused on completing the only task he had been trained to do.

Crocotta's merciless laughter followed him into the forest.

A Storm is Coming

"But you said my training would begin today!"

The wooden sword was held slackly in Keavy's arms, for she wanted to feel it no more than a rope of dead pig intestines.

Vorian stood opposite her, holding his own wooden sword. On his expression he held a patient countenance learned over the course of fourteen years. "It will. I do not break my promises."

"Then why must I practice with the wooden sword?" Keavy demanded. Last night had already become a dull memory pushed aside by a youth's excitement. "Yesterday, I held God's Breath itself!"

Vorian smiled faintly. "And nearly impaled yourself in a faint."

Keavy's pretty face wrinkled into a frown and grew hot. She held the wooden play sword by the hilt and examined the splinters in the makeshift blade until the feeling subsided. "What about the cockatrice?" she asked her sire glumly.

He responded with a short sensible laugh. It was the laugh of a father. "Despite your luck, dearest, you are not yet ready to deal with the sword of Idris."

Keavy watched as Vorian twirled his own hand crafted wooden sword slowly with his two fists on the hilt. In the midday sun, his muscular arms glistened with workman's sweat. When shirtless, Vorian's hardened life became unmistakable. His bronzed body was weathered and stained with the scars of many battles, but the worst of these had been obtained on the day he had taken the child with the ruby eyes in as his own. His right shoulder came decorated with pink patchwork matching the jaw line of a blachund.

"I never said that you would train with God's Breath today," he shrewdly reminded her. The wooden sword spun ever faster in his grip. It was now going so quickly that a *whooping* sound was issuing from it, and a transparent brown circle appeared in its twirling path. "God's Breath is not meant for the novice."

"Novice? I have used swords since I was twelve! Bow and arrow since I was nine! I am well educated in the craft of battle!"

Long black hair danced as he nodded his agreement, the spinning sword a mere blur now. "Yes, and practice, as they say, makes perfect. But you haven't been practicing, and that is my own folly. I did not expect to begin hard training for you for another year."

Vorian flipped the twirling sword into the air and watched as it remained suspended above their heads for just a moment before plummeting back to land. He raised a hand to catch it, but Keavy's was faster. She snatched the sword right out of the air and rested the shaking timber blade on her shoulder. Her own, she balanced on the tip of her middle finger, and a cheeky smile graced her face.

Vorian reached out a commanding, but tender hand, back to which Keavy tossed his training weapon. Once he had it back, the man thought by the people of Nodens to be a half crazed idiot for living in the deepest part of the woods changed his stance and readied his blade for battle.

"*Soha!*"

Keavy instantly took his cue, and together they laid their wooden blades together and fought as if death would be the punishment for losing. For another hour, they practiced until at last Vorian smacked the sword from Keavy's sweating hands and held the tip of the blade to her throat, signaling the end of the fight. Keavy's yellow shirt was damp at the neckline and armpits, and she was panting too heavily to care that she had been beaten by her sire yet again.

Vorian lowered the blade and dropped it at the ruby child's feet. He had barely begun to flush. "Your grip is too tight. Your hand must guide the blade while not melding to the hilt."

Keavy bent to pick up Vorian's sword, and found that sitting down on the ground was a much more logical choice. Head braced between knees, she groaned in exasperation.

Vorian nodded and gave her a little smile. "Perhaps it's time we stopped for the day. Go finish your chores. Afterwards, you may do as you please."

"Many thanks." Keavy moaned without raising her woozy head.

"Just one will do." Vorian ruffled her hair as he passed her, and finally she looked up to see him walking back to the bungalow.

An impatient neigh brought Keavy to her feet. Annick needed tending to, and he would demand it loudly until he was.

From one of the only two windows in the bungalow, Vorian watched the ruby child saunter into the barn. Despite the shape he was in, every muscle on his body ached restlessly, particularly his right shoulder. It hadn't been the same since the blachund had bitten him all those years ago. He unconsciously rubbed it now as his worries cast a shadow on his mind. Although he no longer remembered his exact birthday (he was sure it was sometime in winter), Vorian knew that he was not getting any younger. He would have to increase the youngling's training if he hoped to have her ready for her journey before he was too old to teach her. A series of premonitions within his dreams had told Vorian in the recent months that the time to release her to her own care was soon to come. He could only hope that the gods would allow him just a little more time to train his youngling for her only destiny.

Keavy spent much of the morning's remainder cleaning out the barn while the playful tricorn watched, blowing and pawing at the latch of his stall, hankering for a romp. She looked up at him and rolled her eyes. The tricorn copied her, rolling his and nodding his head. He blew through his nose and grumbled his impatience.

"If you wouldn't drop so much dung, you'd be out running right now," Keavy told the impatient steed.

In response, Annick whinnied and flicked his large ears. Keavy put down her shovel and went to him, running her hands along the length of curly mane on his neck and patting the end of his horny snout.

"Thanks for coming back," the girl whispered into one of the long velvet ears. She laid her head against his neck and breathed in his scent, that of hay and sweat and hidden wildness, and home. She became so absorbed she almost fell over when he lifted his head suddenly and raised his ears in the direction of a sound he had heard but she had missed.

Last night's fears that lay silent all morning came leaping back into her like a cat upon a mouse. With lurid reflexes, she bent and withdrew a serrated hunting knife from the inner left leg of her pants and spun with it, ready to impale a manic blachund or, worse, that horrendous thing that had charged her in the forest. Instead of connecting with flesh, her knife hand was seized at the wrist and stopped in mid-stab. Keavy's other hand came up and immediately found itself in the same position. She was pushed backwards against the stall door, and completely vulnerable to her attacker.

"Whoa there, easy!" Keavy's assailant voiced in alarm. He held her steady against the splintery barn wall. Annick swung his deadly head at the threat, and the intruder let go of Keavy's wrists and jumped back just in time to avoid being impaled by one of the horse's long horns.

The girl stepped forward, knife raised and ready. She got a good look at her attacker and frowned. With arms passively raised, he stepped back into a ray of sunlight invading through the barn ceiling. A sly grin sliced the edges of his mouth wide open while his youthful green eyes twinkled in the sun's glimmer. Around his sharply cut face, baby strands of sun-kissed blonde hair floated freely, while a thick bunch of it hung down the back of his long neck, imprisoned in a leather tie. He was dressed in a white button shirt and gray dress pants cinched tight with a black belt. Over his shoulders he wore a brown wool cloak made with the care only a mother could provide. Though a thin cover of fuzz sprouting upon his cheeks signaled his advancement into manhood, manhood had not yet fully shown itself in this handsome lad. Keavy knew this fact better than anyone.

Keavy found herself burning at the cheeks as the boy broke into a donkey's braying laughter. She sucked in her lip and pushed him as hard as she could out of shear childish resentment. "I could have killed you!"

"On edge today, oh supreme *hrotage*?" the lad muttered through his jarring giggles. The slightest touch of trepidation peppered the cords of an adolescent who mostly spoke with daggers of sarcasm imbedded in each word.

Keavy bent and put her knife back into its leather holder under her pants on her right inner calf. She was not at all amused by her visitor's jeering teases, despite the fear she noted in his voice and his flushed cheeks.

"Don't call me that. I'm no hero."

"That's not what the town is saying," he sang playfully, then swept a finger into the air and appeared to erase his own words with it. "Correction, that *is* what the town is saying to each *other*, that you're no hero, that what you did was simply fool's luck. After all, whose lives did you save but those of a few stinking wateroggs and a fat waster?"

He issued another cruel bray of laughter at which Keavy almost flinched. She took Annick's head in her arms to calm him. His eyes were marbles rolling about in their sockets and he blew continuously through his nose until she assured him, still a bit doubtful of this trespasser in the barn.

"*Actually*," the lad continued, seeming to enjoy the sound of his own voice. "Most would say that your meddling did more harm than good, but alone, in their homes, as they gather 'round yonder dinner table, they are looking at their shy harmless daughters and secretly wishing they had raised a plucky young creature such as you."

Keavy gave Annick a last pat and picked up her shovel, sighing "What do you want, Alder?"

Alder sauntered to her and took her wrist again, in a far gentler manner this time. With his free hand, he removed the shovel from her grip and let it fall to her feet, a gesture that seemed much more intimidating to Keavy than his surprise attack. Keavy turned to him, and for an uncomfortable moment, the two stared into each other's eyes.

Keavy both hated and admired Alder Devnet, the son of Nodens' only blacksmith, Glynn Devnet. The Devnets were renowned for their talents for making weapons, which had run down their bloodline for five generations. Alder, of course, would be the sixth to pass on the blacksmith trade if he indeed found a woman crazy enough to give him a son. He was more than happy to do it, and quite arrogant about it as well. At only seventeen, Alder had already gained a craftsman's hand and an eagle's eye for detail about which his father (and he) boasted any chance he could. The Devnets had provided Vorian and Keavy with all of their weapons, excluding God's Breath. In fact, the hunting knife which had nearly killed Alder had been crafted from his own hand and sold to Vorian. Keavy had received it as a gift from her sire for her fourteenth birthday not six weeks before.

Keavy was fiercely jealous of Alder for many reasons, the main of these being his gender. Being male entitled him to a level of respect she feared she would never reach, even if she slaughtered every monster in the forest. For another, he was stronger in both body and spirit. Had it been Alder on the path last night, he probably would have dispatched both the blachund and the large beast with a cool hand and a sarcastic comment and gone home to brag about it in stride. Keavy wouldn't have been surprised at all.

"I have chores to do," she muttered, these envious feelings running their course, allowing her to break the uncomfortable eye contact. "State your business and be off."

Alder nodded his understanding and backed away. "The first presentation of Barra's Wonders is tonight," he said readily. "I came to suggest the pair of us take it in." His frown turned into another of his heckling smiles that Keavy so despised. "That is, if yonder monarch hasn't forbade his only subject from cavorting with the common herd."

At this, Keavy scoffed crossly and again picked up the shovel, hoping that the motion would give Alder the hint to be off. "This *subject* can do as she pleases, thank you."

Alder, however, didn't back off this time. He leered scathingly and jabbed her rare crimson eyes with his plain green ones. "And what exactly does she please?"

Keavy leaned upon the handle of her shovel and sighed, and unable to deny her unruly pride, she bit down upon the bait Alder dangled before her.

***

Pishnee Ralo spent every waking moment of his life regretting his past mistakes. It was his wily teenage years as a street thief (and a slow one) that had landed him in this hell hole the establishment had called "forced employment" in the first place. One wrong veer into a dead end had turned his serene days of free living into an everyday struggle to keep his sanity. Pishnee spent his daylight hours driving a beaten up wagon and a pair of mangy donkeys down long dirt roads, usually following along behind the larger more impressive carriages which carried exotic beasts who occasionally found it entertaining to piss on him through their steel cage bars. His own load was a splintered old coop housing an oversized rooster with a spoiled set of manners.

During Pishnee's evening hours, when he wasn't helping to pitch tents and arrange props, he was mucking cages and feeding the miserable monsters Barra called his wonders. Tonight was their first night in Nodens, the first of seven performances. In a week it would be time to pack up and move on to the next peasant town to make even less money. Pishnee found it a waste of his life to be trundling along with the insolvent circus which could barely pull in a skia, when he could make a sweet skopa pinching from vegetable kiosks alone. Alas, it was his only redemption, and Pishnee meant to carry on the rest of his term without protest. The more he complained, he found, the further his sentence reached.

So, clutching a feed bucket, and hobbling on a badly lacerated leg (which he had sewn himself and bandaged), Pishnee entered the animal tent and lit up a lantern. The cages came into view, lined up in neat rows, most of their inhabitants resting up for tonight's big show. Barra had many wonders indeed, all wild creatures his wanton crew had trapped themselves, risking limb and life for the collector's spectacle. There were a dozen varied creatures to grace Barra's stage so far, but he had told his crew that he wanted to own a collection exceeding one hundred. He planned to change the name of his circus to Barra's Horrid Hundred, and turn it into a blood bath, pitting creatures against each other for the amusement of the crowd. Pishnee thought it absurd, but a part of him longed for that far off day, when he could proudly boast that he had helped capture each and every ferocious brute Barra had desired. It was sure to get him girls, if not skopa.

His first stop was Whipsaw, his own cart's impatient passenger and the reason he was limping. The cockatrice that had yesterday ransacked the market was at the present moment, snoozing with his ugly head tucked under one leathery wing and his giant talons hidden beneath his feathery body. The green scaly tail was coiled around him and twitching with each of the bird's croaky snores. Pishnee reached his hand through the bars slowly and removed the food dish, dipped it into the bucket of moldy grain, and replaced it without the animal stirring once. He had learned quickly from this one after being assigned as its personal chauffer.

Next, was the unicorn, whose stilted pen had been sealed with a containment spell to keep her from wishing her way out, not that she even tried to escape anymore. She was a gaunt old thing, her silky coat once of snow white had now fallen an ashy gray and was missing in patches along her flanks and neck. The unicorn's magnificent spiraled horn had cracked and weakened to the point that it quivered upon her head and threatened to fall off at any moment, another reason the containment spell had become a waste. Unicorns could not perform any kind of magic without their fabled horns. Pishnee looked forward to the death of the old thing, so he wouldn't have to smell her. The mare was riddled with parasites and mange which caused a riot inside his guts every time he inhaled too closely to her. For the unicorn, he also provided a dish of moldy seed along with a sprig of mint for her rotten breath. The mare didn't even flare a nostril at the meal, but lay with her scabby knees tucked under her body and watched her keeper move on to the next waning prisoner's cage.

Pishnee finished seeding the dishes of his first six responsibilities and left the tent for but a moment to fetch the gut bucket for the real entertainment. The carnivores were the only aspects of the show Barra spent his hard earned (and closely guarded) money on. The circus kept on hand a sty of fat pigs to provide fresh entrails for them every day. Pishnee was lucky he didn't have to slaughter them himself, for he paled at the idea. That was the cook Detani's job. He just had the leisurely duty of feeding Barra's precious monsters, which was not always a safe task. The beast keeper had scars to prove it. His cockatrice wound would just be one more color on the palate as soon as it healed.

Resting on top of a bale of hay in the center of the room, a box small enough for a child to carry sat. It was quite impressive despite its compactness, because it was made of extremely strong steel that not even fire could melt through, and was solid save for the tiniest of air holes scattered across its top. Barra had spent quite a skopa on reinforcing the locks and structure of this one, for within it was the volk. Pishnee made sure he cleared his throat loudly and stomped as he walked to assure that the volk was aware of his coming. To surprise a volk meant dire consequences, perhaps death, depending on what form it decided to take on. Pishnee stopped at the quiet buzzing sound coming from the metal box. Yes, it was awake. It was safe to proceed. With a shaking hand, Pishnee unlatched and lifted the lid of the volk's cage and peered inside.

It was no bigger than a mouse, and in fact, had decided to take on the form of one. This mouse, however, had the wings of a fly, the tail of a scorpion, and was green. A new one, Pishnee noted. The volk was always surprising him with new forms and powers. All the more reason to throw in a chunk of meat and close the lid before it decided to play a trick on him. Though it had been collared and chained to the floor of the box, the volk had enough slack to leap out and sting whoever it so pleased. Pishnee had not been the first to care for Barra's wonders.

Making sure the volk's latch was securely fastened; Pishnee picked up his gut bucket and approached the barred and wired confines of the two cyclops. They too, were in a smaller cage, though not as small as the volk's. The twins had enough room to stand without hitting their heads, but they could not build up enough running speed to bash through their bars. Although only toddlers, Min and Hog were exceptionally strong, and for this reason, their legs had been shackled together, and Min's right wrist had been chained to Hog's left. With soft ginger skin and a single big brown eye in the middle of their foreheads, Min and Hog were almost cute. That is, until they tucked into their bloody meals. Pishnee hurried past them, shuddering at the squibbling of sibling rivalry behind him.

The next cage was quite tall, reaching to the ceiling, also made of fire-proof steel. Siavon should fall if the creature inside accidentally cut himself and melted clean through his enclosure with his nasty acidic blood. He was sitting up on the highest of his metal branches, glaring down at Pishnee as the beast keeper loaded a slop of guts into his bowl. In a flash, it was upon the meal. Pishnee wrenched his hand out through the bars just before he would lose it and cursed his surprise. He watched the creature gobble the guts and scramble back up onto his branch in under a minute and wondered again how Barra had managed to capture this speedy little scoundrel. The bogle, long limbed and limber, resembled a skinny plum colored monkey. It had long tasseled ears which stood high upon an arrow shaped head, a wrinkled yellow face with a flat nose, a mouth full of needle sharp teeth, and gold eyes that squinted in a permanent expression of loathing. And bogles were known for their adaptability as well as their speed. A colony of them could make a happy home underground or in the trees, sometimes even in one's very home without one ever knowing. They were rarely seen by people and, usually, people liked it that way. The destructive and foul smelling bogles had about as much respect as the household cockroach.

The gryphoness was next, her containment system as oddly mixed as her own biology. The part bird, part cat atrocity lived in a stable lined with soft hay, but outlined with barbed chicken wire that covered every open space excluding the animal's direct living area. If the gryphoness decided to try and fly out of her enclosure, she would be ripped to ribbons. Parts of her large tawny wings were in fact scarred and knarled from previous such attempts, and she was all but missing her left eye. As Pishnee approached her pen, the gryphoness jumped to her feet, flared her enormous wings, lashed her tail, and let out a fearful cry that made him picture a lion growling with its mouth full of squawking eagle, a sound he called a squowl. Even so, Pishnee didn't even flinch as he flung a fistful of bloody entrails over the wires and watched the gryphoness snatch and gulp it down in a single bite. She squowled at him again as he passed her enclosure to make his final stop in front of the newest edition to Barra's Wonders.

***

Pollen wafted up from under Tulley's shoeless feet as he charged out into the garden, coughing and wrinkling his small pink nose in preparation for a sneeze that just wouldn't come. For hours now, the old catman had seen nothing but signs of a storm brewing over the horizon. Fat dirty clouds hovered ominously overhead, graying up the sky and casting a perfectly shaped rainbow from one end of the land to the other, forming a rather picturesque frame around the distant hills and forests that that he could see in the backdrop of his own happy home. The wind hissed in warning, a sign of the upcoming thunderstorm that he was now trying desperately to beat. A single large drop of cold rain surprised him when it plunked down hard onto his orange head. The rings in his ear tinkled together as he shuddered, accenting his dreadful feeling. He prayed he'd be able to gather together all of his ingredients from the garden before the sky got angry. There were certain things about thunderstorms that Tulley didn't like. He wasn't quite so bothered by the feeling of being wet, as one might expect of his species, but the sound of thunder did bring out a few old memories he wished to pack away. Some time ago, the outdoors was beyond doubt Tulley's true love. Nowadays, however, the old catman had been puttering away his life in his stuffy hut reading and remedying, and the most time he'd spent outdoors in the past decade was the few hours it took him each week to tend to his garden and go into town for supplies. He was truly a housecat.

A cut of lightning broke through the sky directly above the distant hills, and Tulley braced himself for the thunder that would follow, but flinched anyway when it came seconds later, that sound like the crack of a whip tearing across the atmosphere not something he liked hearing. Tulley extended his front claws and dug into his garden with the speed of a gopher. His efforts at thwarting away the storm with prayer proved faulty, because immediately after their large predecessors, a sea of drops fell from the sky and paddled the ground fiercely. Tulley groaned in disgust, for his fur and clothing had gotten instantly soaked and begun to stick to his skin and weigh him down. He thought of fighting it, but decided now was as good a time as any to forget his dignity and crouch down to all fours to shake out his coat. After he had done so, he heaved himself to his feet and peered through his glasses to see the horizon though the rain.

There it emerged, as in the prophecy; a rise of dark clouds began to take on a life of their own as they emerged in the atmosphere. Tulley shut his bad left eye to give his right one the upper hand, and that's when he could begin to make out a frightful shape. The swirling clouds stretched and curled until they had created the malicious form of a beast. The red skyline of the dying day was all but blotted out by the depraved features and high curled ears of Crocotta's ugly side, except for the break where the eyes and mouth would be, colored in by the blood red horizon underneath. Tulley could see minute sparks of electricity caress the evil shape, and then suddenly, the image was again nothing but clouds. Tulley began to think that perhaps his age was getting the better of him before a roar bellowed across the land, sounding very unlike natural thunder.

Another jolt of lightning raked the sky above him with awesome blazing light, spreading an unholy crack across the already shaken skyline and following with a low monotonous rumble that surely was unmistakable for anything but thunder, but was all the more intimidating to Tulley, who forgot entirely about his garden and dashed back to the house. The storm threw drops at him with a force like a thousand bees stinging him through his thick fur coat. Tulley squinted against them to protect his eyes, even though his glasses were taking most of it. They were in fact, so spotted with water from the short period he had spent outside that the catman could hardly make out his front door, which he threw open fiercely and burst through.

Inside, out of the ghastly rain at last, Tulley went right to his shelves. He moaned and mumbled to himself as he began rummaging through his organization of potions until he came upon a squat, dust covered jar no bigger than his own hand. Inside it, a bright yellow grainy substance sparkled with the luminescence of mica. Tully carefully unscrewed the lid and sniffed it. He had to turn his head to sneeze and jammed the lid back on before his spilled it. Carefully, Tulley made his way to the side of the dying fire and sat down in front of it, coughing.

"Show me," Tulley spoke to no one. "Show me what mine eyes cannot see."

And the catman lifted the lid from the jar and promptly dumped its entire contents into the fire. For a moment, nothing happened. Tulley leaned forward and watched the embers dance and die on the burning logs. The yellow powder had sizzled into nothing before his eyes in a none too exciting display. But Tulley was born to be patient, and so he simply watched. For nearly an hour, Tulley sat in front of a dim orange fire and did nothing, said nothing, only watched. He watched until slowly, ever so slowly, the image of a young man on a gray horse galloped into view within the growing flames.

***

Outside the oversized blue and white striped tent, a pear-shaped man stood high upon a wooden box in a crisp clean white frock. His face had the blotchiness of a recent shave, his black hair had been slicked back with its own natural oil, and he was all toothy smiles and waving arms as he shouted out his previously memorized lines to the curious onlookers who came near to explore the new folks in town.

"Ladies and gentlemen, children of all ages, we welcome you to Barra's Wonders!" the plump man boomed. "See magnificent beasts from around the world! Watch the Wiles in their famous disappearing act! Gasp and shiver as Barra himself slays a monster on this very stage!"

"Scared, youngling?"

Keavy peered to her left at the sly young man beside her and did her best to hide the blush on her cheeks. He looked very handsome in his slacks and crisp white shirt. His cloak, he had draped over her shoulders to keep her warm. Her eyelids lowered haughtily.

"Do I look scared?"

With a smile, Alder bowed before her and beckoned her ahead of him into the tent. After she had gone inside, he tossed a couple of coins into the pay box beside the hawker's stand and joined her. Neither Keavy nor Alder took notice to the servant riding a donkey toward the side entrance. Both had much more important things on their minds.

Pishnee had readily volunteered to bring in the galerush for the final act, even though his jobs were done for the night and he would have been free to entertain himself. He lusted secretly for a bigger cut of skopa, and so he was the first to volunteer for every unwanted job. The sooner he improved his behavior, the sooner he'd be free of this hole.

The cockatrice wound in his leg throbbed with each move the donkey made underneath him, but Pishnee showed no sign of discomfort. This little task would earn him an extra coin or two come next week. Behind him, the cart which the donkey pulled rattled as the beast inside moved about. It was covered with a large tarp for now. No one was to see the creature until Barra himself revealed it on stage. Pishnee was very familiar with the antics of this monster. He had nearly been mauled by it several times, and he was the only one brave enough to take on the task of readying the beast for its nightly shows. He was not looking forward to this evening especially, for a storm was brewing and that could only make the creature more dangerous than ever.

Outside, the sky was darkening, and it was about this time that Tulley had begun to see the bestial form of Crocotta in the clouds.

***

Dusk had fallen on Nodens, along with the increasing storm. The townspeople in the East Village had begun packing up their kiosks and heading inside from the rain. Overhead, the clouds had begun to take on a frightful form that few noticed, because something else had captured their attention. From the horizon, galloping urgently down the muddied road was a young man on a gray horse. From his lungs, panicked words took flight.

"I am a messenger from Bedivere and I bring word from Siavon! Make way! I come with the lexis of disaster! Come hither, come hear. I beg for your ear!"

In spite of the increasing drizzle, a crowd gathered round the worn out young messenger as he came into town slowing his dusky mare. The horse shook out its mane as the rider climbed down from upon the saddle and clutched at his rapidly beating heart. Though his breath was wheezy and ragged from pneumonia, and his soaking wet body shook with the cold, the young man cried to the townspeople with every ounce of vigor he had stowed up inside his gaunt body.

"Gather 'round good people! This messenger comes with terrible news!"

A man with a black beard stepped forward, his wife and daughter behind him clutching each other fearfully.

"What be your business, boy?" He demanded gruffly. "You are frightening the women."

The boy began to speak, but doubled over with awful wet coughs instead. The people closest to him took a few steps back, fearful of infection. The boy had the ill pallor of one near death. When he had steadied himself, he raised his voice again. "And frightened they should be! For I come with frightening news!"

"Spit it out, lad!" Another man growled. "Don't put your breath to waste with talk of doom."

"Yes, spit it out!"

"What be your news?"

"Garric the Elder," the messenger's sickly breath trembled. He lifted his head and peered sorrowfully towards the sky, where the City of Souls shone down brightly with the moon. "Has been taken from Siavon."

71

Gasps of alarm surrounded the wheezings of the quickly deteriorating messenger, who had obviously traveled far and suffered for it.

"The protective field has been broken by the Danaan," he hissed hoarsely. "The conquest has begun!"

"You lie, boy!"

The messenger frowned and shivered violently against his illness. "I do not! Look for yourself!" A trembling hand pointed skyward to the horrid shape that had taken form in the crying sky. A sound unlike any thunder snarled through the air with a great invisible force. The crowd rumbled with rising panic.

"It will not be long before Crocotta shows herself in these parts," the lad hacked. He clung to the reins of the gray mare for support, face drained of life. "Take your children and—"

It attacked without warning, without a single soul sensing its presence. The dying messenger's last words were interrupted when long fangs pierced through his throat and destroyed his message forever. His body sank to the ground before his killer like a soft doll from which gushes of arterial blood flowed. An old blachund almost completely hairless from mange crouched over its kill and snarled at the horror stricken crowd with immense hatred. Behind it, the mare reared up, whinnying, and turned to run, only to be cut off by four more drooling blachunds which ravaged it at once and tore its belly out from under it. They fell upon the dropped entrails and gobbled greedily, snapping at each other as more and more of their pack appeared on the street and closed in on the panicking crowd. The streets were filled with the screams of impending death as the blachunds marauded through the villages and slaughtered all that entered their sight.

***

The fire was dying down now, and its images were fading, but Tulley did not wish, nor did he need to see more. The time had come much sooner than had been expected. Tulley had packed full his leather satchel with all that he could carry and he plunged through his front door, unmindful of the wet weather now. Adjusting the satchel on his back with one furry claw and clutching tightly his weapon of choice in the other, he drew back his lips and called for his ride.

"Igor! Come, you flea-bitten ass!"

From behind the hut, the scruffy old donkey trundled to him, shaking his head in the rain. He patiently awaited Tulley's mount, then galloped as fast as his knobby legs would allow towards the outskirts of town with the catman digging his front claws into his neck for encouragement. The bitter rain beat down upon them, and the thunder roared furiously above.

***

The Wile triplets in their beautiful red dresses rematerialized in a puff of gray smoke which was obviously meant to hide the trap door in the stage. However, due to the storm wind coming through the tent opening, most of the smoke ended up in the audience. The Wiles could easily be seen hopping up from their secret hiding place and waving at the audience with large smiles on their sunken faces.

The crowd booed for the third time tonight. An hour into the show, and the only standing ovation had come from the customers who left early.

Barra was desperate. He stood in the center stage and sweated in the torchlight in front of the few dozen people who had decided to stay. A sea of jaded faces bore down on him with the weight of a hundred boulders. Barra gulped audibly. He was a fat man, bursting at the seams with expensive fruits and meats. A pair of bushy black eyebrows decorated his swollen face, constantly furrowing like terrified caterpillars. He wore a long red coat and a set of white (or what had originally been white) slacks, and on his feet were brown sandals too narrow for his fat feet. Slapping on yet another shady smile, he raised his flabby arms high above his oval head and bellowed, "The Amazing Disappearing Wiles!"

A couple of hisses floated into his tiny crumpled ears, along with the laughs of several dissatisfied customers. Barra gulped again. The next act was being prepared behind him. It would be his best shot at keeping a good reputation. Pishnee was guiding his donkey cart out onto stage. The sheathed cage behind him was silent and uninteresting. Seeing the growing annoyance in Barra's face, Pishnee jumped down from his mount and kicked at the side of the

73

cart. The covered inhabitant gave an ear shattering squeal that caused a stir in the audience. Pishnee grinned at the approving smile splitting from the master's red lips and, happily counting his future spoils in his head, scampered off stage.

"Ladies and gentlemen," Barra began in a hushed manner. "For my next act, I in good conscience must warn those of you in the audience who suffer from a weak heart to consider leaving or your condition may be worsened."

Keavy sat rigidly with Alder on her left and a scrawny old man on her right. The dull clothing she was wearing, a tan button-down shirt with a pair of faded white slacks made her feel out of place amongst the finely dressed onlookers around her. She didn't own a dress, finding them too difficult to practice swordplay in. Secretly, she worried that Alder would judge her poorly for it.

Underneath her, the bench was cold and hard, and her legs had lost feeling ages ago, but that wasn't the only reason she was uncomfortable. They were in the fourth row from the back, having an excellent view of the unexciting excitement in the ring below. Keavy had cheered for every act as if she had never been more entertained in her life simply for Alder's benefit. He looked aghast and embarrassed for bringing her to such a hokey show. Keavy felt a rise of affection for him despite this, or even possibly because of it. She slid herself closer to him and allowed his warm arm to slip around her shoulders. A shiver coursed through her, but not from the cold.

Not a soul heeded Barra's warning. In very fact most had laughed loudly at his ridiculous attempt to frighten them. In the midst of the evening, he had presented them with such disasters as a ring of fire that wouldn't light, a clown show that wasn't funny, and an old unicorn that defecated on the stage and stared dully at Barra as he desperately attempted to command her. Barra's Wonders were certainly not turning out to be as wonderful as promised. This was the show's last chance to prove itself, and it had a lot to accomplish to do so.

Barra kept the silly smile glued upon his red face despite all the retreating customers. Nearly half of the audience had gone or was going, but they would be sorry they missed this. The galerush act always brought the customers back, and their meager skia too.

He approached the covered cage and grasped the edge of the tarp with sweating hands. This part of the show never got any easier.

"Ladies and gentlemen," he began proudly. "I present to you one of the most spectacular and dangerous creatures to grace Aryth, the ferocious galerush!"

One snap of the wrist had the tarp upon the ground. Barra held his hands high above his head in triumph, anticipating the reaction of the paying customers. Without a hitch, they did exactly what they always did, despite their previous reaction to the show. The audience stayed stoically silent for a moment, then a rise of alarm and fear grew into its veins. Those who were standing to leave had plunked down upon their seats with open mouths. Barra's reddish complexion reddened further, and he lowered his arms again and approached the uncovered cage.

It had been still when covered, but when the tarp fell, the beast inside the steel cage rose up on two strong legs, opened magnificent red webbed wings, and created a throaty scream. The sound was so loud inside the enclosed tent that many of the children who had fallen asleep at their mothers' bosoms awakened and began to bawl hysterically. A woman let out a cry of shock, which startled a number of people around her into shrieking as well. The rumble of fear increased. In the fourth row from the back, Keavy had broken Alder's embrace and was now leaning forward on her seat, her ruby eyes wide in astonishment. Alder beside her had gone rigid.

The beast inside the cage was, to say the least of it, a dragon. It was this simple fact that had initially gained the reaction from Barra's audience. Dragons were rarely seen in a captive state, and usually when one came upon a dragon in the wild they did not return to speak much of it. The last dragon the citizens of Nodens had seen had appeared fourteen years ago and nearly destroyed the town. The phoenix dragon had been a minion of Sephora, the castaway daughter of Garric the Elder, and ruler of the Danaan witches. It had disappeared into the forest where some believed it still lurked.

Barra's dragon had brought about this memory for many, though it was much smaller than the giant that had terrorized Nodens all those years ago. Comparable in height to a donkey or even a large pony, the galerush had a long lean body with muscular limbs ending in four fingered claws in the front and three toed claws in the back. Its smooth skin was dominated by a stormy hue patterned with thick black stripes up and down its long neck and curved back. On the flanks of the creature was a peppering of tiny black specks in between the stripes that led from the tail up to the face, where they ended in a masking spot around each eye. The eyes themselves were perfect yellow globes quivering with intelligence, above which sprouted a sharp protrusion that was not quite a horn, but an addition to a pair of thick bony crests upon the snaky reptilian head.

As the audience leered in complete fascination, and Barra stood smirking beside the cage, the galerush cocked its head from side to side and sized up its situation with its large forward facing eyes before it rose up again and another awful scream erupted from its throat. A few people became jarred from their seats and started to head quickly for the exit. Keavy was not among them, though Alder had to bite his tongue to keep from suggesting an early night.

Barra was an intelligent man and had anticipated panic from such a lowly community as the burg of Nodens, and so as the swell of panic began to rise in the audience, he looked to the left side of the stage and whistled to the hand waiting there to come forward embracing a sheathed sword like a lover. The commotion died as Barra took the sword and motioned his assistant away. He turned again to the audience and unsheathed the sword in a slow, disturbingly dramatic manner. The slick sound of metal against hide griped the atmosphere with a chokehold. Every wide set of eyes watched Barra pull out his bent iron weapon and hold it high above his head.

"I have in my hand," he boomed proudly, "the very sword Garric laid down before the warrior Idris Rotonzael after he created Aryth, God's Breath!"

If a giant bug had bitten her rump, Keavy could not have jumped out of her seat any further. She opened her mouth to object but Alder was quick to pull her down again and lay a hand over her mouth. He ignored her glares and shook his head, mouthing a warning to her.

Keavy pulled away from him and crossed her arms hatefully. It was a lie! God's Breath rested on her sire's mantel, not in the fat hands of the conceited ringmaster! What blasphemy for him to claim ownership of such a weapon! And to allege that the poorly made sword in his hand was the sword of Garric the Elder's own making was a very stake to the soul at that! Even though Keavy's distress was eminent, her fellow townspeople seemed enthralled by the fat man's speech, dazzled into believing anything by the sight of the glorious creature in the cage beside him.

"With God's Breath at my command," Barra's windy speech dragged on, "I shall summon the spirit of Idris to possess my hand, and I shall slay this devil's creation as I have slain hundreds before it!" Barra lifted the sword high into the air and bellowed victoriously, "With God's Breath I shall rid the world of Sephora's minions one at a TIME!"

The previously silent audience broke into frenzied applause of newly found affection for one they had laughed at mere moments before. Only Alder and Keavy remained still, both with expressions of disbelief as they watched Barra turn to the dragon's cage and proceeded to lift the latch from the door. He pulled the rusty cage door open and jumped back, awaiting the creature's attack with a hilariously over-extended fighting posture.

Keavy could have pointed out a million things wrong with the picture. He held the sword as one holds an ax, high above his head in a chopping position, he squatted so close to the ground that his giant rump nearly touched it, and he was dipping his head up and down like a crazed chicken. Keavy managed to laugh despite her rage. A dragon slayer indeed! No doubt the beast within the cage had been drugged. It stumbled out of its prison on rubber legs, uttering low warking vocalizations. It dragged its snout across the ground appearing to be wiping its nose, which was running with thick snot. Paying little attention to the crouching Barra, the dragon plunked its haunches down on the floor, swishing its arrow plated tail back and forth, and blinked in confusion.

The galerush looked at the quickly hushed audience, then at Barra, and promptly sneezed, a glistening string of mucus drizzled down from its flaring nostrils which a black forked tongue licked away. Alder gagged at this, and Keavy laughed again. The short bout of promise in tonight's show had turned out to be a bust. Around her, the other people had started to catch on to the lunacy of the situation and joined her laughter. Not long after, the entire audience was booing and hissing.

Barra reddened. Curse that useless Pishnee! He had overdosed the stupid beast with soothing powder again! As soon as he found a way out of this mess, Barra meant to give that youth the

77

lashing of his life! First, however, he had to win back his audience. It was time for dramatic action.

With a quick hand, Barra dove into his trouser pocket and came up with a small red sphere. Screaming with determination, he let back and threw the sphere straight into the dragon's lulling face. At contact, it exploded in a pop of red smoke and flecks of white light, and the half-slumbering beast's head shot up, its eyes widening with anger, and its wings opening to reveal their bloody hue. The galerush reared up on its hind legs and roared horridly and then, at once, it charged Barra with its head lowered and its spiked crest aimed for his chest. The audience shrieked as the sword made contact with the animal's armored skull. Barra had taken on his ridiculous crab squat again, and was now keeping the enraged animal at bay with the shaft of the sword braced against its crest. He and the snarling dragon began to circle each other in this position, occasionally separating to swing or snap at each other.

The audience ate it up, but Keavy was still not convinced. She was looking at the dragon rather than its so called slayer. Its bright yellow eyes had formed a milky film over them, and in fact the beast seemed to be charging in defense rather than anger. Barra was the one actually attacking the beast, for every time it separated its head from his sword he gave a battle cry and slammed back into it. The blinded monster was backing away from him, snapping madly with its fierce jaws, and yet Barra pressed on. Keavy cast a concerned glance to Alder, who shared in her unease.

"That poor creature," Keavy whispered.

"Yes, and look." Alder was nodding his head towards the dragon as it reared up on its hind legs again. "Do you see its chest?"

Keavy did indeed see that the creature's chest was littered with scars over scars as it rose to slash blindly at its attacker again. The scars reminded her very much of healed over sword wounds. She had seen her share of them, having grown up with a master swordsman as her sire.

On center stage, the battle raged on between man and beast. Barra was drenched in sweat, but his character never wavered from possession of Idris' warrior spirit. In front of him, the galerush moaned its distress. It was tiring. Now was the time to end the battle.

"Fall before me vile one!" Barra shouted, in as loud and heroic a voice as his dry throat would allow, "Enter thee into the pits of *Hell*!"

He zeroed in on his mark with eyes burning. The galerush warked again and rose up, wings beating furiously. The film over its eyes was clearing quickly. He had to do it now. Barra took the hilt of the sword with both hands, and, screaming manically, drove the tip of his version of God's Breath's blade into the panting dragon's chest, into the tangle of scars. The animal fell to all trembling fours as Barra ripped the bloody sword out of its chest and posed over it, waiting patiently. Eyes now completely clear, the dragon peered up at its killer, then back at the audience. For a moment, Keavy looked directly into its large yellow eyes and the face of true misery. She looked away as it collapsed, motionless, at Barra's feet. The cheers of the audience thudded in her ears like a headache.

Barra allowed the cheering to waver a little before he spoke again, in a voice not his own, for he was an excellent mimic. In his best imitation of Idris, he addressed the good people as a warrior.

"My children," Idris in Barra's body sadly sighed, "My spirit has grown weary from battle, and I must rest and take a moment to reflect. Returning to the air of the living has weakened me, and I cannot stay in this body for long."

Behind Barra, three hands had appeared to drag the body of the galerush out of the ring. Alder tapped Keavy on the shoulder.

"Something is very wrong," he said.

"You and I think the same."

Idris continued to assure the awestruck audience that Barra would return to them once he allowed his soul to depart from his body, and the two teenagers deftly made their way to the back of the tent and lifted the flap to exit without being noticed. Down on the center ring, Barra took a final bow and made his own exit.

Keavy and Alder snuck around the side of the tent and hid behind a stack of crates just in time to see the three stage hands dump the body of the galerush onto the softened ground outside. Another cage was in position on a mule cart, with a hand already at the reins. The rain was beating down furiously now, and at once they resembled drowned rats as they rolled the animal onto its back to reveal its wound. Barra joined them and squatted down in the mud, muttering something in an indecipherable language and digging into his other pocket. He withdrew a leather purse which he swished a finger into, and brought out a dollop of yellow paste. Muttering more absurdities, Barra smeared the paste into the open wound on the animal's chest, wiped his hand off on the shirt of the nearest stage hand, and darted back inside the tent to be greeted by more applause.

In fascination, Keavy and Alder watched the monster's mortal wound glow brightly in the dark as it sealed itself over, leaving nothing but a few traces of dried blood and yet another white scar for the collection. The dragon's spotted chest inflated slowly while the stage hands loaded it into the cage on the cart. It reached full consciousness and rolled onto its feet just as the door was locked behind it.

Keavy could not believe what she was witnessing. The magic behind the trick was all so very simple. Barra performed a quick healing spell on the beast so as to keep it alive, and by the time it was well enough to be dangerous again, it would be safely locked in its cage, put away until the next time it was to be slain for entertainment. The trick would work every time provided Barra had perfected his timing. With the modest healing paste he was using, it was probable that he had lost a beast or two in the past before he'd trained himself for targeting a non-lethal area.

"I do not believe this is that dragon's first slaying," Alder observed.

He had a point. As the stage hands departed, and the rider egged on the scruffy mule, the galerush peered out of its bars and dragged the spikes on its crest across them, creating a sharp clinking sound. Its yellow eyes shown eerily in the dark, poignant, but unafraid.

"He has been through this many times; so many that he is no longer fearful." Alder said Keavy's very own thoughts aloud. "Barra has killed him tonight as he has killed him many other nights."

Keavy sighed. "And he will resurrect him every time."

"You there!"

Both youths spun around. Keavy automatically dropped a hand to her belt, reaching for a sword that wasn't there. A rumpled old man wearing a blood spattered white apron over his low set belly stood before them. Over his shoulder, the butchered corpse of a piglet hung limp and dripping.

"What are you doing out here?" The grotesque man's chew blackened teeth and blistered lips snarled. A corroded cleaver glinted in his fist. Alder nudged Keavy and huffed through a curled lip one simple word.

"*Run.*"

And run they did. They sprang out from behind the crates and whooshed past the mule cart carrying the newly resurrected galerush. Spooked, the mule reared and backed up, unmindful of its rider's objections. When its rump hit the crate, the animal became more spooked and it tried to turn, straining against the halter that connected it to the cart. A low painful creaking noise fluttered up from the cart as the mule pulled it onto two wheels. Then, with a crash, the cart fell on its side, bringing the mule, its rider, and its precious cargo to the ground with it.

Keavy and Alder made furious haste heading toward the spattering of small green tents where the show's unneeded employees had begun to hunker down for the night. The butcher tossed aside the dead piglet and brought up his cleaver. It barely missed Alder's ankle when he threw it. Enraged, the butcher bolted around to the other side of the master tent and came up panting before the two hulky guards at the tent entrance.

"Intruders!" he squalled. "They must not reveal our secrets!"

The larger of the two guards looked to the other and nodded, and his comrade placed a hand on the ram's horn hanging from his neck.

The bleating note of the horn sounded the alarm clear across the camp. Lights began to appear in tent openings as Keavy and Alder dashed past them and, soon after, they had gathered a number of pursuers, each one arming themselves with all manner of weaponry, from pitchfork to cattle prod.

Keavy made it back onto the path first, with Alder hot on her heels, screaming, "You better have a good plan, youngling!"

"Don't I always?"

Keavy stopped short and swept up her pant leg to reveal the dagger Vorian had given her, safe in its sheath. Taking her cue, Alder dug into his belt and removed a set of slightly larger knives, spinning them deftly in his grasp. Keavy glared at his display, but he had already turned away from her. Their attackers were making it

81

through the tent village and joining them on the path, and most of them looked very angry.

A short chunky fellow got to them first, yielding a rusty old sword that rattled in its hilt, but a sword none the less. Alder caught the long blade between his two meager ones just as the guard was throwing it down upon him, and landed a swift kick into the squat fellow's abdomen. Instinctively, the man bent over, giving Alder the opportunity he needed. He seized the sword between his blades and slung it out of its owner's hands and over his own head. Keavy caught it with one deft hand at the same moment she threw her dagger into the forehead of the next advancing attacker. More guards and hands were approaching fast. Alder was finding his skills in footwork quite handy. He danced about on delicate feet as two of them attacked him at once, one with an ax, and the other with a fire poker.

Keavy swung madly to keep the rest at bay. She found herself in combat with a witchy looking woman whose form was as tangled as her hair. Keavy leapt back as the cackling bitch charged her, her pitchfork's business end first. As she braced herself to fend off the attack, the presence of a wheezing advancement behind her caught her ear. Quickly, she pointed her blade forward. Her muscles tingled at the weight, but Keavy was able to swing herself in a perfect circle, taking out her female adversary as well as the pursuer behind her. Alder kicked back from his own battle and raised his eyebrows at her, observing the damage she had caused. She shrugged and began to run, cueing him to follow. Together they darted through the camp as more and more hands and guards sped after them.

"You're a rough one to impress!" Alder laughed nervously. "Another girl would call it a fine night out if she received a flower and a goodnight kiss!"

"When you meet this other girl, give her my best regards!"

They weaved through another section of tents and looped the last one, finding themselves on another dirt path leading through the large common area of the camp. Pit fires that had recently been distinguished still smoked in their stone fortresses. Large tents the size of bungalows loomed before them, dark save for the torches poking out of the ground in front of them for those who had to work late. Those like Pishnee, who was leading the blindfolded cockatrice out of the carnivore's tent on a rope and humming to himself. Imagine his surprise when two younglings nearly ran square into him as they turned the corner. Shouting in alarm, Pishnee stumbled backwards into the currently placid bird beast behind him. It squawked and lowered its head to butt at whatever had threatened it, and in a last attempt to steady himself, Pishnee's flailing hands accidentally tore the blindfold from the bird's eyes. The cockatrice shook its head, blinked, and scowled at the stunned teenagers in front of it.

"Pardon us!" Alder shouted, and he and Keavy ran past the confused bird and even more confused handler. Angered, the cockatrice began to pursue them. Pishnee limped after it.

"You oversized pullet! Get back here!" he wailed. "I said get back here, Whipsaw!"

At the sound of its name, the cockatrice turned its snaky neck towards Pishnee and crowed. Pishnee's haggard face paled. The bird now had decided that chasing after its long time tormenter was a much better idea than pursuing the teenagers.

"No, Whipsaw!" Pishnee bawled relentlessly, as the creature tailing him snapped at his backside with its long sharp beak and missed him by an inch. "You and I are friends, remember?"

Whipsaw took another snap at him and didn't miss.

Pishnee's screams followed Keavy and Alder, now exhausted, into the next tent they saw. They crouched in the opening and watched the raving cockatrice chase down its handler and dig its vicious talon deep into the back of his neck. His screams stopped short and drained into a thick splattering sound, from which Alder turned away. However, the sight behind him was not much better than the one in front.

All around them, cages filled with beasts loomed. In one corner, a pair of baby cyclops were hitting each other and wrestling, in another, a bogle bounced about on its branches, uttering a high pitched maniacal giggle. Alder's jaw muscles went limp and his mouth fell open.

"Keavy," he choked "Do you see— "

"Watch out!"

Keavy slammed into him, and the pair of them hit the ground hard. Cursing, Alder shoved her away only to see that the spot where he had been standing was now occupied but the front talon of a gryphoness reaching through her cage bars. His face fell hot instantly and he helped his rescuer to her feet.

"Thanks."

Keavy began to speak, but the deep resonation of rumbling men spoke for her.

"Pishnee is dead! I'll bet this is the work of those youngling brats!"

"We shall split up to look for them. You two! Search the carnivore tent!"

"Yes sir!"

"From the looks of it, *this* is the carnivore tent," Alder observed. "We have to hide."

He pulled Keavy with him and bid her to duck behind a hay bale underneath the cage of the gryphoness just as two guards burst into the tent, brandishing torches before them. The gryphoness squowled and bashed about in her enclosure, cutting her already scarred wings on the barbed wire that entwined the bars of her prison. Biting down on a quivering lip, Keavy waited for both guards to look the other way before leaping up and sliding out the pin of the creature's door lock. Alder pulled her back down just before the shorter of the two guards cast his torch light in their direction.

He mouthed at her. *What are you doing?*

Keavy shook his hand from her shoulder. *I have an idea.*

She began to crawl forward on her hands and knees, following just behind the light of the torchlight, heading for the next cage.

You're mad!

Get the rest!

They began to crawl about on the floor, out of sight of the two guards, waiting for the opportune moment to unlatch the cages without being seen.

"Come out with your hands above you!" The larger of the two grunted. "We know you're here!"

Keavy, against Alder's objections, stopped to lift the lid of the small metal box upon a dusty crate in the middle of the room before both of them snuck for the entrance without being seen.

"Boris, something is wrong," the shorter guard murmured. He scratched his bald scalp with the cool end of his torch, leaving upon it a streak of black soot.

"Shut up!" Boris snapped. His big toothed grin filled the room, and he squinted in the dark looking for the hideaways. "This is not a game, younglings! Come out peacefully or suffer the consequences!"

A squeaking sound had both men pointing their lights to the dead center of the room. On the lid of a strange metal box, a tiny green mouse sat washing its paws. A scorpion's tail was wrapped unthreateningly around its round body, and fly's wings fluttered open so the mouse could lick them clean with sharp mousy movements. It ignored the approaching men completely, even when the louder of the two brought his face very close to it and spat when he talked.

"What the bloody hell is *that* thing?"

The other guard was not as trusting. "Let's get out of here, Boris."

"It's gotten out of its cage," Boris snorted. "If we don't put it back, Barra will have our hides." He transferred his torch to his left hand and reached for the tiny beast with his right, "Little rascal."

The little critter stopped washing itself and appeared to glare, and Boris paused long enough to witness the astonishingly quick shift of power between man and mouse. In a speed that would have given Crocotta a shaky test, the volk's tiny body lengthened and thickened, the queer rodent features sunk into the changing head. The wings sucked back inside the body with a zipping noise, and the tail became fatter, the poisonous end shifting into a thick hard rattle. In less than a minute, there was an enormous green snake coiling itself around the modest metal box which had been its prison. Thick scaly coils crushed it into a flat hunk of scrap, deeming it forever unusable. Two large heads raised high above the terrified guards and smelled the air with fat forked tongues, then each other, then finally they caught whiff of the guards bellow. A spiky white frill sprang out around each neck and both snake heads opened their large, toothy jaws and hissed in symphony. The men had no time to scream before both heads struck and devoured the two of them at the same time.

The other animals, paying close heed to the large serpent slithering out of the tent, began to test the doors of their own cages, and in no time at all, they had joined their escaped comrade in the unsuspecting circus settlement.

***

Keavy and Alder ran towards the end of the road, which was high upon a hillside, where they would be able to see the lighted town below. Despite (or possibly, because of) their fear, they were laughing. After all, they had reached the end unscathed, and discovered a great use for their years of training. It hadn't sunk into either of their minds that they had killed tonight, not yet. The chemicals of their brains were seeing to it that they got as much of a high out of their recent brush with danger for as long as possible. Later, it would be time to become children again, for now they were soldiers just happy to be alive.

Alder made it to the top of the hill first. Keavy's steam had finally run out, and she lumbered in beside him heaving and laughing at the same time. She peered wistfully down at the starry village below. They were still far enough away that the horror unfolding within was not yet visible, especially through the heavy rain. To the two soaking wet teens, the sight was of just a sleepy burg dotted with torch lights.

"We made it," Alder said stoically. "I'm impressed, youngling. You didn't pass out."

Keavy's laughter wavered. Her mouth closed and she looked at him with the careful curiosity of the guilty.

Alder smirked and gave words to her thoughts. "Your faun friend has a large mouth for one so small."

Curse you, Nessa, Keavy thought to herself. Aloud, she snorted in contempt. "I did not pass out," came the lie. "I fell and took a blow to the head, that's all. And, stop calling me youngling! You're not so much older than I!"

Alder bowed his head, smirk still present. "My apologies, oh supreme *hrotage.*"

Keavy tried to shove him, but this time, Alder caught her by the wrists and pulled her into him. Their faces came as close as two faces could without touching and Alder was making it quite clear that he wanted that to change. Keavy pulled back suddenly, and his expression became first hurt, than angered.

"Why do you tease, you shameful girl?" he snapped. "You are poorly raised, boorish, and distinctly curt. You dress as a ragged young boy and not a woman. You have no manners and you live in the woods like an animal! You're nowhere near the proper lady you should be to be wed off to an honorable name as mine, and yet I foolishly pursue you still! Why do you push me away when I am the only man who will have you?"

Keavy stepped back from him as if she'd been slapped. "You speak to me so?" Her ruby eyes flashed. "You speak as though I am property to be auctioned off to the highest bidder? Perhaps I have not yet had the pleasure of finding this so called *honorable* name, because there are no men left in this world worthy of bearing it!"

For a moment, Alder tensed, his fists became rocks and then at once they released. He stepped back from her and inclined his head. "I have insulted you," Alder sighed, embarrassment, what little there was, somewhat apparent. "Forgive me, Keavy. It was wrong of me to speak to you that way."

Keavy's eyes did not show the tolerance that her tone adopted. "You are right about some things," she said. "I *am* boorish and unladylike, and I do live somewhat as an animal does. But you will *not* say anything of my sire. Vorian protected me after my family was killed by Crocotta's minions. He trained me for my only destiny. He has taught me all he knows, and I am happy to have been reared under his watch. You will not call me poorly raised again."

"My apologies." He did not add "oh supreme *hrotage*" to this but, even so, she still detected that hint of Alder's home brand of sarcasm that she hated so much.

Keavy turned away from him and, as she did, the sight of the lonely village blanketed with stars became blocked by the heads of two approaching guards coming up over the hill. They had been cut off! Keavy and Alder's argument was put upon a dusty shelf for now, and the two took no time in turning tail and running back toward the settlement.

It was mayhem. The freed beasts had now gained the upper hand in destroying the campsite of their former keepers. The lightning illuminated the scene for just a moment, long enough for the teenagers to see what was going on in perfect clarity. The twin cyclops, still chained together at the ankles, were taking turns throwing dung at the people trying to shoot them with arrows. The old unicorn, a long time prisoner of Barra's Wonders, now gleefully trotted through the mud, a new shine of youth in her eyes. One desperate worker made an attempt to restrain her by leaping upon her back and clinging to her mane, but this did not slow her up at all. She shook him loose and made a hopeful leap into the air, and with a flash bright as the lightning itself, she vanished.

Keavy and Alder stood in fascination as the beasts of Barra's Wonders disappeared in their own way one by one. Some ran, others flew, but all had regained the freedom they deserved. The scene was so enthralling that Keavy almost missed Barra haughtily strutting back from his act. He appeared just in time to witness the volk, now in the form of a green bear harboring deadly porcupine quills upon its back and stalky antennae eyes on its head brush past, mewling happily at its newfound freedom. His mouth dropped open.

"M-my wonders!" he sputtered. "What has happened to my wonders?"

A great sound broke the air, sounding a mix of a lion's roar and an eagle's cry. The gryphoness, able to stretch her scarred wings in flight for the first time in years, was but a flash in the lightning as she swooped down upon him, just missing his scalp with her fierce talons. Barra ducked, but he was not able to avoid the second attack wave. When he stood again, his balding head had been painted a creamy white. The cold rain merely washed the dung down over his face. The fat man moaned and wiped it away from his eyes with the back of his hand, not noticing the small plum colored creature crouching at his feet until it sank its teeth into his right ankle. Barra screamed and withdrew his bent version of God's Breath from his belt, but before he could sweep down upon his attacker, the bogle was long out of range. It was the last of the creatures to scamper out of the camp, giggling and bouncing about in the mud puddles as a handful of circus hands clumsily pursued. Barra's Wonders was no more.

Barra roared with anger at a sky that roared back in the language of thunder. His ruddy flesh had become a deep dangerous purple. "Who is responsible for this!" he cried. The white droppings oozed in two tracks between his bloodshot eyes. A flash of lightning lit up the fat man's seething face. "Who did this to me?"

In the midst of the confusion, Keavy and Alder lost their wits. Abruptly, they both found themselves lifted from their feet. The two burly guards had seized them under both armpits and now carried them back into the camp, their well hardened grips no match for the youths' kicking and squirming.

"These knaves, sir," Keavy's captor was happy to tell the circus master. "They are the ones to blame."

Keavy was furious. She kicked with the vigor of an untamed mare. "Release us!"

Barra stalked through the mud, his head almost washed clean of its white paint. The rain comically bounced off his bald head. "You have ruined me!"

He made a beeline for Keavy first, swinging a meaty slab of a paw. Her head flew back, her body was nearly knocked from the burly man's grasp. She lifted her head, stingers in the shape of Barra's palm biting at her cheek.

"You shall die for this!" Barra snarled. He drew back his iron sword and licked his lips, hungry for her blood. The end of the rusty piece of garbage he had dared to call God's Breath glinted in another blaze of lightning.

"No, leave her alone!" Alder demanded in a crackling voice ripe with terror.

Keavy closed her eyes, wishing only for a quick death. She reminisced of her short life, glazing over every regretful decision she had ever made, particularly over the past few days. How disappointed Vorian must be in her. She would never even begin to learn what she must do to complete her destiny. She had failed. Some *hrotage* she had turned out to be. Keavy changed her mind and forced herself to face her death head on. She would at least die with dignity.

Barra was not moving.

Upon his fat red face, an expression of alarm had replaced the hate. His eyes bulged from their sockets, veins dark against the whites. His chirpy mouth was a perfect O, the purple tongue lolling from it like a dead worm. He didn't react when the last trickling bit of gryphoness dung rolled into that O and dripped down onto his tongue. Keavy could have gagged and would have if Barra hadn't begun to shake violently where he stood. Sparks of electricity caressed his body in brilliant streaks quicker than lightning. The veins in his eyes darkened and then burst, covering his eyes in sheens of blood. The O vanished, and Barra's teeth chomped right through his dying worm of a tongue. A torrent of blood rushed out of his mouth, following the severed chunk of meat into the mud, and still he trembled and shook and pulsated where he stood, not making a sound until at last, he lurched forward. Then, the circus master sighed his last breath before he fell face down on the ground in the pool of his own blood. Smoke curled from several small holes in his charred back.

And that was when the galerush rose before them, standing taller than even the large bulky guards restraining Keavy and Alder. His claws were splayed, Barra's blood dripping from them, the normally black nails glowing silver. The dragon's tail was swishing back and forth excitedly, the arrow plated end also glowing silver. Its eyes were not at all milky, and certainly not blind. It was no longer drugged; no longer restrained. Its massive wings popped open and revealed their astonishing red insides. Keavy felt herself being dropped. The guards had wisely decided to leave the knaves to the dragon and take off. The galerush slammed back onto all fours and roared after them and they shrieked and disappeared back over the hill that Keavy and Alder had first met them on.

Alder tugged at her arm. "Keavy! Let's go!"

Keavy shook him away. The fear of death had somehow become a lazy memory to her. She was lost in the galerush's enormous eyes. It stared at her and folded its wings back over its body. Keavy tentatively raised a hand in front of her within biting range of the animal's jagged mouth.

"Keavy!"

The galerush lifted its neck out and rubbed its snout against her hand uttering a low rumble that reminded Keavy of the sound Tulley sometimes made when he nodded off at the fire pit.

"Thank you," she said, and stroked the beast with no fear. "You are free now."

A bolt of lightning cut the sky and the galerush looked up at it longingly and then back at Keavy. The sadness had escaped its face. Blinking, and with a final chilling cry, the dragon opened its wings and leaped upwards into the sky, catching its flight on the wind. The youths watched as it flew above the deserted circus camp, higher and higher, until it seemed to brush the belly of the storm itself. Lightning chased after it and struck the metallic plated tail of the creature, and suddenly its whole body seemed ignited and it shot off into the dark, leaving after it a trail of white energy behind it.

"We saved him," Keavy explained, watching the storm consume the trail of the galerush. "He knew that."

Alder sighed and slipped an arm around her waist. "Come on, let's get you home."

As the two teenagers headed back to retrieve Alder's horse, something watched from the safety of its hiding spot, clicking and clacking, and swishing its furry brown tail.

***

A sea of white ears perked upon hearing the smooth *shling* of the mighty God's Breath being unsheathed from its master's side. The closest blachunds somehow found a way to pull their slavering jowls from the carnage they had created to surround the magnificent black tricorn and its mysterious cloaked rider. Beside them, a scrubby donkey with a catman upon its back honked and whimpered and tugged at its reins while its mount cursed and tried to control it. The mud sucked at the animal's hooves and the rain bounced off its back like thousands of tiny rubber balls.

"Igor!" Tulley, fur mud streaked and matted from the rain, scorned his terrified donkey, "Keep your head you miserable burro!"

"Steady now," Vorian murmured to the better trained Annick. The tricorn's blue eyes rolled despairingly in its sockets. A scrawny gray furred blachund snarled and snapped at the horse's front legs and, in response, he reared and came down upon its head. It squashed flat like a pumpkin under a boulder, brains and blood squirting out from beneath the steed's heavy hooves and mixing red swirls into the brown mud.

The second attack came from the left. Snarling and drooling buckets, the beast leapt with claws and teeth shining fiercely in the glint of moonlight. It ended up leaping straight into the tricorn's long black horns, meat still squealing on the end of its spit. Annick shook the dying thing from its face and uttered a challenge to the rest of the fiends surrounding them.

"Soha!"

The call to battle rose from Vorian's lips with great gusto, and at the same time, the thunder roared above, as if coaxing them onward. He sliced another leaper open at the belly, the intestines pouring forth in a slimy tangle at its own feet. Two smaller blachunds, juveniles by the unproven way they moved, took no time in bearing down to eat from its still beating organs. Beneath them, their dying comrade bawled tortuously until one of the juveniles ripped the voice right out of its throat. Vorian jumped down from Annick's back. With a swift swing, he beheaded both juveniles, and then spun to meet the next leaper in midair, hacking off a quarter of its jaw and then plunging God's Breath into its chest, killing it instantly. Yet, still they came at him, and still he killed them one by one, two by two. God's Breath quickly became wet with gore from the tip of the blade to the hilt. Vorian's cloak was soaked from the wrist to the elbow with the hot blood of his enemies. The rain-soft ground at his feet lived with it.

Annick fended off the fiends without haste, blinking away the rain and blood that fell into his watery blue eyes. Whatever beasts he could not pierce with his horns, he kicked with his powerful legs, dislocating shoulders and jaws, shattering ribs and limbs. The blachunds that did not die instantly were soon dispatched by their own kind and devoured on the spot.

Igor panicked considerably under Tulley and bucked the old cat from his back, but Tulley landed gracefully on his feet as his kind had always been known to do. Three snarling blachunds went for the braying creature immediately, and there was nothing neither Tulley nor Vorian could do to stop it. The first long set of jaws crushed the left rear leg of the old donkey while the second and third sets sunk deep into the animal's neck. Igor went down with a squelched cry and said no more about it.

Several of the beasts surrounding Tulley backed off and instead found greater pleasure in snarfing up his old companion's spilled guts. Still, Tulley had not been completely overlooked. One large blachund charged at him with bloodlust in its manic yellow

92

eyes. At once, however, it backed off with a whimper, tail swept up between spindly legs. Tulley had raked his bared claw at the dog's eyes and popped the right one like an overdue pimple. As it doubled back, the old catman, still fluffed and hissing, brought his flanged mace down upon the blachund's head. It yelped and backed off, shaking its ugly head in confusion, and before it could charge him again, Tulley swung his mace into the side of the animal's head and brought him down for good.

Another beast barked as it ran at him, foam flying from its jaws at every angry enunciation. Tulley snarled back and the pointed end of the mace bit right into his attacker's neck, its frenzied barking morphed into a shrill yelp of pain and it backed off, only to be overpowered by hungry pack mates that had smelled its spilled blood. The next, its jaws agape and smeared with donkey blood, was already leaping over its dead form not thinking for a moment that it could not take down the small orange creature that had just dispatched two of its pack mates. Tulley jumped back and clunked it over the head as it landed. The head of the mace smashed down onto the gangly dog's bony black head and knocked it cold.

"For Igor, you sons of bitches!" Tulley shouted. "For the people of Nodens!"

Annick's distressed squeals brought Tulley quickly to his aide. With Vorian tied up in his own battle, he could do nothing about the four creatures surrounding his steed, snapping hungrily at his legs and belly, getting closer each time. Finally, one blachund made it onto the tricorn's back and despite the horse's best efforts to throw it, the monster sunk its teeth into the back of his neck. With a running leap, Tulley charged through the pack, bounced off the head of one of Annick's surrounding threats, and from there, leapt to Annick's rump. He dug his front claws into the steed's flesh whilst gripping the wooden staff of the mace between his teeth, and scrambled onto Annick's back just as the blachund turned to face him.

"Here, boy!" Tulley shouted, "Fetch!"

His mace smashed into the creature's open jaws. It fell yipping from the tricorn's back, and Vorian ran God's Breath into its thick neck. Tulley jumped down on top of the gurgling thing's head from Annick's back, driving its long snout deep into the mud. He wheezed heavily, but he held his bloodied mace at the ready, by the side of Vorian Tranore and God's Breath. Despite their odds, they would not give up.

Crocotta's horrendous roar broke through the cry of the storm. All at once, the blachunds ceased their advancement on the warriors. The sea of white returned, swiveling in unity towards the monstrous sound. The pack parted for their leader as she came forward out of no place that Vorian nor Tulley had seen. She was a terrifying sight, towering above even the enormous blachunds with her wily striped fur and massive jaws. They lowered their heads and drove their tails between their legs as she passed them. Some of them growled softly, eager to resume the fight. Crocotta growled back at them, and they slunk down, giving her a clear view of the tired warriors standing in the middle of an empty rain beaten town.

"Call off your hounds!" Vorian demanded. Though he was soaked to the bone and heaving, he held fast to his commanding presence.

Had Crocotta currently had the ability, she would have smiled. The shift came, in just as revolting a sight as before. Her fingers were twiddling the chain of her necklace even before they had fully formed. The crackling of moving bones preceded her unruffled response. "You will send the child, then?"

"We will do nothing of the sort!" Tulley snapped. "It is not the proper time!"

Vorian quieted him with unspoken conciliation. "He speaks true," he told the witch calmly. "You gave us eighteen years, Crocotta. It has only been fourteen."

Crocotta had regained her womanly form and now stood before them in her gray dress, black hair in dancing spidery braids. She now could smile furtively at Vorian, almost pleasantly. "Sephora's plans have changed. She requires the child now. "

Tulley scoffed haughtily. "It appears as though your mistress is keeping her unruly bitch on a short leash!"

Crocotta's head made a sickening snap as it changed into that of the hideousness she so concealed, an awkward, heavy lump which snarled at Tulley from the shoulders of a beautiful woman. Tulley's hackles rose and he hissed.

"I want the girrrrl, Vorrrrrian." Crocotta snarled through her reversal. "Sssend Keavy and I shall call the blachunds back forever."

Vorian looked upon the town, where the blachunds had done their damage. The mangled corpses of townspeople were scattered everywhere. Fruit carts and carriages lay on their sides, mud and blood spattered against every building. The air stunk of death and fear and evil. Crocotta's now placid blachunds, though obedient, were looking to it with desire. Tulley sensed the thoughts of his long time friend almost as clearly as if he had spoken them aloud. A small hand tugged at a mud spattered pant leg.

"Vorian," he said. "She is too young."

"I have no choice," the recluse sullenly replied. He closed his eyes briefly, but only briefly, and opened them to Crocotta's grinning human face. "I will send her on her quest, tonight."

"Very good, Vorian!" she cheered. "You have grown wiser since your…reconnection with nature."

Tulley looked up, first one tattered then one pierced ear swiveled in the witch's direction while eyes examined Vorian.

"I will keep my word, Crocotta," Vorian promised, ignoring the catman's asking glance. "Now, keep yours."

"Very well."

Crocotta changed once again. When her monstrous form was complete, she fell to all fours and roared a command to the blachunds. With only slight hesitation, the blachunds turned and trotted from the streets, peering over their shoulders in disappointment, their jaws drooling. She snapped at the heels of the stragglers, sending them yelping into the darkness. Then, Crocotta's vicious stare met Vorian's.

"Until our pathsssss crossssss again, Vorrrrian."

"Until then." He sheathed God's Breath and nodded.

The rain stopped.

***

When the storm abruptly ended, the youths were riding Alder's fawn colored gelding, Lorcan, on the forest path to Keavy's home. The horse began to protest his rider's commands, and stopped short on the rocky path, whinnying with fright.

95

Alder groaned. "What's the matter?" He gave Lorcan a stern kick, and the animal reared, but he did not continue onward.

"He's afraid," Keavy said. "He senses something."

Alder dismounted and placed a reassuring hand on the gelding's soft nose. The bushes rustled to the left of them, and at once he had his blood stained daggers in his hands, waiting for whatever dared to surprise them. Keavy joined him, dismounting quickly and withdrawing her own weapon.

The animal that came from the shadows was an abomination. Almost the size of a pony, its body a sleek long thing with shaggy brown fur sprouting from the tail, belly, neck, and chin. Its sides and back were covered with large square scales, dirty yellow in color and textured like brick. The back legs were very powerful and ended in sharp spaded hooves, while the front legs ended in two thick black talons. The neck was long and muscled, supporting an oversized head from which two beady black eyes blinked underneath long black lashes. Long skinny brown ears stuck out horizontally from its head, between them two short knobby horns. The nose was wrinkled and piggish, protected by an even rougher set of yellow scales. A coarse clay tinted beard hung from its wide protruding jaw which remained locked in a permanent expression of perplexity. What looked like two strange black growths tumoring out of its cheeks revealed themselves as two pairs of strangely insect-like pincers. These snapped together on their own independently moving muscles, creating a hollow clacking sound. The pincers oversaw menacingly long fangs that protruded from the top lips even when they were closed. Even more sharp white teeth snarled from the mouth when its chasm of jaws gaped open.

A fat blue tongue licked out from between the thing's deadly overbite and lapped at the terrible fangs. The pincers on its face vibrated rapidly against its scales, producing a hollow rattle. It fluffed its tail out and raised it over its head, then bowed down before the stunned youths like a playful puppy. Rather than yipping happily however, the monster opened both sets of pincers wide and hissed. With opened mouth and pincers, the thing appeared to have three strange sets of angry jaws hungry for human flesh.

Alder hesitated not in hurling one of his daggers into the weird monster's left eye. It let out a surprised bleat, ducked its big head, and batted at its face with the wrists of its front feet. When it

96

finally loosened the blade from its destroyed eye, the horse and its two riders had gone from view.

Rut moaned helplessly through the ache of the healing process. His blind eye oozed thick blue liquid down in between the scales on his snub nose. The stench of a dead skunk's musk filled the forest. The liquid clotted around Rut's damaged eye and began to sizzle until smoke appeared, and Rut bleated his anxiety until the blue liquid had dried over the eye itself, regenerated whole in its socket. Rut blinked away the remaining crust with his long eyelashes. He tested his new eye by winking several times, and then lifted his wrinkled nose into the air. He lumbered off, his pincers shuddering together, snaky body held low to the ground. Somewhere, Crocotta was lurking, and if she knew he had failed, anything she did to him now would not regenerate. Death could not heal.

The riders galloped the gelding full speed through the glistening forest, cutting through the brush, the saplings, the thistles, the thorns, until Lorcan's legs were bloody and he was foaming from the exertion. Keavy clung tightly to Alder's waist and peered over her shoulder, expecting the strange thing they had encountered to be snapping and snarling on their tail. It was nowhere that she could see, but that scarcely made a difference to her apprehension. Strange things had been going on in the last few days. The blachunds, the giant beast, now the odd thing on the path. It was as if the creatures of the forest were agitated, sensing something; a change?

Suddenly, Alder let out a cry and pulled back harshly on Lorcan's reins. His legs squeezed tightly around the geldings side, and his entire body tensed under Keavy's grasp.

"*Halt!*"

Lorcan nearly lost his legs and nearly sprawled head over hooves at the suddenness of his master's grip. He whinnied loudly, reared and bucked, and finally came to a full stop before he could toss both riders from his back. Eyes rolling fearfully, the gelding snorted his annoyance when Alder and Keavy dismounted him. Keavy gave him a quick rub to apologize, and followed Alder ahead of her. When she neared his side, she saw what, or rather, who they had nearly trampled.

Nessa was crouching over another faun, her brother Masiko. He was motionless upon the ground, tiny body enveloped in blood. One of his antlers had been broken clean off. His belly had been ripped open, and his innards were exposed, but life clung to him. Wide black eyes quivered inside their sockets, and coppery saliva bubbled from his open mouth. Nessa held his hand and did not acknowledge either human's presence. In any other situation, the faun would have scampered out of the way of the horse before it had been close enough to see, but this time she would have been run over had Alder not seen her.

"Nessa!" Keavy cried in horror. "What happened!"

Nessa's ears flicked toward the sound of her friend's voice, but she did not look back nor did she stir from her dying brother's side.

"Blachunds," she stated like a well known fact. "Blachunds attacked our clan as we were foraging. We scattered in the panic. Masiko and me, we got cornered, we did, Innes, she…she didn't…" The little faun trailed off, but Alder and Keavy could guess the rest of the story. Slowly, Keavy crouched down next to her friend and watched as the older faun slipped away.

Masiko was a rusty colored buck nearing his years of maturity. The buds of his antlers had just begun to branch out. In another year or so, he would have grown into a fine specimen of wood faun. Now, however, he lay on the ground under his sister's watch, intestines coiling out of a ragged wound. Masiko's left antler had been broken off down to the quick and the blood flowed profusely. His sister delicately cleared it from his eyes, and he reached out to her to take her blood covered fingers.

"Little sister," Masiko bid her, his voice soft and fizzy through the foam around his mouth. "You must leave me here."

Nessa clasped her brother's hand between her own and held it to her chest. Fauns were not capable of crying, but they did emit musty smelling oil from glands on their temples when deeply troubled. Dark tracks of the oil were present on both of Nessa's cheeks. "I will not abandon you."

Masiko smiled warmly. "Me heart beats its last beats," he told her. "There is no one left for you to go home to. All the others is dead." A squint from the pain. "You know this as well as I, you do."

Nessa's ears flickered in agitation. She shook her head. "No, some must have lived! Some besides us, yes? Papa? Mama?"

Masiko continued to smile, though the spirit was already gone from his eyes. "Do not take that chance. Go with the humans. Do not let me leave this world before I know my youngest sister is safe."

Only now, his own empathy oils began to flow in globs from his temples. Quite possibly, this overflow of oil was his body's way of shutting down, but Nessa did not see it that way. She placed her brother's hand on his chest and crossed the other one over it just as his chest hitched for the last time.

"At peace, brother." Nessa closed his eyelids with two trembling fingers. "Your soul awaits mine in Siavon."

"Nessa."

The faun looked at Keavy for the first time since she had nearly been run over by Alder's horse. "We must return to the burrowing grounds." Her eyes were brash. "We must look for my family!"

Keavy reached her hand forward. "Come with us. We will take you there."

Reluctantly, Nessa left her oldest brother's side and did not look back as they rode away.

The burrowing grounds of the wood fauns had been dug out by the pack and destroyed. The food stores had been plundered and the pottery smashed. The strong odor of a mournful clan's empathy oils lay heavy in the air. Aside from the wrecked wooden furniture that the blachunds had apparently seen as chew toys, there were scattered body parts strung across the ground in bloody clumps and several large piles of blachund dung. This was a horror that none as young as the trio should ever have had to see in their time. Alder hunched over, hands on knees, and vomited at the sight of the carnage, Keavy resting her hand upon his shoulder. The girl's ruby eyes hid from the scene against his back. Nessa's oils flowed freely as she sniffed about the destroyed burrows for any sign of a living relative.

The trio searched the grounds hesitantly and found not a single creature alive amongst the destruction. The only recognizable part they discovered was a lock of Senga's silver hair wrapped around a broken table leg. There was no more they could do for Nessa's family. She was alone.

When the young faun finally gave up and allowed Alder to lift her onto Lorcan's back, her face and neck were soaked in oil. Alder tried not to react to the awful smell her hurt was producing, but it was overpowering to his already queasy gullet, so instead of riding Lorcan, he walked and led him by the reins. Keavy held her small friend and rode upon the gelding's back while Alder took them back onto the path. They did not speak again until they reached town.

***

Tulley and Vorian saw the last blachund slink off, a scrawny thing missing one of its ears and about a quarter of its tail. Vorian stomped a foot down hard as it passed him, and it showed him its teeth before it hurried after its pack, leftovers of tail swaying behind it.

Annick was snorting agitatedly. The smell of fiend's blood was upsetting to most animals, and it was everywhere, even splashed all over the horse. Vorian went to his side and stroked him comfortingly.

"Good work," He told his horned charger. Vorian pulled from his satchel a clean cloth to dab at the wound on Annick's neck while the animal, though obviously in discomfort, stood patiently and allowed it.

Tulley rested heavily on the safe end of his mace, using it as a crutch. A fist pressed up to his heaving chest. His earrings tinkled together at each ragged cough he produced.

"We are far too old for this, my friend." The catman said good-naturedly.

Vorian replaced the dirty rag in his satchel, patted the tricorn, and snuffed a breathy laugh. "Undeniably," he agreed. "But the gods have been good to us."

"Bloody good, I'd say!" Tulley chuckled. He found his balance and laid the mace over his shoulder. "We should thank them many times for our strengths."

"I will hold my thanks until the last Danaan witch falls under the blade of the ruby child."

100

Tulley was a wise creature who had known Vorian for a very long time. When he had first traveled to Nodens as a younger individual, weak and tired from a long journey, Vorian had been the one to welcome him. The man everyone considered an unstable hermit had taken the ill young cat into his home, revived him, and helped him build a home right off the Ardor Flower Valley. It was Tulley who truly knew the man of the blade. He asked his next question with the added caution it required.

"Vorian, do you truly think it was wise to agree to send Keavy so soon? After all, she is still just a kitten."

Vorian looked down at his significantly shorter counterpart, his hood fallen to his shoulders. "She is still a kitten," he said with a wane smile. "But as you well know, Tulley, sometimes the smallest kittens have the sharpest claws."

"Vorian!"

The ruby child had appeared, riding upon the gelding of the blacksmith's son with the young wood faun. The Wheat Moon was high and bright in the dark sky, its beams caressing her auburn hair, reflecting from her eyes a reddish gleam that so reminded Vorian and Tulley of the blachunds that both of them nearly withdrew their blades again. Alder led Lorcan, his smile spelling his thankfulness to see trustworthy adults, until the condition of Nodens caused him to stop cold.

The streets of the East Village were painted with the blood of both victim and fiend. Scraps of clothing fluttered from the bodies of their wearers, full of life in a dead world. The bodies of man, woman, and child alike lay everywhere, so reminiscent of the wood faun clan massacre that Nessa's musky empathy oils began to flow across her coarse fur once again. She looked a mess, her face, neck, and shoulders sticky and greasy. Not a live soul inhabited the streets save for Vorian, Tulley, and Annick. Nearby, sprawled the body of Tulley's old donkey, rendered and already drawing flies.

Alder moaned and leaned, trembling into his anxious horse's side. Keavy jumped down from Lorcan's back at once and ran to the waiting arms of her sire.

Vorian embraced her with immeasurable relief. "Thank the gods you are safe!"

"What is happening?" Keavy cried into his chest, unmindful of the dank smell of his sweat.

Vorian hid her face in his blood soaked cloak and held her, saying nothing.

Tulley, once again using his mace as a crutch tottered over to Alder. The Devnet son still held fast to his horse. His face was pale as the corpses that surrounded him. The old catman cleared his throat so as to attract the lad's attention, but it was Alder who spoke first.

"I must look for my parents." Alder's expression was blank, and his words came out in a forced sigh, a hopeless sound.

Tulley placed a clawed hand on Alder's arm. "My lad," he murmured softly. "I am afraid that it is not in your best interest to do that now."

That hopeless voice rose again in dire inquiry. "What do I do?"

Tulley frowned. He glanced back at the man of the blade embracing the child of the prophecy, a young girl of only just past fourteen years of age, a youngling who was far too inexperienced and naive to take charge of the sword of Idris Rotonzael and defeat the daughters of Garric. She was a valiant fighter, and Tulley had spent many sleepless nights peering into her future to crack open the secrets of her fate. He had failed to find the answer he so hoped for, but had discovered that destiny did not change. Tulley had his own to realize just as Keavy was due to fulfill hers, despite the consequences of her unripe age. No matter how one attempted to change the law of destiny, destiny itself was written in stone. Keavy's chances had been restricted by Crocotta's demands, but not destroyed. Her failure, however, would mean the end of Siavon, Aryth, and possibly all of the known existence.

"You must go with Keavy." Tulley said. His face had grown far older than his true years. The bent whiskers and wispy orange fur on his face had lost their healthy sheen, and even his good eye glazed over. "You must accompany the ride of the ruby child through the four holy cities under the Danaan."

He looked first at the once smug young lad close to collapsing against the side of his horse, then at the orphaned wood faun still perched upon Lorcan's back, stinking of grief. "Both of you."

"Us?"

It was the first time Nessa spoke since the death of her brother. She leapt down from Lorcan's back and landed daintily on her haunches. When standing, she was small even compared to the catman.

"We are no use to Keavy," the faun respectfully disagreed. "Master, we is no children of prophecy, no."

"Yes, what help are we to her?" Alder snorted. He was bathed in the light of jealousy for his younger female counterpart for the first time. Tulley could see into him as an owl sees into the darkest forest.

"You are her friends," The catman replied furtively, green eyes pointed in Alder's direction. "That is enough."

Vorian brushed the wild hair out of the ruby eyes of the child he called daughter. He knew he could no longer consider her his own, because now she was bound for her journey and his job was complete; the blade at his side was becoming warm against his thigh, signaling her time for release from his protection.

At the sword's command, Vorian carefully withdrew God's Breath from its sheath and inspected its hilt. The ruby stone embedded there was emitting a dull glow, and as God's Breath left his hands and went into the small wary ones of its true owner, the dull glow grew to a hot piercing red.

Keavy held the sword in her hands, her face alight from the stone's living radiance. "Sire, I can't!" she objected tearfully. "I'm not ready!"

"God's Breath says otherwise."

Vorian's caring arms left her, and a solid wall of command slammed down between them. She was gone from him while only a few inches away.

"You have no choice." He told her in unsympathetic aloofness, sternly and impatiently. "Your time is now."

Keavy broke into full outright tears for the first time in front of Vorian since she had been a tot. She fell to her knees with the weight of God's Breath and dropped the sword in the dirt. At once, the stone went dark. "I can't!" she wept, "I don't know what to do without you! I don't know anything!"

Vorian stood over her. His long black and silver hair whipped around his shoulders in an unseen breeze. His hard eyes blinked forth not a single tear. "You will know what to do when the time comes. It is your destiny. It is your fate."

To Keavy's horror, Vorian turned and began walking away. He was leaving her as he had once upon a time told her that she would leave him. He was abandoning her to her own quest. His purpose was complete, and now the Man of the Blade, the hermit of the forest, would return to his life of solitude to forget the child he had raised as his own.

Keavy staggered to her feet and chased him. "Vorian, no!" She fell upon his cloaks and pulled them, jumped onto his back and was shaken off, crawled, sobbing hysterically after his boots and snatching at them like a hungry beggar, and still Vorian walked away from her, fading into a reflection of his former self.

It was not the first time Keavy had seen Vorian use this gift, though it was a rarity that he ever did. Vorian did not believe in abusing the magic he had acquired over the many years of his life. This time, however, he began to use them to his full ability. Keavy stopped chasing him and sat on the ground, sniffling as she watched him fade away. He stopped at the end of the path, turned his head slightly and whispered something that she could not understand, but behind her, Annick was pawing at the dirt, his ears flicking toward his master's voice.

"Aona rapek kato'ick."

The tricorn heard the Language of the Blade as it left Vorian's mouth as clearly as if he'd spoken them directly into one of his silky black ears. With a gentle nicker, the tricorn approached Keavy and nosed her shoulder with his soft muzzle. She climbed to her feet obligingly and held the animal's large head to her cheek, her sobs subsiding into the hisses of a serpent.

"What did he tell you?" she demanded of him.

Annick only blew a puff of air through his nose. Angered, Keavy pushed his head away.

"Tell me what he said!" she yelled. "Why does he leave me? What is my fate? Why does he speak to you in Blade?"

The animal, of course, could say nothing of use to her, but Keavy sensed that even if Annick had possessed the ability to speak, he would have remained silent. The Language of the Blade was sacred and spoken only among those who had earned the right. Beyond this, Keavy knew nothing of its purpose or origin.

By now, Vorian was a blink on the path. The only parts of him Keavy could still see were his fierce blue eyes and the blackness of his long hair.

"I hate you!" She bawled at the twinkle of her sire's presence. "I shall hate you forever! You have betrayed me!"

Tulley touched her arm. Wild in the eyes and crying, she scowled down at him. The catman did not meet her glare but remained still, watching his friend fade into nothing.

The faintest of voice reached the old catman but none else heard it, not even Nessa's excellent ears. "Tulley, accompany my child," it said. "*Yeela swoll.* Teach her all that I have not."

"*Za mas teh oja hrotage.*" Tulley spoke aloud, ignoring the strange looks he was obtaining from the unhearing rest.

"What are you saying?" Keavy demanded again. "Tulley, tell me!"

"We must take our journey to End of the Path," Tulley said mournfully, his eyes closed. The ragged look had dispersed from his features. The old potion master now looked tranquil and even dared to smile as he spoke. "Once we are there, we must leave the horses and go on foot. The grounds there are dangerous and it is imperative that we be extremely heedful of the flora as well as the fauna."

"You are being watched, youngling, be vigilant."

Keavy yelped in alarm. Vorian's voice was close again, sounding a fraction from her ears. The others looked at her with confusion, for they heard nothing.

"We will meet again soon."

Keavy reached a tentative hand in front of her, but could not feel him there. He was truly gone.

"Farewell," the ruby child tearfully whispered. "My father."

End of the Path

Garric's oldest lived in friendless isolation upon Bedivere's highest of mountain peaks. Once upon a time, she had been a treasure of beauty. Now she was a twisted evil recluse, unbearable to the eye. Garric had struck her with the worst of curses, to appear as a harpy as a last punishment for her wicked ways. She could remove the charm from 'round her neck and become beautiful again, but only at the expense of her powers and immortality. Sephora chose power over beauty, and so she was doomed to live this way, with only a whisper of the shape she had once been. Though her body had suffered, it was her face that suffered the most from her father's curse and, because of this, Sephora kept no mirrors in her palace.

Through the vast and endless corridors of an icy fortress, the birdwoman straggled on legs no longer shapely. Watching with hateful eyes were the caged minions of the witch's rule. With outstretched claws, they begged and cried at her as she passed them, hoping to gain her good favor and perhaps a reward for their loyalty. Sephora's heels clicked on the marble floor as she brushed past the enchanted bars holding a phoenix dragon just like the one that was destroyed years ago but this one far smaller and younger. The infant charged the bars and hissed hatefully at its captor as she passed close to its prison. Its will was almost broken, and then Sephora would be able to control it. For now, the beast remained locked away, receiving only what it required to survive. Rewards would come only when it submitted to her control.

The last pen at the end of the hallway was where Sephora stopped to observe, for it held no dragon or demon, only a frail old man in rags. He was chained to the floor by enchanted silver locks as fat as a python's full belly. He was thin and pale, and though he appeared helpless, Sephora knew better. She could not grin, for her mouth was a curved beaky extension from which came rows of sharp toothy protrusions. Instead she opened her beak slightly and blinked huge black eyes. The old man looked at her sadly for a moment, but showed no fear. Sephora snapped her beak shut and teasingly chinked it back and forth across the bars of his prison. The old man looked down again and closed his eyes.

Sephora reached the end of the corridor and stood before a heavy black door. She uttered a scratchy phrase in a language unmanageable by any human tongue and it opened before her as if someone on the other side had simply pushed it. Before her lay a vast circular room surrounded by a crimson river of churning lava. A stone bridge allowed her to cross and stand in the center of the room, where she squawked an additional avian curse. The door slammed behind her, and suddenly, the river began to bubble and spurt. Sephora grinned as the lava rose from its basin, suspended on her word, forming and changing, becoming a raging wall of liquid fire. Within this wall, lumpy images began to form. To Sephora's right, the lava gave birth to a woman's face. Following it was a torrent of long swirling hair, then a graceful neck and generous breast. The lava puckered and hissed into the contours of the merwitch, Sorka. To Sephora's left, the sly face of Crocotta was materializing, even through the lava appearing to be sneering, and at last, in front of her, the vampire Vetala emerged, hanging upside down from the rafters of an old church, eyes burning in the darkness.

The Danaan sisters had come together inside this small chamber, and it was Sephora who addressed them in her raspy squawk.

"Show me your amulets."

At once, the charm around each sister's neck began glowing brighter than even the molten fire that their faces were visible within. Sephora's beak gaped into a vicious smile.

"The plan is under way," she croaked, "The ruby child has severed ties with the knight." The birdwoman swung a profoundly scaled neck in Crocotta's direction, and she gaped again. A dry bark of laughter issued from her leathery throat. "Congratulations Crocotta. You have earned yourself a biscuit."

The other women snickered at the comment made in their canine cursed sister's expense. Crocotta was not amused. Her molten image morphed and broke through the wall. At once, the redness of the lava disappeared and allowed Crocotta to appear in all her colors. Her hyena's head reached out and snapped at the likeness of Sorka, rippling it into chaos, and then sucked back into the fiery wall, immersing itself in lava once again. Sorka's face oozed back into place with a sloppy smacking sound.

Vetala snorted and fingered the charm on the choker around her neck. "Come off it, Cottie. Learn to take a joke."

"I almost felt that for real!" Sorka cried.

Crocotta bared her small white teeth, looking almost for a moment like her bestial form again. "Wait until we *meet* for real."

"Ladies!" The harpy's harsh screech silenced them all. "Do not fight amongst yourselves. I have brought you together to dispense some good news. The souls entering Siavon have increased in number, and you know what that means. Without Garric to welcome them to the next world, the souls will collect and combine, and together we can absorb their power and break free of our charmed prison forever." A leathery brown tongue licked the exposed fangs on the outside of her cracked beak hopefully. "But first, we must eliminate our greatest threat."

Sephora lifted her arms, the dingy gray rags clothing them falling back to reveal her feathered limbs and the three walls of lava swiftly slammed together in a hissing bubbling mass, obliterating the faces of her sisters. When the liquid steadied, a new face began to take shape.

"So, our child of prophecy." Sephora muttered a garbled noise that barely passed for human. "The true beholder of God's Breath is a mere youngling girl not yet past the age of learning."

The smiling face of Keavy slid back into its three separate images of the Danaan sisters. Their amulets glowed as bright as the noonday sun.

"I do believe fate is on our side," Sephora huffed in good measure. "Do you think so, ladies?"

Sorka clapped her hands and giggled merrily, beside her, Vetala's luscious red lips parted to reveal the winking tips of bone white fangs, and Crocotta stretched her ugly head to the sky in a blissful roar.

***

Rut peeked in the entrance of his mistress' den apprehensively. She stood in front of a full length mirror in a dress of emerald green brushing her long black hair with a boar's ivory hairbrush. For once, it was not in braids. At full length it reached the backs of the witch's knees. She could see the frightened kylin in the reflection and inclined her head slightly to invite him in, graceful smile ever present. As ugly as she was, she was still quite the beauty.

"*Ratah*, my darling, do not be afraid."

Rut slunk forward, plopping down on his behind at his mistress's side, hanging his head. Crocotta reached a long fingered hand out to pet him, from which he at first dipped back. When she showed no intent to strike, Rut tentatively lifted his head out and laid back his ears to receive what little kindness she would offer him.

"I have a new task for you, one that even in your animalistic stupidity can be accomplished easily." The witch said, stroking him lovingly under the muzzle.

Rut rattled contentedly.

"The girl is in good company and has access to a weapon more powerful than even I," Crocotta muttered curtly. "So, I cannot possibly expect you, a simple kylin with the heart of a coward and the brains of a pullet to fulfill your duties without a bit of help."

Crocotta put her hairbrush on the vanity and picked up an unmarked bottle of liquid that resembled dingy dishwater. As she spoke to Rut, she unscrewed the cork and took a long whiff of the chemical fumes before holding it out to him. Rut sniffed at it and recoiled at the vile odor it produced, yakking. Crocotta grabbed him by the hairs of his muzzle, and in spite of his rattling and bleating, she managed to pry his sharp jaws open and pour the rank fluid down his throat. He backed away from her, yakking, mewling, and swatting at his face. Crocotta laughed at him and stood smiling as the kylin began to change shape.

Rut scampered backwards from her, dragging his haunches. Inside, his guts began to gurgle and the kylin started to slobber. His bones disintegrated inside him with a noise like dry rice being crushed in hand and he fell to a motionless fleshy pile on the floor, bleating piteously. Vital organs popped in sickening audible squishing sounds within a diminishing body. Rut's fur and scales shrank inside his flesh and at once his entire self slipped into an entirely new structure. The process took less than a minute, but afterwards, Rut lay on the floor in his new shape, panting in his terror.

Crocotta stood over the former kylin, no trace of sympathy evident. "With this form, you shall destroy the ruby child and all who aid her, and then my dear Rut, you shall be free from my keep."

Hearing this, Rut lifted his new head hopefully and attempted to clack his pincers, succeeding only in uttering a wet spitting sound. His pincers were gone, as were his long protruding fangs. He tried to stand on four legs, but found it quite difficult, being forced to push himself to his back two, swaying in an awkward manner that made Crocotta laugh cruelly at him. Rut stopped wobbling immediately following the halt in Crocotta's laughter. She approached him casually, now much taller than he was. He lowered his head in submission.

"I shall keep my word *only* if you do not fail me again," she warned. "However, Rut, if you do...."

The crackling sounds within Crocotta's body was all Rut needed to gain the ability to stand properly and bow to her in total and unconditional obedience. Crocotta nodded.

"I see we understand each other."

Rut watched his mistress circle him, nervous of her examination of his new form. She pulled at his skinny arms and legs, grabbed his chin and peered into his pincerless face, yanked on his tiny ears. He took it in silence, suppressing the instinct to withdraw.

"Yes, very nice," the witch complemented her own doings. "You shall be recognized by none."

Crocotta threw her head back and roared. The bottles of perfume upon her vanity rattled fearfully and Rut covered his ears with his new hands. In almost no time at all the outline of a gangly brute of a blachund hovered at the entrance, drooling generously when it saw that the kylin had become a very easy prey item. One domineering look from Crocotta, however, had reduced the prowler to a whimpering coward with its scraggily tail thrust between its legs.

Crocotta's womanly tone adopted the gritty croak of her other side, and she spoke to the blachund in its most easily understood language. In response, the animal crouched and awaited Rut to climb upon its back. Crocotta went outside and watched her minion scamper off into the distance carrying with it her backup plan.

"So obedient, my children," she sighed to herself, feeling the weight of her powers in the palm of her hand. "Oh, but one little doggy strays from the yard, doesn't he? Scampering about alone and scared in a deep dark wood. Well, fear not my lost one." She began to change rapidly, in little time becoming the monster she truly was. "I will find you and end yourrrr sssuffering."

***

The ruby child and her companions were on their first real travel day, having spent the previous night in town and the morning gathering from the North and South villages what modest supplies had gone undestroyed in the attack. It was nearing dusk, and few words had passed between them all day. Keavy rode high upon Annick's back, her expression slackened by her thoughts. Her eyes, normally bright as the stone imbedded in the sword at her side, were dull and listless and dry of tears. She could no longer cry for the man who had pretended to love her as a daughter in order to fulfill some lost prophecy. Keavy could imagine it now: Vorian, sitting at home wrapped in his fox skins, sipping musket tea and reveling in the silence he had at last obtained. His role in the prophecy done with, he could now regain the life he so loved, a life of solitude, a life without her.

Dancing along on all fours between the tricorn's hooves was the recovering wood faun, sniffing away at the ground like a hunting hound. She was still sticky with empathy oil, but it had stopped flowing from her temples hours ago. Despite the trauma Nessa had endured in the last few hours, she still retained her species specific ability to bounce back. Yet she was quieter and less probing than ordinary, possibly in respect for Keavy's grief.

Tulley rode behind on Alder's horse, nodding off every so often with the rhythm of the gelding's working haunches and the soft tinkling of his earrings clinking together. His satchel was stuffed to the stitches with potions from his own storage as well as supplies borrowed from the market. "Borrowed" was the word he used. Looting was such a harsh and very unthinkable term for catfolk to use, especially one of his stature. He hated to think himself a

111

scavenger. In these times though, scavenging could very well be their only means of survival. Tulley's eyelids drooped again. He pushed the glasses up on his nose and twitched his whiskers, purring himself into a doze.

Far ahead of all of them, Alder scouted on foot with a newly obtained bow and arrow he had plundered from his father's shop. Against Tulley's warning, he had searched his family's home for his parents, but had found not a sign of their existence or lack thereof. The hope that they had escaped with their lives was what kept Alder in high enough spirits to go hunting for the group's first fresh meat. Looking back to make sure the others were far behind and could not see where he was going, Alder stepped off the path and charged into the thick forest.

The others had not seen Alder in quite a while and still assumed him to be far ahead of them on the path, so there was no pressing concern when he did not reappear after they decided to rest the horses and dismount for a quick nibble of jerky rations from Tulley's satchel. Keavy refused the snack and, instead, took the chance to clean the dirt out of Annick's hooves with her knife. Tulley and Nessa sat cross-legged on the ground chewing slowly. Nessa had a difficult time with the salty meat. Her species was primarily herbivorous, so she excused herself to forage the leaves and roots growing within sight of the path. Tulley sat alone, gnawing thoughtfully. His bushy crooked tail swished contently back and forth in the dirt.

"Fair universe, Keavy," he lightly addressed her, "You are going to pick the shoes right off of that poor horse if you don't ease up."

Keavy grunted and released Annick's front right leg, letting the newly cleaned hoof thump to the ground again. She moved to his back legs and continued, ignoring the catman's advice.

"If I don't scrape out his hooves, rocks will slow him down." she muttered brusquely.

Tulley swallowed his last bite of jerky and stood, brushing off his clothing with the fastidiousness of every feline, part human or not. "Try not to hate Vorian, dear," he said softly. "He has done only what he was meant to do."

Keavy grunted again and dug her knife into Annick's last hoof. The tricorn snorted at her. The blade had gone just a little too

112

deep for comfort, and he now turned his deadly head back at her with blue eyes rolling in agitation. Keavy patted him on the rump and continued cleaning out his hoof with a lighter touch.

Sighing, Tulley stretched his back and craned his neck to crank out the knots. He was walking better now, the catnap had done him good, but he was still sore and greatly drained by his exertions from the previous night. Tulley was no stranger to aches and pains, being as old as he was. Forty-four years had passed him by, and although to humans this was middle aged, to catfolk, it was nearing the end. The catfolk that did not succumb to genetically related deaths early on usually made it to their fifties before transitioning to the City of Souls. Tulley had been one of the lucky few to make it this far and, if he did not say so himself, he still looked and moved quite well. It was as if Garric himself had preserved his youth long enough to allow him to aid the ruby child on her journey through the major cities of the Danaan. If he passed into Siavon as soon as the prophecy had been foreseen, Tulley would have no complaints.

"I fear I have not told you enough about the importance of your purpose, Keavy," The catman said with a self-contemptuous sigh. "It is imperative, absolutely *imperative* that those entrusted with your upbringing follow through. Vorian Tranore's purpose has been fulfilled. I believe he has succeeded in raising a fine young warrior. Now it is my turn to guide you, and I pray to Siavon above us that I can do half as good a job with you as Vorian has. He has worked very hard on you, dear."

Keavy scowled back at him. "And now that his job is done, he can regain his cherished solitude and forget about me."

She had turned her attention to the wound on Annick's neck and proceeded to dab it with topical salve. Annick blew his discomfort through his nose, but stood still.

Tulley's earrings sang with a shake of his head. "Vorian did not take you in just because he had to, Keavy. His role was to protect you, to teach you. The prophecy said nothing of loving you."

Keavy merely sniffed and averted her eyes from the potion master once again. She stroked Annick's neck listlessly, laying her auburn head against his jet black hide.

Tulley smiled warmly, whiskers twitching. "Do not think that he does not care for you," he told her. "That is very untrue. Very untrue indeed."

An hour passed between them in silence. Tulley groomed himself with a wooden bristle brush, working out the knots and mats that got into the longer bits of his fur. Keavy spent this time with Annick, treating his wounds, speaking to him softly, using some of their fresh water to rinse the dried blood from his legs. Nessa, stuffed full of shoots in very little time, made her appearance just as Tulley was about to shout for her. She looked plump and happy, much different than she had earlier.

"Me loves the roots in these parts, me does," the faun tittered, white tail wagging. "Do I wish I weren't filled to the top now or I'd take another nibble at them, I would!"

"Don't get too fat, Nessa." Keavy joked. Her sullen mood lifted slightly since their first stop, especially in her orphaned friend's presence. "We might just roast *you* up should Alder not be able to track us down any deer."

"Where is that lad?" Tulley mumbled aloud, scratching behind his frayed right ear with one extended claw. "He hasn't joined us in hours."

Alder was indeed far from his comrades, deep in the forest with his bow at the ready. A rabbit had made an appearance some distance away, and Alder was stealthily readying himself for the kill. He had the creature lined up in his sites and was about to let his arrow soar when a rising figure in the foregrounds of his vision made him lose his concentration and shoot far over the rabbit's head. Startled, the little creature made a bolt for its hole and vanished from sight. Alder would have been angry at the loss, but at the moment, he was entranced by the unblinking eyes of the blachund standing several feet away.

"Is he close, Nessa?" Keavy asked her friend hopefully.

Nessa huffed and snorted around in the path's dusty soil and sneezed to clear her sinuses. She rose to two legs at last and rubbed her runny nose.

"Me thinks he went off the path, yes," she said fretfully. "Some time ago. The scent fades in the breeze."

"Can you tell which way he went?"

Nessa bowed her head, shamefully. She toed at the dirt with her hoof.

"We will give him the night to find us." Tulley spoke up. "Tomorrow, we move on, with or without him."

Keavy gaped in surprise. "You're suggesting we simply *leave* him?"

"Alder is an expert tracker." Tulley pointed out to her. "We will waste a lot of time and energy wandering about looking for the boy when he could easily catch up to us on his own. Furthermore, it is dangerous in the woods."

Tulley frowned at the looks the rest of his party was giving him, including Alder's loyal horse, Lorcan.

"We cannot risk your safety, Keavy," he explained softly. "I am sorry."

"What about *his* safety?" she shouted. "We cannot just feed him to the blachunds!"

The old catman sighed with the patience of one accustomed to the tantrums of younglings. "Keavy, you must get to End of the Path as soon as possible. The longer we wait, the worse things will be for everyone, including Alder. If he is alive in the forest when Crocotta falls, he will no longer face harm from her minions. And if I am not mistaken, it is *you* the blachunds are after, not Alder."

"The master is right, he is." Nessa reluctantly agreed. Her ears were drooping at the sound of own words. Leaving a member of the clan behind was not the way of her people.

Keavy ventured a gaze into the woods, peering between the twisted branches of the scaly trees and prickle bushes. She could see very little in the fading light, and without a torch, Alder would be seeing littler still. He would be an easy target for hungry predators, whether or not he posed them a threat. Keavy knew this, and was positive Tulley knew it too.

"So we are going to abandon him with those…those *things* out there."

Tulley reached forth his hand and took hers. "I am confident that young Alder will find us," he assured her, though his attempt at masking his own doubt with heartening words was very close to translucent. "Don't you worry, dear. No blachunds would dare to face Alder Devnet with a bow and arrow."

The blachund stood in the open ground, crouched and staring. Its large ears swiveled back and forth, flashing their white inner hairs like beacons. This blachund was different than most of those Alder had seen in his lifetime. Its eyes were blue, not yellow, and its fur was crisp and dark and not spotted with mange. It was large, waist high at the withers, but not the largest he'd ever seen. Its build was lean and sinewy, less solid than a typical blachund's. Had Alder not known better, he would have taken it for a large domesticated cur. The heavy jaw and spiny mane said otherwise. This was definitely a blachund, and there was only one thing to do when faced with a blachund. He raised his bow, pulling an arrow back, gritting his teeth. Knowing what bows and arrows indicated, the animal swiftly turned tail and ran, leaping gracefully over obstacles as Alder pursued deeper into the rising shadows after it.

***

Crocotta stalked silently through the underbrush without hurry, the pricks of the thorny bushes but a mere tickle to her thick hide. The traitor was within her range, unmindful of her presence as it feasted on the remains of a dead rotting raccoon. Inwardly, she found herself laughing. What a mighty hunter this one was! Resorting to a feast of carrion rather than attempting to hunt down fresh prey. *This* was the one that had betrayed her influence and ruined her attempt to destroy the chosen one? Crocotta was almost embarrassed.

She took another carefully placed step forward in her hiding spot, mindful not to jingle the chain which held her powers in a mere bauble, waiting for the right moment to spring. The lone blachund lapped at its meal, unknowingly facing a painful death. Oh and it would be painful! Crocotta would see that the traitor's death would be prolonged for hours. First, she would pin it down and chew each of its paws off one by one, savoring in the crackle of bone and the screams of torture her prey released beneath her. After she had immobilized it, she would rip off its ears and pluck its eyes from their sockets. Eyes were quite sweet, the witch remembered from many earlier kills, and suppressed the urge to drool. She would also devour the poor brute's genitals and tail at her long leisure. Afterwards, she would go for the belly, ripping out the entrails. If by

116

a wicked twist of fate, it still lived after that, Crocotta would go for the throat and end it, then leave the rest to her loyal pack. No one who crossed her would be granted the luxury of a quick death. Crocotta lost her inward struggle and drooled listlessly, taking another step and tensing her excited muscles for the spring.

The blachund jerked its head up, perked and listening, and Crocotta froze. A noise had disturbed him, but it had not come from her, she was sure. It was from some distance behind, the loutish crackling of twigs underfoot that could only mean a human in their midst. Crocotta remained hidden. Perhaps this night would offer two main courses instead of one.

The blachund merely watched Alder make his appearance with his bow and arrow drawn. He was sweating and covered with sap, heaving in exhaustion, but the unmistakable gaze of hate was drawn upon his boyish features.

"Why do you not attack me?" Alder inquired impatiently. "Why do you run?"

He watched the blachund warily, awaiting a sign of aggression, perhaps even *hoping* to be attacked, but it stood watching him with curiosity. Alder decided to even the playing field a little to show the beast he was a fair fighter. Perhaps it did nothing because it knew it was no match against a bow and arrow. He hung them over his back and grabbed the knives from his belt, twirling them teasingly in hand. He drew back and threw one at the beast, but it evaded the attack with ease and the dagger stuck deep in the ground, hilt quivering.

"What trickery is this?" Alder threw the other dagger, and again, the blachund evaded it and did not move toward him. "Attack me!"

Crocotta could stand it no longer. The opportunity was too great. A snarl rumbled from deep in her belly and she stepped forward, revealing her presence at last. Alder gasped and took a step back, but the blachund did not look particularly alarmed at her appearance. Instead of whimpering or cowering, it trotted, tail in air, in between the path of the frightened boy and the witch, staring deeply into Crocotta's manic eyes.

The blachund's ears flattened against its skull. Its tail became ramrod straight behind it, and then it did the unthinkable. A low threatening growl slipped out between bared fangs, a voice of challenge. No blachund had dared to challenge her before. Though bloodthirsty, they were also stupid and cowardly, especially in the presence of their alpha. This was unnatural behavior. It was protecting the lad, Crocotta realized. This would be its last betrayal!

The witch lunged first. The blachund jumped out of her way, and she found herself biting dirt mere inches from Alder's foot. He cried out in alarm and made a run for it, but Crocotta was fast. She looped in front of him and bristled angrily, her stripes pricked up all along her hairy back. The lad would die first in front of his failed protector. She would remove his head with a single swipe and swallow it whole. Alder fumbled for his bow and arrow, but his hands shook too badly. Crocotta inched forward, teeth gnashing as he backed away from her. At last, he tripped over a rock and fell on his bottom and could do no more than raise his hands up to protect himself. Crocotta rose to her haunches and bared her claws. One swipe would do it. She would dispatch the boy and then hunt down the traitor. Two of her enemies would fall before her like quivering saplings.

The blachund sprung at her, barking wildly. Its jaws clamped down on her one raised black claw. Screaming in pain, she flailed and shook the beast off, seeing that it had taken two of her digits with it. While she watched, the blachund jerked its head back and swallowed them, then licked its chops contently and glared back at her like she was just a meal. Blood furled from her mangled paw and dripped down onto the ground below.

The boy had climbed out from under her and was trying to run again. Roaring, Crocotta chased him, but the blachund leapt in front of her once again, ears back, blood spattered teeth bared. It charged at her and grasped her by the throat with a lethal grip that would have killed another blachund, but to Crocotta, it was but a mere annoyance. The blachund's fangs were no match for her thick hide and she reached up with her good paw and slapped it off again. Crocotta swung her head around, looking for Alder in frantic anger. She spotted him several feet ahead, but he was not running. Instead, he had finally drawn his bow and was pulling an arrow back into place. Crocotta charged at him, and he let it go. It whistled through the air and pierced her right shoulder deeply, but it was not enough to slow her down. Crocotta continued to beeline for him, bleeding, frothing, and roaring with hate.

The blachund landed hard on the back of her neck, and this time, she could not reach it to fling it off. Crocotta slid forward in the dirt at the sudden impact and fell, jaws snapping shut and severing the tip of her lolling green tongue when her head hit the ground. While she yelped painfully, the blachund seized one of her soft ears in its teeth and tore off a mouthful of it, causing her yelps to turn over into a scream. She got to her feet again and tried to shake it off like a drop of water, but its teeth took a solid grip on the ridge of flesh where her left eyebrow would have been. Her eye became clouded with blood, and the witch roared and reached up to tear the animal from her face.

Another sharp pain hit her in the chest, disrupting the witch long enough for the blachund to jump from her back safely. She sat back on her haunches and looked down at the arrow embedded in her. Just as she gripped it in her claws to pull it out, another arrow flew from Alder's bow and struck her dead on in the heart. The paralyzing pain in her chest went numb. She screamed. Another of Alder's arrow whistled through the air and hit her again, and another came soon after it. Gravely weakened, Crocotta went down to all fours and whined. Her chest resembled a porcupine's back. She focused her wheezy growls at Alder as he picked up his daggers from the ground and stood over her triumphantly, the blachund watching quietly behind him.

"You have made a powerrrrfully ssssstupid misssssstake, boy," she informed him with her wasting breath. Her legs quivered under the weight of her dying body, and reluctantly, she lay down by the feet of her slayer like a subservient before her king. Her bare toothed expression though, was far from meek.

"Drink your last daysss in deeply, for my hounds will ssssleep upon your sssskin after filling their bellies with your tender ffflesh."

"You should concentrate on dying, bitch."

These words accompanied Crocotta to her death. Alder plunged both daggers deep into her neck and stepped back, a thought coming to his mind as he watched the witch jerk and moan in death's grip. He reached down to grab her amulet, meaning to pull it over her head and watch her die in human form. Visions of glory raced through his mind when his fingertips brushed the silver moons lying against the slowly rising and falling fur covered chest, but the spark of vibrating pain that laced through his hand steered him into far simpler ones. He cursed and pulled back, fingers tingling. The beast could not smile, so she bared her teeth at him, her eyes wet and gleaming. Her mocking laugh came out as a low rough growl. She closed her eyes then and breathed no more.

Crocotta's body began to sizzle and smoke. The amulet around her neck began to melt and drip down into the carcass until it had become part of what had been Crocotta. The flesh seared from her bones until they were completely clean, and then the bones themselves crumbled into a pile of simple ash in the vague shape of the fallen Empress of the Forest. Only dust leapt up from the remains. It was over, for now.

He had killed her with his own hand, but Alder knew that Crocotta was not truly dead. It would only be a matter of time before Sephora would resurrect her to finish what she had started. He turned to the blachund that had saved his life, crouched quietly behind him with the whites of its ears facing forward and muzzle dotted with the witch's blood. Cautiously, Alder crouched down and lifted out a hand to it. The strange blue-eyed blachund came to it, wagging an eager tail, and licked the offered hand affectionately. An ally had been made.

***

Siavon hung high and bright over the end of the day, and Tulley was busy preparing a fire in its assuring light. Keavy brought forth the rabbit she had killed and cleaned and passed it to him to be roasted over a makeshift pit fire of sticks and stones. Nessa was feasting on shoots again; armed with Tulley's flanged mace at his advisement. He was taking no chances after the disappearance of Alder, especially since he had not returned as hoped. Continuing onward instead of searching for him was not Tulley's proudest decision, but he had promised Vorian he would protect Keavy at all costs. Her life was the only one that mattered. Should Keavy die, all hope would be lost. Tulley only wished it was easier for her to understand that. She hadn't spoken to him since yesterday. It was reaching nightfall, and at the closing of their journey's second day they were very near to End of the Path. The group needed to cast aside their hard thoughts to make room for larger concerns.

Tulley sat by the fire, his tail wrapped around his feet for warmth. He held up the torso of the skinned rabbit and nodded, then proceeded to drive a sharpened stick clean through its anus and out from between its long ears and hold it out over the flames. His wet nostrils flared at the smell of roasting meat. Keavy took a seat across from him, but did not look his way. She merely picked up a branch and poked lethargically at the fire.

"I know you are angry," Tulley spoke up. "And so is your right. Alder's disappearance is regrettable. It is your duty, however, to continue onward and complete your quest despite the pain you endure along the way. Vorian would want you to be strong right now."

At the mention of her sire's name, Keavy glanced up, looking at Tulley with eyes full of suffering. "He just left. No hesitation. He just *left* me." She dropped her branch and drew her knees up to her chin, blinking away the emotion. "Gutless wretch."

Tulley gasped and dropped the cooking rabbit into the fire. It hissed and sputtered within the flames, the fat shriveling up like a slug in seawater. "Watch your tongue or I shall cut it from your insolent mouth!"

Keavy fell silent and turned her eyes away. Tulley at once regretted being so quick to anger. The child of prophecy she was, but she was still only a child. Her heart overpowered her head, and this was something that Tulley had been charged with breaking her of, however reluctant she was. Tulley realized that the only way he was going to gain back her trust, was to trust her in return. That meant, his story had to be told. The old catman sat back down slowly. His popping knees seemed to echo in the woods beyond.

"I never told you, Keavy, how I came to live in Nodens, have I?"

Keavy shook her head mechanically.

"Well, perhaps now is the time," the master sighed. He picked up the rabbit again and shook off the ashes, then pulled it from the flames and sat it on a flat cooling stone.

"I have never relayed this story to anyone before you," Tulley admitted somberly. "I beg your pardon, for the memories are ragged and painful to relive."

Hearing this, Keavy looked up again. Tulley had placed one knuckle to his temple and was fingering his whiskers with his other hand. His large green eyes were alight with remembrance, and the tweak of a smile curled the corner of his oddly split mouth.

"I used to make my living on the island of Murias as a fisherman," he began. "I was born there and I believed I would die there. The Talla Muro was a beautiful place before Sorka arrived. The ocean was warm and clear, teaming with life. The beach held pearl white sand upon its back like a warm blanket. It was lovely. I shall always remember it that way."

"I met my wife in Murias. Her name was Leona Cero, and she was from a farmer's family. I could not help but gawk at her, she was so elegant. There was not a fault nestled in her silky white fur. Ah, she had such lovely blue eyes."

Tulley smiled. The tip of his tail flicked.

"Together we had four sons and two daughters, all of whom were crew on my boat, *Maiden's Kiss*. I taught them everything I knew of the seaman's craft." He chuckled. "They learned well. I would have trusted any one of them to captain a ship blindfolded. We ran up and down the coast collecting a profit with our efforts. Leona stayed at home and grew a garden. Our family sold her vegetables and the fish I caught to keep comfortable for a number of years."

Tulley paused to test the heat of the rabbit with one finger. Finding it bearable, he sliced open the creature with a small hand knife and sectioned it out between Keavy and himself as he told his story.

"One year everything changed. While the children and I were away, my wife took ill. You would not know it by looking at her, but she was riddled with internal turmoil. Bad genetic illness had surfaced inside her. When we came back a month later, she was

122

near death and no healer had the proper medicine to cure her. I chose to stay home to try to concoct a cure for her myself using various ingredients I was able to barter for or buy. Our children continued to fish and bring home an acceptable profit, but about that time Sorka came to the islands and made the waters angry."

Tulley's voice caught on the ragged edges of looming sadness. He disguised it with a low cough and stuffed a piece of rabbit meat in his mouth to chew on for a moment. Only after he'd swallowed a few more bites did he continue. Keavy leaned forward, enthralled. She found herself wishing she was back at the master's home by the Ardor Flower Valley, listening to one of his lessons instead of this.

"*Maiden's Kiss* sank in a dreadful storm," Tulley continued. "My children were drowned," he huffed despondently. "All of them."

Tulley cut out another section of meat for Keavy, which she took and ate, though it tasted overcooked and chewy.

"Try as I did, I was unsuccessful in producing a lifesaving cure for Leona. She died in my arms, shortly after I relayed the news of our children's deaths. To this day I wonder if it was the illness that took her or the heartbreak of our loss."

"I grieved at the bottom of a barrel. I drank away what little savings I had left until I had nothing of my former life in Murias. I abandoned my home and drifted from island to island, mixing up potions and selling them to earn enough for grog. Eventually, I was discovered by a sailor from Gallus who brought me aboard his ship with his mates. They treated me well, fed me, clothed me, and then revealed what they truly were, pirates. And I was forced to join their crew."

"Tulley!" Keavy blurted.

He nodded, confirming her worst beliefs. "For twelve years, I sailed under a brigand flag. The things I saw; the things I *did* just to keep my own skin intact...My dreams were never peaceful after that."

Tulley offered her another piece of rabbit, but she shook her head. Her appetite had diminished.

"I attempted escape, but was caught. The captain was kind enough not to kill me only because I had..." Tulley winced. "I had been so *useful*."

He let out a ragged cough from deep inside his chest. Keavy would have leapt to his aid if he had not settled her with a raised hand. When he was finished, he swallowed hard and resumed telling his story.

"They cast me out into the open ocean in a beaten up dingy. It gets very hazy after that. I should have died. I *deserved* death. I keenly awaited it to come to me as it had come to my family. But, death would not even take pity on one such as I. Eventually I reached shore after many days in the sun, delirious, injured, and ravaged with sickness. That was when my savior, my *hrotage*, pulled me from the wreckage."

Keavy bit her lip; her eyes were now spilling tears generously. She was overtaken with an immense feeling of guilt as the catman spoke.

"Keavy," Tulley said strongly. "Vorian Tranore found me and brought me back to Nodens. He took care of me and taught me all he knew. When I was well, he helped me build my home in the valley, and there I finally found solace. I used the knowledge I had accumulated over the years to teach gifted children, and I recorded my findings in my books. Vorian gave me a second chance. He saved my very soul. And all he ever asked in return was that I be your guide."

The catman grunted as he climbed shakily to his feet, proudly puffing out his orange and white chest, one claw raised to his heart and a scrappy expression showing through his spotted lenses.

"Here stands Linneaus Marcus Tulley!" he laughed dryly. "A nearsighted, shambling, belligerent, old hairball! Widower, drunkard, vagrant, pirate, and now advisor to the ruby child herself. It's amazing how the gods work their magic upon the world, isn't it?"

Keavy sucked in her lip. All at once, her anger had melted away. "Tulley, I…I don't know what to say."

She found herself heavy with a new respect for not only Tulley, but Vorian as well. Since the witches had risen to power, the consequences were brutal for those who dared to break the Law of Idris. The very mention of helping pirates, even former pirates, could have one drawn and quartered before the day was through. Vorian had risked all to save Tulley, just as Tulley had risked all by settling in Nodens. If word spread of Tulley's true beginnings, he would surely be driven from the civilized world into the unknown wilds of Wendoa, if not stoned to death in the streets.

Nessa returned from her grazing, just as fat, but not as happy as before. Her long ears drooped and her big eyes shook in their sockets. She clasped Tulley's mace tightly in her three fingered hands like a child with a doll.

"I don't like it here, I don't," her voice trembled. "Evil gets thicker in the air here, yes. Me heart's afraid to beat!"

Tulley approached her and gently pried the mace from her hands.

"Ah, right you are, Nessa," he agreed. "Evil is certainly present in the air here."

The old catman examined the pointed end of his weapon with squinted eyes through his gold rimmed glasses. His face became distinctly feline as he licked the remains of his meal from his lips with a rough beveled tongue. Then, Tulley patted Nessa reassuringly on her small head and her ears perked up again at the gesture.

"Soon we will reach End of the Path, Crocotta's dark lands," the catman told his students. "Sleep close tonight."

***

She was in the Ardor Flower Valley. The wind was blowing so hard it almost flattened the plants to the ground. Tulley's home was a tiny little dot against the stormy sky, but Keavy could make it there before the shower if she ran. A drop of cold rain struck her in one of her ruby eyes and caused her to flinch in surprise. She wiped it away and started for Tulley's. It was so windy! She could barely lift a foot off the ground without feeling like she was going to blow away. Nevertheless, Keavy quickened her pace and trotted towards the cottage again. The rain began to pour, drenching her to the bone instantly. She flicked the wet hair out of her face and pushed on to get to Tulley's.

Now she could see him standing in his garden, waving to her erratically, motioning her to come in out of the storm, but he still seemed so far away. No matter how fast she walked, Tulley's cottage remained that small little blob in the distance. Keavy was frustrated. She stopped in the middle of the valley and shielded her eyes against the rain.

Nessa appeared before her, standing about ten paces away. It was raining all around her, yet she looked totally dry and smiling. Her arms were folded and she was tapping her hoof in jocular impatience. Keavy smiled at her and waved. Nessa waved back at her and vanished from view.

Thunder boomed like a massive explosion above the valley. A bolt of lightning struck the ground directly in front of Keavy, blinding her in a flash of light. She yelled and dove for the ground, covering her head in an instinctual attempt to shield herself. A familiar jeering laugh brought her out of it, and when she dared to look up, she saw Alder standing over her, shaking his head in disbelief at her cowardice. In another flash of light, he too was gone, and Keavy rolled over onto her back to stare at the sky.

A brilliant sun in the sky burned fiery orange. Keavy smiled and soaked up the rays, thankful for the relieving warmth they gave her from the chilling rain. The sun jittered, jolted to the side, and seemed to lose its balance in the sky. It not so much fell as *hurtled* toward her like a giant frightening fire beast. It moved with the speed of a living thing, pulsating, glowing, rushing down on her. Keavy wasn't worried though. She was just glad that the rain was drying off her skin. She folded her arms behind her head and watched her clothes and flesh burn off of her body. There was nothing to do but lay there and wait to die.

At once, images of her friends and family began to pulse in the sky with the rhythm of her quickening heartbeat. Tulley crouched by his kettle telling his stories, Nessa frolicked with the Mool clan in the underbrush, Vorian drew God's Breath from his belt, Alder sat upon his horse, rearing in a challenge to race. Memories flashed before her quicker and quicker, liquefying into strange and ominous images as the sun neared, growing hotter and brighter. Alder impaled through the heart by God's Breath, Tulley's broken body motionless at the bottom of a black gorge, Vorian's throat in the grip of a blachund, Nessa drowning in a whirling black sea. The sun bore down upon her while Keavy lay upon the rain soft ground. The ground around her melted. The oxygen finally burst into flames around her, and the sun came down around her, swallowing her whole.

With a clotted gasp, Keavy awoke from her dream, lids fluttering open like the wings of newly hatched butterflies. Cold, even under cover of a blanket, she shivered and drew herself upright to gain perspective on her surroundings. The visible parts of the sky leering above the trees still retained the old bruise yellow color of dawn, but Keavy could already feel the warmth of a beautiful day chasing away the chill in her bones. The nightmare mercifully began to fade as Keavy quietly rose and went about the task of collecting wood for the breakfast fire. She wandered about the skirts of the path, keeping a clear eye out for danger as she collected sticks and dry leaves to bring back to the camp.

The sun hiked itself up over End of the Path just about the time Keavy reached the end of the woods and the dirty path slowly merged into a rocky terrain. She stopped at the wood's end and watched the morning come, lamenting inwardly for the people who would never again see another sunrise. A familiar musky smell warned her that Nessa was soon to join her. Not long after, the young wood faun made her approach, plunking her round bottom on the ground, possibly thinking the same as her human companion. The two friends silently watched the wicked grounds of End of the Path come into full view, a barren rocky landscape surrounded by ever present storm clouds over which the sun reigned high.

Keavy looked down at Nessa, and the little wood faun looked up at her. "I've been a fool all this time, Nessa," she said through a sigh. "I thought for sure I knew what I was doing. I skipped my lessons, I disobeyed my elders, I laughed at my fate, and now it has come and I am not ready. I'm not right for this. I can't be the chosen one. Simply because my eyes are this color, I am to be some sort of a divine conqueror."

She rested a listless hand upon the belt which held the sheath of God's Breath, and in return, the sword warmed against her thigh. "I'm a youngling," she muttered darkly. "I'm a *child*. I am no *hrotage*."

Nessa toed the dirt with one shy hoof. "Keavy, you know you is me best friend and all, yes?"

Keavy's brow went up, concerned. "Of course, Nessa."

"Well, then I hopes you listens to me when I says me mind," Nessa replied with a stiffness that was unbecoming of her. "You must trust in yourself more, you must. You have a lot more to offer

127

than you thinks, yes. I saws how you faced down those two fiends in the woods, I did, and you did it fearlessly. You are very brave, Keavy. I feel safe with you."

Keavy's mouth turned up into a smile. The eyes that marked her destiny sparkled in the new light. Nessa smiled back, but soon fell into an expression of apprehension. Her ears flickered, and she turned her head back in the direction of the camp. Keavy followed her example and cocked her head to listen for what the faun's excellent hearing had picked up on. A distressed whinny came muffled by the distance, and Keavy knew the sound of Annick's cry better than anyone. Without hesitation, Keavy pulled out her sword and hurried back down the path, Nessa scampering on all fours after.

Keavy and Nessa arrived back in camp right around the time the blachund maneuvered swiftly out of the way of Annick's heavy front hooves. Tulley cursed and wielded his mace, swinging at its ugly head each time it got too close. He succeeded only in grazing the large dog's shoulder. A shred of fur wrapped itself around the flanged sides of the weapon, but the blachund had been unharmed. Its ears went back and it snapped at the mace as it came up again, and Tulley took a step back and hissed. Lorcan had taken off in the opposite direction, but Annick would not be frightened off by a single blachund. The steed whinnied again and lowered his head to aim his long horns. He charged at the beast and chased it across the path for quite a ways before it suddenly double backed under the tricorn's belly and leapt out of harm's way once again.

"Look out, younglings!"

But Tulley's warning came too late. The blachund was already making a running leap straight for Keavy. Heavy paws connected with her shoulders, and a great stinking weight knocked her flat on her back, throwing the sword from her hands, leaving her vulnerable to a jugular attack. The heavy muzzle closing in on her face, Keavy started screaming, waiting for fangs to sink into her throat. Instead, she felt a hot wet tongue slide over her cheek and chin, and she opened her eyes to the horrendous black fiend's friendly gaze and wagging tail.

"It's all right."

128

The voice came from the distance, along with the thick clopping of hooves upon soil marking the appearance of a rider. The blachund, in its strange actions, responded to the voice as a dog to its master's, and backed away from Keavy to bound toward it, barking excitedly. Keavy sat up in her daze, and there was Alder, leading his shaken horse by the halter and bending down to greet the brute.

"Me stoles and minks!" Nessa sputtered. "Lookies!"

"He is a friend," the unharmed, if a bit disheveled blacksmith's son claimed, a smirk on a face sticky with sap. He patted the blachund on the head and stood, meeting Keavy's dumbstruck stare. "A thousand pardons for my lateness, oh supreme *hrotage.*"

"Alder!" Keavy shrieked, and at once she was running into his arms and embracing him. "You're safe!"

She pulled back and stared at him, and for a moment, but only a fleeting one, her natural inhibitions failed her. She wanted him, even if it meant that her honor would be compromised, even if it meant making a big mistake. Her body rose up on a cloud, making the distance between them just a little shorter, perfect for their lips to meet. Alder pulled her near, his face adopting the cool vulnerability that she rarely saw in him. It was only the grunting and groaning of a tired old catman behind her that broke her of the trance, and them of their embrace. Blushing furiously, Keavy backed away.

"How was your hunting trip, Alder?" Tulley was using his mace as a crutch again as he approached the boy, keeping a weary eye on the blachund panting by his side.

"Long." Alder paused, his softened face rematerializing into its cheeky curves only after a moment more. From Keavy's eyes, Alder's focus turned to the fire, where in front of he plunked down in the way a hawk shot from the sky lands in a ditch.

Tulley backed away, bristling slightly at the blachund. It trotted past him and lay at the lad's side, resting its head on folded paws.

"I can surely imagine," the potion master said, unimpressed. "Do you mind explaining why there is a minion of evil following you about like a loyal pet?"

"I have no explanation for it, but he appears to be utterly tame," Alder replied wanly. He began scratching the beast between

129

its tasseled ears, and the blachund laid them back and closed its eyes.

"He refused to attack me, no matter how I goaded him," he explained. "I do not believe he has fallen under Crocotta's spell."

Alder failed to inform them of his encounter and conquer over the Danaan witch. That would open an entirely new can of worms for which he had no hook.

"Highly improbable!" Tulley scoffed, then with a change in his mind, shrugged off his previous retort. "But not completely impossible. There are some exceptionally strong animals that can avoid the mental powers of Crocotta, although it is very unlike a blachund to approach humans even if not under spell. I am assuming you would object if I suggested you kill the mongrel anyway to be on the safe side?"

Alder tensed noticeably for a second, and then proceeded to continue stroking the napping beast. "I would."

Tulley shook his head in exasperation and rested his mace over his shoulder. "Then I suppose I have no choice but to allow it to stay, however exceptionally against it I am," he muttered. The old catman gave the duo a wide birth as he walked around to the other side of the fire and eased himself to his seat. "But, I reserve the right to change my mind should the situation call for it."

"Fair enough."

"It is settled," Tulley said, and his whiskers twitched in annoyance. He pointed an accusing bared claw at the lad through the waving oxygen over the small flame between them. "Now, as for *you*, if you ever wander away again, I will slice the tendons of your ankles and tie you to your horse, and don't think for a moment that I am joking."

Nessa, perhaps unfreezing herself for the first moment since the blachund had "attacked" Keavy, joined her friends in seating at the fire. Keavy sat down with her, still a bit flushed.

"I won't." Alder said it with an exaggerated sense of apology. Tulley caught him rolling his eyes as he looked back down at the sleeping brute under his hand and his claws flexed out of impulse. Both his bad and good eye appeared to blaze.

"Perhaps I need to stress the importance of staying together a tad more firmly for you empty headed youths," he growled. "The empress is *everywhere*. She need not be in our view to be a threat.

Every creature inhabiting the forest feels her influence, even this so called tame blachund; therefore, we are never safe. We *must* stay together. It is our best hope at survival."

The old catman took in a deep steadying breath to ease his temper, for it was not proper to lose control, especially in front of younglings. He looked to the path ahead of them, at the skyline hanging high above the trees, knowing what lay less than a rolling count yonder.

"We grow closer to End of the Path with every step. Crocotta's influence is stronger there. Luck tipped in your favor this time, Alder. Do *not* wander off again."

Alder glanced up at this threat of sorts, face full of cheek. He stood, chest proudly swelling. "I handle myself well on my own, despite what you may say, and I was not a target of *luck*. I am a *Devnet*. I certainly don't need to listen to idle threats from a common like you."

Keavy and Nessa went rigid, mouths open and ears pricked, disbelieving what they had just heard. Alder had received his last lessons from Tulley not two years ago, and knew the proper way to address the master. To speak to an elder in such a way was unheard of! Grounds for a lashing even! Tulley did not appear extremely surprised by the remark. His ears flattened momentarily, but his gaze did not waver. It seemed as though he would let the comment slide as another audacious youth's insolence. That was why even the horses jumped when the catman's collectiveness burst with the sharpness of a newly crafted sword.

"What you need boy, is a hard dose of reality and a swift kick in the ass!"

Alder was ready with his retort. "You kick my ass if you can reach it!"

Nessa cowered behind Keavy, peeking around her pant leg. "Oh no no, Alder!" she cried. "You cannot talk like that to the master, no!"

Alder whipped his head towards her, his blond ponytail flailing over his shoulder. "Why don't you wash the gunk out of your fur before I spill my cider!" he snapped, much louder than intended.

Nessa crouched down to all fours in the standard submissive wood faun position; tail and ears down. She had never done that in front of them before. It was only customary to react as such amongst her kind. Keavy was shocked and saddened by the look of it, almost embarrassed, as if she had accidentally witnessed something very private. She stood her ground, guarding her friend stoically from her insulter. Alder reddened, and his face shown with absolute regret. All eyes fell on Tulley, rising from his seat and limping stiffly from the fire side.

"I worry about you, Alder," he said tersely, his own hard to read feline features stiff but composed again. "You have been fooled by your upbringing into believing that you are untouchable. I fear that this may be your downfall some day."

And with this, the old catman leaned heavily on his mace and left their presence, continuing his journey to End of the Path ahead of the rest, with the wood faun rising and following quietly soon after.

Once they were alone, Keavy and Alder faced each other. One face had been stripped entirely of sentiment while the other retained its inward battle between pride and compliance.

"What stains your tongue?" Keavy asked darkly, quaking with contained wrath. "You have no business speaking to Tulley that way."

The battle in his mind ended, with the victor being Alder's old family pride. "And why not?" he spat, "What has that castaway pariah ever done to deserve my respect? My family took their roots in Nodens back before the realm of the Danaan had even been established! We made weapons for ancient royalty! We are practically royalty ourselves!" the lad ranted, growing bolder. "Tulley is one step above a barn cat and one step below a waterogg! My father said we never had catfolk in our town before Tulley arrived. He's starting to think the scrappy kittens in our shed may not be the work of the neighbor's tom!"

Keavy slapped him, her ragged fingernails scraping his flesh. Caught off guard, Alder jumped back a step and clutched at his blazing cheek with one hand. She braced herself for his response, lifting up her chin in invitation when he raised his much larger fist to her in threat.

"Strike me!" she invited, "I would rather fight you now and lose than listen to anymore of your pompous drivel!" She stepped forward, closing the space between them, goading him still. "What's the matter? Afraid to be beaten up by a girl?"

Alder drew back, but instead of punching her, he opened his fist flat and slapped her back. The force was just enough to send Keavy tripping backwards over a rock and landing on her backside, where she sat for a moment, holding her cheek and fighting away the urge to cry. Alder stood over her with folded arms. He was poised now, returning her hateful glare with a smirk. Keavy jumped to her feet and tackled him, bowling him over, and they began to wrestle and scrap, shouting and spitting at each other in juvenile rage.

"Fourteen years of training and you barely pull your weight in a fight against me!" Alder taunted. He rolled over, throwing her onto her back and grinning. "What are you going to do with Crocotta, mighty *hrotage*? Throw a stick?"

"At least I know how to handle myself in real danger!" Keavy snarled back. "I didn't see you coming to my rescue at the circus, you coward!"

She brought her legs up and threw him off of her, turned to her hands and knees and stood. Before she knew it, Alder had seized her and locked her head tightly against his side, laughing of all things while she snarled and brayed beneath him.

"Had enough?"

Keavy growled and elbowed him hard in the gut. Gasping, he released her and hunched over, holding his stomach, but not for long. As she backed off, Alder butted her in the belly. She fell down, groaning, and at once kicked his legs out from under him and landed him on his ass, releasing a harsh huffing breath from his lungs. Before he could stand up again, Keavy pushed him over and pinned him on his back, her knees driven into his thighs and hands clasped firmly around his wrists.

"I don't know," she finally panted in triumph. "Have *you*?"

Alder smiled right before he brought his legs up and flipped her off of him, and before she had realized he'd used her own move against her, he had pinned *her*, being careful to keep her knees back by locking her legs with his own, curling them together in a chaotic jumble of limbs.

"Thought you had me, didn't you?" Alder teased, his sweat dripping onto her face. Keavy cursed and struggled but he held her down with far superior strength, laughing hysterically "Whoa there, wild pony!"

Keavy writhed, squealing "You are a spoiled brat! I hate you!"

Alder grinned and waited until it was apparent she was tiring to loosen his leg lock on her. Keeping a firm grip on her wrists, he slid his body down onto hers, bringing his handsome dirty face down close.

"You fight well," he whispered hungrily. "Almost as well as a man. *Almost.*"

Keavy scowled, but accepted defeat at last and went limp in his grasp. Alder kissed her. Keavy whined under him, alarm overtaking her in a brief wave. Alder would not have her escape him again, and so his grip tightened on her arms, and his chest heaved against hers, pinning her further still. Keavy brought her knees up again, but instead of pushing him off, she wrapped her legs around his waist. Alder released her arms and she flung them around his shoulders, bringing them closer together, sighing quietly against his lips. When they parted, she smiled seductively at him, clasped his cheeks in her hot hands, and butted him. The pain that he felt was sudden and raw. Alder rolled off of her, clutching his forehead and cursing her name.

"Cunning shrew!" he wailed, rolling piteously like a log down a hill.

Keavy stood up, brushed her clothes off and rubbed at the dull ache in her own forehead, replying "We shall call it a truce."

Anger melting into laughter, Keavy reached down and helped Alder to his feet, and then she saw that the blachund sleeping by the fire had awakened. His big head was raised on his muscular neck and his large ears were erect but relaxed. The animal's eyes penetrated her own in that haunting blue gaze and Keavy was overtaken with the serious feeling that he was not simply observing her activity, but truly *watching*. It was as if he could smell the air of destiny about her.

A small chill ran a course over her spine and she looked away. For the first time since her journey had begun, Keavy started to discover a real sense of purpose in herself. This was real. This was happening. The others could not protect her from it, and she could not deny it. Vorian Tranore was gone and she had a destiny to fulfill. She was on her own.

***

"We have reached End of the Path," Tulley announced, his voice full of foreboding. He stood on the line of the ending dirt path, pads gingerly feeling up the gray pebbly surface of the changing landscape.

The difference was vast and immediate. End of the Path was a much danker land; the air seeming to hang with leaden elements, smelling of decaying flowers and rain. The ominous skyline barely held back a storm. The stale soil was dotted with large jagged gray rocks and razor-sharp pebbles, high perilous hills, craters of molten fire, and steep divots. Spewing out of the virtually sterile ground the sickly snake shrubs grew, their sticky black tendrils, lined with needles, and motionless, starring out around their spiky mouths, awaiting careless prey.

The travelers dismounted a few steps back, for the much wiser horses could smell imminent danger and were stubbornly refusing to go any further. The blachund, whom Alder had begun calling Avalo, a royal name meaning Righter of Wrongs, whined and peered nervously at the angry ground.

"The ground grows quite treacherous after this point. Annick and Lorcan must stay here," Tulley stated morbidly, knowing they would not cross even if he had threatened them with branding irons. He turned to Nessa standing beside him on her hind legs and still barely reaching his waist. "Nessa, you had better stay too. A creature of your size stands no chance against the fiends in these parts. Even the shrubs will prey upon you."

An insulted expression crossed across the faun's face. Her nose wrinkled and she flipped her mane back in a slighted gesture. "I want to help, I do."

Tulley nodded. "Then keep a lookout yonder and take the horses into hiding."

Nessa was appeased with this task and went to work immediately, heading back to the two large mounts and grasping Annick by his dangling reins. He complied, turning around to be led away. Without being asked, Lorcan followed the larger horse.

"Guard them well, Nessa," Tulley called to her. "We will return as soon as Crocotta's lungs cease to draw in one more gust of Aryth's air."

Alder, recovered from his tantrum, gave a snort, trying to sound amused but unable to cover his rising fear. Avalo knelt quietly by his feet, watching him closely.

"What plan do we have for this endeavor?"

"All of Garric's daughters keep with them their sacred amulets in order to retain their powers," Tulley told him. He tugged at the back of his pants, allowing his mangled tail to fit through a carefully positioned hole more easily. It had only been a few minutes since his argument with the lad, but he was in no mood to hold a grudge. There were many more important things to worry about, and reminded of this, he pulled the satchel from his back and opened it. Grumbling to himself, Tulley began removing items and setting them aside, he searched for something hidden away.

"Crocotta wears hers around her neck," he continued, further emptying his bag. "If we can remove it, she will no longer be able to change shape, and her magical abilities will be greatly faltered. It is then and only then, that you will be able to kill her, Keavy."

Keavy gulped back her rising gorge. She was horrorstruck at the actual mention of her job. Her complacent sigh almost prevented the potion master from lecturing her.

His ears rotating on wooly head, Tulley squinted in that all knowing gaze. "This is but a single part of your destiny, child," he told her, "You will not complete your purpose until the last Danaan falls and Garric is returned to the throne."

"Good luck, Keavy. I shall pray for your safe return." Nessa had come back, minus the two mounts.

Keavy hunched down and took the faun's rough three fingered hand, wondering if her friend would be safe with just Annick to protect her. "Thank you, Nessa, and take care."

Nessa nodded, shot a weary glance to the predator by Alder's feet, and scampered off again.

"Ah!"

The exclamation made both Alder and Keavy jolt with surprise. Tulley had found what he was looking for, and was holding it high above his head in triumph. He showed it to them, squinting proudly in his cat-like way. It was a small red sphere no bigger than

Tulley's own fist, and before they asked what it was, he told them, and they both secretly hoped that his plan for it would follow through without hitch.

For if not, it would almost certainly mean death for all of them.

***

The slaughtered ram lay bloated and rotting upon the Altar of Second Life. It rested on a marble platform intricately decorated with depictions of Idris harboring God's Breath as he faced a golden dragon. Below, Sephora stood on the steps leading to it, a staff of fire in her hands. Without a word, she touched the carcass of the ram until its wool began to curl and catch flame, and waited patiently for her black magic to do its work.

Several seconds passed and the carcass burned and sputtered upon the stone slab, its internal organs hissing and whining inside of it, boiling, ready to pop. At last, the ram's flesh burst open, sending flecks of sizzling fat up into the air like dancing sparks. Sephora watched, her horrid black eyes glazed with sullen interest as the carcass upon the stone slab began to shift and squirm. A slippery squishing sound preceded the wolfish groan that rose up from the carcass, and then a small twisted head poked up from the gore of the ram's gut, squealing in distress, its eyes empty sockets, its mouth a sticky mucus lined trap. The pathetic creature lifted a single twisted claw out from the viscera and then another, all the while crying out in pure agony. With Sephora watching, the malformed beast began to take shape from the entrails of the ram. Her toothy beak gaped.

The deformed creature seemed not to pull itself out of the ram, but to morph from the insides of the ram itself. As the beast lunged out of the carcass, revealing bent shoulders, a sleek long back, dagger like claws, and a stubby tail, pieces of the ram began to suck back into its body, absorbing into the beast like an essence, its blood covering it from head to toe in thick clots, and then at once, it disappeared into the monster's very flesh and became striped bristly fur. Crocotta's form twisted and shifted until at last she knelt naked on hands and knees on the slab, trembling from exhaustion. Her amulet shone polished and new around her neck.

It was then that Sephora finally spoke in her serpent's hiss. "Welcome back, Crocotta," she said. "How disappointed I am to see you here. I did not believe killing a few children would be so complicated for you."

Crocotta climbed shakily down from the marble slab and grabbed onto it for purchase as her wobbly legs found their strength. "Forgive me, sister," the witch mumbled piteously, eyes to the ground and shoulders slumped, an omega before her alpha. "I was…taken by surprise."

Sephora's black eyes narrowed hatefully. She watched her sister walk uneasily down the alter staircase and crouch submissively at her feet.

"And by one of your own fiends, no less," she scoffed. "I am disappointed in you, Crocotta. I thought that being a mongrel yourself would give you the upper hand in containing the minds of your lowly hounds."

Crocotta, still naked and slick with sweat, rose, facing her sister hiding the fear from her eyes as best she could. Her strength was quickly returning, and so was her dignity.

"*He* is different," she replied tersely. "His mind is strong and repels my influence, try as I do to penetrate him. It is unusual. The spell does not fully envelope him as it did the others."

"This is not acceptable!" Sephora snapped forward, surely removing Crocotta's nose had she not flailed backwards away from her. "You will go to End of the Path and destroy our enemies, and you will not fail again, or the next time you resurrect I will kill you myself, over and over and over again. Do you hear me?"

And before Crocotta could respond, Sephora waved her stick, and banished her sister from sight, banished her back to her own lands. She had given her new life, and now Crocotta would go back to End of the Path prepared.

***

Tulley's ears, though failing with age, were just sharp enough that they picked up on the slithering sound of an advancing snake shrub in the knick of time. He evaded its pointy tendrils easily as they lashed out at him, snagging at his feet.

138

Tulley brushed off his burlap pants vainly and sneered back in the direction of his attacker, warning the younglings ahead of him "Snake shrub needles are poisonous. Keep a watchful eye."

And without warning, Tulley found himself suspended high in the air, a set of human hands clamped around his middle. Hissing in the direction of his assailant, Tulley failed to notice the seedling snake shrub lifting a set of preformed tendrils high above its gnashing teeth, reaching for Tulley like a baby for its bottle. Alder lifted him out of the way before he was bitten and put him down aside of it.

"Watch out for the little ones."

If catfolk could blush, Tulley would have been strawberry red. He cleared his throat and mumbled his gratitude to the lad before digging his mace into the rocky ground once more and trekking ahead.

End of the Path proved a difficult hike. There was virtually no flat land on which to rest their tired feet here, only large loose rocks and boulders. The little ground that did show was showered in broken glassy shards of black and gray obsidian. Tulley was having the most trouble of all in his bare feet, but he scarcely made a cry when his pads were cut to hellfire by the jagged ground. It wasn't proper for a master, particularly one of catfolk heritage, to show weakness in front of his pupils. However he did call a stop long enough to tie ripped up strips of fabric around his feet to not only ease the pain, but to conceal the bleeding. He was still mistrustful of Alder's tame blachund. The smell of blood could prove too much for him to ignore.

The fire craters, their crusty rims slicked with hot red lava, gurgled and hissed at the travelers as they marched past, wishing them to slip and fall into their smoldering chasms. The obsidian shards littering the ground winked in the little sunlight managing to peek through the glum haze of clouds. It was extremely humid. Their clothing, their hair and fur sucked close to their bodies, stifling them, suffocating their flesh. The air was almost too hot to breathe. Every step they took was potentially dangerous. If they weren't getting cut by the broken rock or staggering over holes and craters, they were dodging the deprived tendrils of poisonous snake shrubs. By the end of their first hour in End of the Path, they were close to giving up. Three of them (Avalo having a better sense about his feet than his bipedal comrades), from the knees up were covered in scratches underneath the rips in their pants. With Tulley in the lead and Alder close in second, Keavy resentfully flagged behind, blachund trotting at her side.

"I need to rest," she admitted bitterly, though it ate at her ego to do so.

"Soon, dear," Tulley jadedly answered. "I believe it would be wise to find a safe place to do so first."

"How far yonder does End of the Path stretch?" The query was from the brooding Alder, who still wasn't completely over Keavy's endless rejections.

"The rough estimation is five rolling counts across."

"Five counts!" came Keavy's gripe, "Tulley, we'll be—"

The ground beneath Keavy's boots simply crumbled, and in the time it took to unsheathe a sword she was gone. Only Avalo saw it occur, and if he hadn't begun barking, Tulley and Alder may not have even noticed her absence. In a hurry, they both ran toward the site of their precious ruby child's disappearance and crouched over it. A plume of dust billowed up from the ground where she had fallen.

"Keavy!" Alder called.

There was no immediate answer, and Tulley and Alder looked at each other with the same frenzied thoughts running through their minds. The ground had appeared to give way into a narrow chasm, the bottom of which their eyesight could not reach. The mutual fear between them was that the child of prophecy lay dead at the bottom of a jaggy grave. Avalo paced in front of the hole, head lowered on long neck, ears pricked forward listening for life.

Finally came the slight sound of movement, feet sliding against gravel, a dust clogged cough, and at last an echoed voice.

"Tulley? Alder? Can you hear me?"

Their fear slid into blessed relief. Tulley sighed and clutched his chest, hacking back an answer as the dust from the disturbed ground filled his lungs.

"Are you okay, Keavy?"

"Yes, I'm fine."

"Can you climb back up?" Alder shouted to her.

"I don't know. I'll try."

A few moments of pained silence, and then there were sounds of scraping and grunting. A groan of exasperation preceded *"It's too steep. There are no footholds."*

Alder reached behind him and unhooked the bow from his back. He placed it aside and opened his coat to remove his daggers. "I shall go for her."

He was beaten to it. Tulley had already opened his satchel and pulled out a thick stumpy torch. He ran to the nearest fire crater to light it and, feline reflexes flaring, slung himself over the side of the hole with both claws extended and hooked them into the purchase of damp exposed earth making up the wall of the chasm, the torch clutched between his teeth. With a groan of exertion, he arched his spine, dug his back claws into the wall for purchase, and began to scale downward as swift and agile as a cat half his age. It wasn't long before Alder lost complete sight of the potion master altogether. He could only follow the glow of the torchlight as it shrank into the darkness below.

Keavy stepped back for Tulley to jump down from the wall. He landed on all fours before her in an ankle deep puddle of cold water, torch still clutched in his mouth. He almost looked like a dog bringing back a fetching stick. Well aware of this, Tulley stood up, brushed off his shirt and pants and removed the torch from his mouth. He held it up so he could see the child's freckled and dirt streaked face. Her clothes were wet but she appeared to be unharmed.

"Any injuries, child?"

Keavy shook her head.

Tulley nodded and looked around. In the torchlight, he could see the bouncing shadows of the fire off the chasm's walls. Behind Keavy was a large cavity maybe twenty feet across and ten feet high. The puddle of water streamed through it into a small flowing creek leading off into a cavern lined with dripping limestone stalactites and stalagmites. Clinging to these hanging rock formations as well as the ceiling and walls, were dozens upon dozens of large white insects as big as squirrels. They looked like moths with stubby knobbed antennae, round squishy bodies, underdeveloped wings, and no eyes whatsoever. The insects were not particularly unusual to look at in and of themselves. What was astonishing was that each insect's fleshy abdomen was exuding a fluorescent blue light, painting the dingy cave walls with luminous color.

Tulley harrumphed his understanding. "It looks as though these insects have developed to live an entire existence in darkness. Quite intriguing."

The color in Keavy's eyes flashed. "I wonder where this cave leads to," she muttered aloud.

"That is not important right now, dear. We need to get you out of—"

She disappeared again, this time down the path the glowing insects made for her through the cavern. Tulley called after her pointlessly, knowing very well that silly curiosity would conquer conformity. Younglings!

Alder's sharp silhouette formed at the bright circle of sunlight high above him. His voice echoed down soon after.

"*Are you two okay?*"

"Bloody damnation, she's run off!" Tulley shouted back. "I am going to fetch her, Alder. Stay put!" The catman growled in frustration. "As if *that* is a fair expectation."

And, holding his torch high and hating the dampness, he stumbled after her, grumbling to himself all the way.

"I am through with these silly children! Bloody through!"

Things in the dark scampered out from underfoot as the human girl rambled through their bathing pool, followed by the grumbling old catman. One of them, smelling the wounds on his feet, lashed out with tiny webbed claws, just barely missing his ankle as he splashed by without noticing. It glared with lustful black marbles and, with many others following its example, dove from its perch upon a small stalagmite into the cold murky water after them.

***

Avalo issued a troubled whine which the lad silenced by scratching him under his chin. Alder was sitting down upon one of the few larger boulders nearby. He was impatient, but he did as the master ordered and waited. The minutes passed by and turned into an hour. Alder grew more agitated with each uneventful second and began entertaining himself by throwing rocks at the snake shrubs.

Avalo pattered off, snuffling at the ground, perhaps in search of prey. Tulley's earlier order had been not to feed the beast of their meager rations. It was the catman's hope that hunger would eventually drive him away. He had remarked that feeding Avalo may cause him to perceive *them* as prey. Alder had snuck his companion a handful of jerky anyway when no one was looking. It wasn't enough to satisfy the beast's appetite, but Alder hoped it would keep him near.

He trusted Avalo, regardless of his previous experience with his species. The beast had saved his life with no hesitation, and treated them all like pack. Blachund or not, he was an ally, perhaps even sent by the gods as a guardian. His eyes, blue as a spring sky, reminded Alder very much of his father's dogs at home, when he had had a home that was. They were eyes of domestication. Alder speculated the possibility for blachunds to cross with regular dogs, and if that was part of the mystery behind the animal's loyalty and strange looks.

Musing over this, the young blacksmith picked up another rock and peeled back to throw it at the gathering of eager snake shrubs he had been tormenting for the last ten minutes. They were growing well out of range, but even so were reaching for him with their tendrils, tangling up in each other and gnashing their spines. Alder snickered while they fought to pull in their prey, ripping each other apart in the process. Severed tendrils and spines whispered into the air and landed delicately around them. The largest plant finally claimed the rock for itself, greedily pulling it into its ugly mouth. Deeming the object inedible and rolling it away, the plant reached stupidly for him once more.

Alder laughed again and got up to pick up another rock when something grabbed his wrist tightly and stopped him. He panicked, thinking at first that a hidden shrub had sprung up and seized him. When he looked at his arm however, what he saw grabbing it was not a black tendril, but a white fist.

"Don't tease the plants, Alder," Crocotta cooed menacingly. She crouched over him, her beautiful face surrounded by dancing spidery braids. "They hold a very unpleasant grudge."

A throaty growl sounded behind them. Avalo sprung to attack. His tail stiff, his ears flat, and his teeth bared. The look of pure murder flashed in his blue eyes. The witch, without even turning to face him, waved her free hand in the beast's direction. Avalo's pounce was intercepted by an invisible force which sent him hurtling backwards through the air. His furious growl twisted into a shrill yelp. He flew head over heels and landed hard against the boulder Alder had been sitting on. The animal whined feebly and fell still.

Alder gasped as the witch's tight grip tightened further.

"Where is the girl?" she demanded shrilly, "Tell me now!"

Crocotta's other slender hand lashed out and clutched him at the neck, and despite his larger size, Alder was unable to loosen himself. He cried out as she cut off his air and glanced helplessly at his weapons lying out of reach by the ravine's opening.

Crocotta's eyes followed his to where the girl and cat had disappeared. Her nose crinkled and deeply took in their scent.

"The caverns!" she exclaimed "Well, it looks like I won't even have to get my claws dirty."

Crocotta licked her lips and peered at Alder, bringing herself so close he could smell the blood on her breath. He hopelessly pulled at her iron grip to no avail. The witch stood, lifting him completely off the ground, hissing, "You boy, are coming with me!"

***

Nessa eyed up the clusters of delectable red berries hanging abundantly from the vines of pink flowered shrubs. They were grape sized, bunched together in fours, and bulged with ripeness. The young faun hesitated to move from underneath Annick's belly, but it was so hard to resist! It had been a long time since she had eaten berries, and fauns were noted for their love of sweets. She had been hiding the horses amongst these shrubs for quite some time now. The aroma of their flowers and berries was overpowering, and would hide the scent of prey. With ears pricked and eyes quivering, Nessa ventured forth to try them. One tiny nibble and her concerns were forgotten. They were delicious! More succulent and sweet than anything she had ever tasted before and just right for the picking! Nessa tittered happily as she stuffed them two at a time into her cheeks, dribbling juice down her chin, waggling her tail, losing herself in the banquet.

She ate and ate, forgetting the time, forgetting the horses, forgetting her friends in End of the Path. Her belly grew swollen, but Nessa didn't care. The berries seemed to get sweeter with every bite. She salivated uncontrollably, and snarfed in another handful. When she had cleared one side of the first shrub, she scampered to the other side, digging in as happily as ever.

Her stomach gurgled in distress. With a bubbling cry, Nessa crouched and vomited. Threads of red juice and pulp poured out of her in rivulets. She stumbled forward with the weight of her stuffed belly and landed on all fours, screaming at the searing pain in her guts. The shrubs began to look more blue than green, their flowers a deep purple. The berries shone a nauseating dire yellow. Nessa backed away from the plant fearfully. Everything around her seemed to pulse and change color in her blurring vision. Poison!

Nessa panicked and spun around looking for the horses. They weren't there, and her prints told her that she had been wandering from shrub to shrub, traveling further and further from their safety. Her senses fading, she could not smell them. Her sight grew blurrier, the colors swirled and changed before her, and then she saw him.

Gnal Mool was an impressive buck; dark agouti brown, white mane swaying loosely around his sharply cut face. On his head was a rack of beautifully developed three point antlers covered with fine velvet. He had not yet lost his velvet for the breeding season, when males of their kind would engage in ritual combat before mating. Though true deer were not monogamous, wood faun mated for life. Fighting rarely got serious and was simply a test of dominance within the pecking order. Gnal had won every battle since Nessa's birth, and had earned the right to lend his name and leadership to the clan for many years. His right ear was shredded and flapped uselessly from his head. From his right shoulder to his middle was a thick mass of curled ripped flesh that had healed oddly and broken up the pattern in his fur. He was quite unsettling in appearance, but Nessa looked at him with overwhelming relief.

"Papa?"

Gnal's husky voice echoed back, distorted and unnatural. "Nessa, is it you, daughter?"

Nessa tried to hop to him, but fell on quivering useless legs. "It is, Papa!" she cried out happily. "It's me, it is!"

Gnal stood before her, making no move towards her, but twitching his ears in her direction. "Thank the gods!" he said, "I thought I had lost you."

Nessa tried to stand on two legs again, and fell to all four. She dragged her belly on the ground as she went to him. "Papa, help me! I am poisoned, I am. The berries—"

A hot jab of pain knocked her over again. She curled up on the ground in a tight ball and shrieked, "It hurts! Oh it hurts!"

"Nessa, listen to me closely," the older faun told her briskly. His body seemed to wriggle as if she gazed at him through fire. His colors came in rich and true in the rainbow chaos around them. "You must eat of the roots. Eat of the roots, Nessa!"

Nessa groaned. Her vision wavered; her weakness left her unable to stand. Dragging herself toward her father, she begged pathetically, "Help me, Papa. Help me!"

Still, Gnal made no move to approach. In fact he seemed to slide back each time she got close.

"Why do you go?" Oil ran in slick trails from Nessa's temples. "Papa!"

"Nessa, the roots!"

Nessa craned her neck and turned around to look at the poisonous shrubs with their ghastly colors, the shrubs that were killing her. She cringed in revolution and vomited again. The little faun then somehow managed to turn around and drag herself back to them. The muscles in her arms tingled. Her vision had grown almost completely black. In her ears, her father's voice was echoic and watery.

Gnal watched his daughter crawl away from him, blinking his remaining eye. "It is not safe in the woods anymore." he said sadly, "Even the flora obeys the empress now."

"It will be soon, it will," Nessa told him with hope in her shuddering breath. "The ruby child has begun her journey, yes, and I is bid to follow, I is. You shall come with us."

She reached the closest shrub in all its colorful repulsiveness. The sweet smell of the berries gagged and titillated her at the same time. She salivated even with her illness.

"Take the root, Nessa."

Nessa, now blind, nearly deaf, and barely able to move, reached the stump of the plant and dug furiously with one shaking hand. When the thick black root poked up from the ground and its earthy smell hit her nostrils, she lunged at it, swallowing dirt as well as root, no longer responding to the pain in her belly.

"Good! Good, daughter!"

Nessa dug and gnawed, chewed and swallowed. She reached forward with her other hand and pawed into the dirt, exposing and eating while her father's voice encouraged her.

"Eat of the root, Nessa. It is the only way."

Nessa pushed her face into the cool earth and licked at the sap oozing from the damaged roots. It tasted awful, like dirt and rot. She fought back the urge to vomit again and sucked it dry, her empathy oils dripping from her temples.

"That's the way. Good."

Nessa groaned and reached into the soil for another piece. She couldn't stand to eat any more. Her stomach was already swollen from her overindulgence of berries, and the roots did not mix well amongst it. Sighing sickly, she collapsed underneath the shrub and lay panting in the cool soil.

"Papa," Nessa whispered tiredly, "Stay with me."

"You will be well soon," Gnal assured her in a soft voice, "Until we meet again, I will wait for you. Now sleep. Sleep, my daughter. We will wait for you by the gates."

Nessa lay her head down and closed her eyes.

***

Avalo jumped aside just as a shrub tendril made its move to grab him. Whimpering, he rolled away from it, stood up, and shook his head. The boy was gone, leaving no trace except his scent. The

147

course fur along the beast's neckline prickled and a growl formed in the pit of his throat. He snuffed in the scent and followed it.

Stepping down on sharp obsidian shards cut his pads to ribbons, but Avalo's nose never lost the boy's trail. Picking his steps carefully, steering clear of fire craters, jumping out of the way of frenzied snake shrubs, Avalo continued onward in search of his lost pack mate. The alluring smell of his own blood drove him to drool helplessly, because tame or not, he was an animal, and a hungry one. His previous hunt had been unsuccessful. Prey animals were too smart to venture into End of the Path.

The day faded and Avalo searched for Alder all through it. It was dusk when he came up over a steep craggy hill overlooking a treacherous valley. Standing atop of it, he could look down and see a large gray slate cave with a gaping toothy entrance smoking up sulfurous fumes ahead. It was surrounded by fire craters that belched up odorous flames in a horrendous spectacle of heat. Evil's stench was thick here. This was *her* den. This was where she had taken Alder. Inhaling the rank scent deeply, Avalo ventured down the hill toward its source.

Rather unexpectedly, the ground beneath him began to hum. The blachund jumped back, sensing something quite wrong with his surroundings. A swarm of tiny red centipedes flooded from unseen holes in the ground around him, organized like ants, attracted to the blood on his paws. They came in thick leggy waves, crawling over each other, raising their mandibles, marching toward him with murder on their simple minds.

Avalo took off down the hill for his life, towards the cave, while the ground vomited up more and more centipedes, covering the gray soil with a red coating. They were extraordinarily fast, even on tiny legs able to move nearly as quickly as the blachund, and there were more and more of them coming out of nowhere to join in the chase. Avalo panted heavily. He was tired from the day's journey, and weak from hunger and thirst. The centipedes were relentless in their pursuit.

At last he reached the bottom of the hill. On flat ground, Avalo could run faster. There was a chance for escape now, and the animal's strength returned to him. He bolted, the centipedes followed, hideous pincers nipping at his cut paws.

The ground moved again and gave way, and Avalo stumbled down into one of End of the Path's many trip holes. He tumbled helplessly into a black abyss and landed hard on his back.

He hurt, but managed climb to all fours again. The centipedes started to flow into the ravine to claim their victim. Avalo leapt at the walls, digging for purchase with his paws, desperately seeking escape. His attempts were futile. Without fingers and thumbs, even a tough animal like him could not escape.

Avalo craned his neck to glare up at the centipedes descending into his death trap. He paced uselessly. There was but one thing he could do now, and if he did it fast enough, he would have a chance to escape, but only one. If he was successful, it would be a close one.

The blachund closed his eyes and began to think a phrase, the same one over and over again, concentrating on this alone while the centipedes swarmed in around him.

***

Keavy was walking through ankle deep frigid water, unaware of the surveying eyes of unknown things swimming at her heels in the dark. She admired the sight of the glowing insects upon the magnificent sparkling rock formations. The cave smelled of earthy mold and acidic limestone, and Tulley raised a first to his nose to corner a sneeze. He had at last caught up to her, winded and holding his torch out to see. His glasses were spotted and scratched, and reluctantly, the catman removed them and wiped them on his shirt. Although he had been blessed with many of his cat ancestor's abilities, most of his senses, including eyesight, had fallen to his human side. The eye shine of several living things bounced back to him in the dark, but before he could get his glasses back on to get a good look at them, they vanished. Keavy slowed down to wait for the master, smiling brightly.

"Isn't this incredible?"

"Hush!" Tulley hissed. He goaded her on with the torch and tripped through the cold water. "Keep moving."

Keavy's smile vanished. "What is it?"

But Tulley wouldn't tell her. No need for the child to know what was after them before necessary. "Keep moving, damn it!"

149

They clumsily hurried through the cavern while the sound of small splashes ricocheted off the walls, accompanied by high squeaking. Tulley turned around and held out his torch again, illuminating one of them.

It was sitting on its haunches on a lumpy stalagmite and appeared to be a rat, or something like a rat, with the same hunched stance, pointy nose, and tiny claws. This rat wasn't exactly the same feral variety he was used to trapping outside his cottage. It was totally hairless, with thin translucent skin mapped out in blue veins. Black eyes far larger than needed for its head sat close together in the middle of its face. Its ears contrasted the eyes, nothing but small slits on the side of its head, but it was the curved tusks protruding out of the rat's jaw that was the most worrisome feature. Drawing webbed claws against its chest, the rat made a leap into the water and propelled itself with a fat rudder tail after them. All along the rocky bank were dozens of its friends, winking in the torchlight, appearing and disappearing in the blue glow. Many of them were squeaking while they dove into the freezing water and swam straight for the two intruders. It was a most unwelcoming sound.

The first one got too close too quickly. Tulley waved his shrinking torch at its tusked face as it darted at him, and the bright light appeared to hurt its eyes. Squinting and squealing, the rat kicked back and flitted away, some of the others along with it.

"Tulley?" Keavy whimpered fearfully. She had seen but a glimpse of the rat in the torchlight, but it was enough.

"Stay in front," he ordered. "They hate the light. Stay in front of me and keep moving!"

Keavy kept moving, with Tulley backing along as carefully and quickly as possible, waving the rapidly diminishing fire at the pursuing cave rats. They stayed a comfortable distance back from the bright light but continued to pursue them in water now knee deep for Keavy and almost waist deep for Tulley. Hyperventilating, following the light trail from the blue insects, and trying to block out the increasingly louder squealing behind them, Keavy pressed on with Tulley fending off their followers behind her.

The god of protection looked away from them, for the worst thing that could have happened did. The torch fire burned down to Tulley's fingers and he dropped it into the water, bringing blackness upon them. The insects were sticking mainly to the high walls, and

150

they could no longer see into the water; therefore they could no longer see the cave rats.

Keavy cried out at the sudden darkness. Tulley pushed into her backside, encouraging her forward through the numbing water.

"Don't stop, Keavy," he told her, rimming on panic himself. "Don't stop!"

The squealing was getting louder by the second as they closed in, more and more of them swimming over each other in their eagerness to feed. The water was waist deep for Keavy and it was up to Tulley's shoulders. The current grew stronger, giving both prey and predators a slight advantage. Keavy could run with it, but Tulley found it quite difficult to keep his head above water. He resorted to swimming with his nose in the air and paddling like a puppy.

Keavy knew very well the old catman needed a lift. Putting her respect for him aside, she practically ordered "Tulley, get on my back!"

"Nonsense!" he sputtered back, as she expected he would. "Keep going!"

Keavy screamed at him "Get on my back, *now*!"

Tulley swam to her and she ducked down into the water long enough for him to climb onto her back. He was heavy against her with his wet fur and clothes. This, along with God's Breath's dead weight at her side, Keavy could hardly stand up to run again. Trying to move fast in cold waist deep water was like trying to run in thick syrup.

They could hear the rats splashing, moving with ease in their natural environment. They were catching up. Keavy found her motivation and kicked herself up from the bottom, paddling as fast as she could in water now so deep she could barely touch bottom. Tulley held fast to her shoulders, his claws inadvertently digging into her skin. He felt sharp teeth nip his tail and cried out, thrashing with his back feet at the horrible thing at his hind end. The current drew them in. Keavy's sobs came in choking breaths.

"It will be fine," the catman assured her in his most optimistic tone. He patted her shoulder, though it was so cold he wasn't sure she felt it. "It is going to be fine, just keep swimming."

Then abruptly, the ground beneath Keavy's toes seemed to disappear. She went completely under, bringing Tulley with her. He released his grip on her shoulders and came up quickly. The cave rats surrounded him, and he furiously batted them away.

"Keavy!" he coughed, "Keavy, where are you, darling?"

Keavy surfaced. She was barely able to stay above water due to the weight of her sword. The current took her further into darkness as the ceiling seemed to grow and the comforting blue light of the insects dwindled. Close to her, a squealing rat surfaced and clamped down on her left forearm with its razor sharp teeth. She screamed.

"Keavy!"

Tulley began to swim, realizing now that the current was becoming erratic. He clawed an attacking rat out of the water and hurled it as far away as he could. He didn't see it hit, but the sick *splotting* noise its body made against the wall was plenty reassuring. The action was met by frightened screeching as the rats around him backed away. The current dragged him forward, and swimming against it was useless. Keavy's screams faded away into the darkness, so Tulley curled his legs and tail into his body and allowed the current to take him to her.

"I'm on my way, child!" he shouting, hoping she could hear him as the current swept them into the unknown. "I'm coming!"

***

Snake shrubs were far stronger than they appeared. This was perhaps because of Crocotta's powerful influence, but it was not so unusual, seeing as how they needed to be able to hold down struggling prey in order to inject their venom. They had earned the right to their names in complete fairness. Hearing Crocotta's unspoken command the tendrils wrapped around Alder's arms and legs. Across his middle, more and more tendrils slapped against him, tightening dangerously at each move he made. He fought listlessly, but the plants slid and slithered out of harm's way and held fast, encasing his entire body against the gritty cave wall and leaving only his head uncovered.

"It would be wise to stop fighting them," Crocotta muttered, back to him. She brushed her hair in the mirror, eyeing him through

152

the reflection. "If they perceive you as prey they may very well stick you with their toxic spines."

Crocotta turned with a smile that was almost sympathetic. She put a sashay in her step and came close to him to caresses his cheek. Alder's glare was full of hate.

"Oh, now don't look at me that way, Alder," the witch begged, "I was a predator on the hunt and you were fair game. You cannot blame an animal for acting on its instincts." She batted her eyelashes. "However I *am* impressed by your bravery. Tell me, Alder, how long do you think you'd have lasted without your...*pet* to save you, hmm?" Her fingers turned into black claws that bit into Alder's cheek, opening his flesh. He grunted in pain, but remained stolid. He would not be intimidated by her. Crocotta's mouth watered at the smell of his freshly flowing blood.

Alder sneered conceitedly, bringing out his own home brand of mockery. "Do what you like with me, bitch, but tonight you will die again and no amount of black magic will resurrect you."

Her eyes burned. "That is a dubious prospect," she huffed back, "However you have spoken true of one thing tonight, Alder. I will do what I like with you, and I will enjoy every moment of it."

The witch stepped back, her braids writhing and her emerald dress glinting in the little light the cave offered. She began to change.

"I have not yet dined this evening and I am rather famished," her rapidly deteriorating human voice croaked. "I have neverrrr had a man for dinnerrrr here before. Thissss shall be a trrrreat."

The woman doubled over and her monster's high broad shoulders popped out of her dress with a sick rip. Alder watched in silent despair as she began to make her transformation, knowing all too well what she would become.

A low growl bellowed from the direction of the outside world, and although he could not turn his head against the writhing tendrils of his snake shrub shackles, Alder knew it was Avalo.

She couldn't morph quickly enough when he rushed at her, the shreds of her dress clung to warped flesh that was just sprouting banded hair. His jaws locked down onto her bare human thigh and he pulled her ruthlessly to the ground and shook her, tearing back a long flap of skin over coiled muscle. Crocotta landed awkwardly, bending back until her spine popped, but she was able to regain balance and find time enough to bud huge black claws from her delicate white hands. When she sprung back up again, poised on her haunches, she jammed them into Avalo's shoulders, stopping him cold. He released a wail as she twisted her nails deep into his muscles and shifted the rest of herself. The cave was filled with the sounds of bones crackling, clothing ripping, and animals roaring. A demonic head sprung out from a graceful neck to sneer at her adversary.

With Crocotta's influence focused on something else, the snake shrubs began to loosen their hold on the young blacksmith. Alder found he was able to push out of the tendrils and rush to the aid of his companion. Without weapons, he was surely powerless to fight her, but even so, Alder dashed toward the fight and grabbed onto the chain around the beast's neck, yanking the amulet against her windpipe like a choke collar, pinching her neck shut until she yelped. The blood covered blachund squirmed out of her grasp just as Crocotta swung a massive claw back and swiped at Alder, missing him by a hair's width. She turned around, rose to her hind legs and slapped him with a huge powerful claw. The lad flew a great distance and crashed into the wooden vanity behind him. The mirror exploded into a rain of shards, the vials resting there popped, and the entire thing crumbled under Alder's weight.

The blachund jumped at Crocotta, but she was expecting it this time, and turned in time to beat him out of the air with a completely formed claw, not forgetting what he had done to her in the forest. While both enemies lay dazed on the stony floor, Crocotta loped past them, a great hulking mass in the dimness of the cave, heading for the outside world.

She was escaping! Alder had to catch up to her and keep her busy until the oh so powerful *hrotage* arrived, *if* she arrived. Truthfully, Alder didn't have a backup plan if Keavy failed to make an appearance. Avalo was at his side, licking his neck, encouraging him to stand up and brush himself free of the splinters. He would be there for him to the end. This, Alder was sure of. The two of them followed the bellowing roar of the witch, trying not to think about the consequences of their actions.

Once they got outside, they were met by a dying sky. The day had faded, and Siavon shone dully through the haze Crocotta

154

had cast upon End of the Path. Hoards of blachunds, snarling and waiting for them, were encircling the cave entrance, with Crocotta standing at their lead. She was bloody, but standing tall in her human form, arms crossed across her bare breasts.

"Do remember this moment," she growled, but not to Alder. Her eyes were cast skyward, to Siavon. "I will take your Knight first."

Avalo looked up at Alder and whined, then, hackles raised, crouched and turned to defend him. Alder huffed a bemused note of mirth and put up his fists. It would be a quick finish, but damn it all, he would go down smiling. After all, he was a Devnet.

***

The cave rat clung to Keavy in the rushing current, teeth deeply imbedded in her left arm. She beat at it with her fist over and over again, crying out in agony as its teeth hit bone. She found one of its eyes and dug her thumb into it hard, and it released her finally. The rat floated eye level to her, paddling its ugly webbed feet to keep up with the current, but when it seemed it would rush at her again, the rat abruptly thrashed its tail and darted away. The others behind it did the same, squeals on top of splashes.

Keavy grabbed onto her injured arm and moaned, but the pain was gone, killed by the numbing effects of the cold water. The cave spoke to her in the language of anxious water. A waterfall was ahead, foaming at the mouth. It was quite dark now, for the insects were nearly gone from this area. Keavy was helpless. She could only thrash uselessly when the falls took her.

She didn't scream on the way down. The thought hadn't even registered in time for a prompt reaction before she was rushing down the endless falls in the pitch darkness with no idea of how fast or far she was falling. She splunked into the freezing water, and nearly drowned just adjusting to it. Her head bobbed above surface with a shuddery gasp, and she immediately began swimming for her life. The light from the insects on the ceiling was far above her now, blue stars winking in the heavens, and now she realized that the current was still sweeping her away. All her determination to fight against it was futile. Using what little strength her numb limbs retained to keep her head above water, Keavy allowed herself to be carried further into the darkness.

Several draining moments later, she caught on a jutting rock and managed to shake herself out of her daze long enough to clutch to its slippery surface. Keavy couldn't see anything at all, for she was far beyond the blue stars now. She shouted for help and shivered violently as she struggled to pull herself further out of the water. Soon, her fingers would become so numb they would be useless in keeping her adhered to her only purchase. Keavy could feel her body disappearing slowly. The frost sickness would set in soon. She had to get out of the water.

Keavy's shoulders screamed in protest as she forced her arms to pull her body up onto the sharp slippery rock. A jaggy rock was poking her in the backside, but she didn't care. She was out of that evil water. Her crimson eyes were even starting to adjust to the blackness. The slightest motion of her hand in front of her face was just barely detectable.

"Hello!" Keavy screamed in no particular direction. "Tulley?"

She didn't expect an answer. Even if Tulley had survived the cave rats, the odds that a creature of his age and size could make it over the falls in the icy water were slim. Keavy hugged the rocks and began to pray for his safety as well as her own. It was rare that she reached out to the gods for anything, for she liked being independent, but this time Keavy was more than willing to give up her pride. God's Breath, once warm against her thigh, was nothing but a cold weight hanging from her belt. Sobbing chants through chattering teeth, Keavy clung to the rock, helpless as a newborn filly.

Her prayers were interrupted by a thick gurgling sound. Keavy nearly fell from her slippery post in surprise. Coming straight for her from about twenty feet away was a yellowish light. It seemed to be floating on the surface of the water, radiating from a perfect orb the size of her head. The sound came again. The light drifted closer and closer with the slight current. Moaning, she braced herself and waited for whatever else was coming for her.

The floating orb came within a foot of her post and disappeared. Keavy was left shivering in the darkness yet again; the only sound that of her harried breath. She relaxed and remembered where she was. It was an underground river system of some sort. That gurgling was probably just water rushing through the cracks in the walls. But what in hellfire was that glowing thing and where had it gone?

Something burst from the water in front of her with a loud *shlop* and knocked Keavy back into the water. Again, the current dragged her under for a few feet before she bobbed to the surface, gasping and desperately trying to keep her head up. For an eternity, Keavy was carried further and further from her only point of reference by a devilishly powerful current. She began to lose hope almost as quickly as she was losing feeling in her body.

Eventually the flow died off and emptied her into a large pool. The ceiling was covered with more of the glowing insects, hanging off of the rock formations just as the ones she had seen earlier. These insects looked more developed. They were larger, had long wispy wings, and curled whippy antennae in place of the short stumpy knobs. These were adults of the same species, most likely. Their light was different, shining a sunny yellow instead of blue. It was like moonshine raining down on the frightened girl's face. Keavy floated pitifully, exhausted and frozen, but still forcing herself to swim. It was quiet here. She had reached the end of the waterway. Now, she just had to swim across the pool to get to the bank on the other side.

Though totally numb, Keavy was somehow able to detect the touch of something against her side. Crying out, she thrashed with her arms hoping to scare whatever it was away. Exhaustion however, did not allow her to do this for long. She was wasting all of her energy on panicking instead of swimming and now she needed to allow herself to float so she could regain her strength.

The touch came again, this time to her other side. Keavy fought the urge to thrash again. It was circling her. She could feel the water around her swirl. Something was investigating her presence. A shark? A swarm of cave rats? Some other unknown horror? Whatever it was, it was in a far better position then she.

***

The beast literally surfaced beneath her. She felt its brawny back push up underneath her bottom, and like a rider upon her steed, she found herself straddling it. Her hands came down on greasy fur growing very close to a bulky body. She could see none of its features, so Keavy had absolutely no idea what she was dealing with, or how quick its temper was, so she ignored her first instinct to pull out God's Breath and impale it. Keavy hunkered down and waited for its next move.

The animal did not seem disturbed by the extra weight it carried on its back, but continued in a slow effortless motion, to glide towards the shore, floating just below the surface of the frigid water as a hawk floats on a warm summer thermal. The insects on the cave ceiling danced lazily in the stuffy air, flirtatiously blinking their desire to mate. Soft buzzing courtship absorbed into the walls until the cave seemed to gently vibrate with it. White powder puffed off their delicate wings and contrasted the modest yellow light their abdomens produced. The animal beneath Keavy lifted a glistening head out of the water and snorted out a blast of spume, but dipped back under when she tried to see by what sort of means she was traveling to shore.

Grunting sounds popped up around her and her carrier, followed by the strange gurgles that Keavy had heard before. Yellow orbs began to bob to the surface of the water. The insects seemed attracted by them and began to blink excitedly as they dipped down close for a better look. Keavy was nervous. She knew that whatever attacked her now would not have to fight hard to overpower her. She was cold, tired, injured, and nearly blind in the cave's dullness. She tensed, expecting any second for more of Crocotta's hideous minions to show.

What *did* show was a big brown animal that looked somewhat familiar. "Sloda" wriggled up from the banks of her memory, though she couldn't recall how she had come across it. Perhaps in one of Tulley's books? She wasn't sure if that was what they were truly named, but sloda was what struck out at her when she first glimpsed the animal in its entirety. It came up from under one of the floating orbs and leapt clear out of the water, opening stumpy jaws filled with shell-crushing teeth. In an instant, it had snatched one of the insects out of thin air and splashed back down into the murk.

Now several more of these oddities began leaping and snatching, all the while blinking lights of their own. In the middle of their oval heads grew ropey stalks ending with a single glowing lure. The lure quite closely resembled the lustrous abdomens of the insects, sized just the same, even blinking as they did. As the insects flitted down in swarms to woo their potential mates, the sloda continued to jump up and gobble them. Their angular eyes came covered by a thin membrane, built in goggles for underwater exploration. Flippers, short flat tails, and almost no neck at all made up the rest of their fat bodies.

They were actually cute in a bizarre sort of way.

Keavy's traverse ended when her carrier made it to the gritty shoreline. It slid onto land on its belly and gave a throaty *wuff*, almost as if to tell her the ride ended here. She climbed off its oily back and gave it a clear path to waddle past. The other sloda came ashore; lights blinking out and stalks coiling quickly back into their heads, leaving just the darkened lures bulging out like tumors. A few were still crunching on prey while they lumbered onto land single file. Keavy ducked back behind a stalagmite and watched them, hand on the hilt of her sword for comfort, moving as little as possible as not to attract their attention. They acted placid enough, but one could never tell in places like these.

The herd of sloda moved with purpose, following the first one through a narrow gap in a solid rock wall up ahead. Keavy was astonished at how elastic the lardy beasts could become. Though wider than the crack, they were able to flatten their bodies and slip through it, contouring to the crevice and flowing into it as easily as a flood of water. She decided to follow them.

Keavy took a deep breath and listened to the sloda wuffing and grunting ahead of her. Maybe they could lead her out of this wretched place. No matter what, she was hopeful that at least she would be safe near the herd.

She could fit through the narrow path with some difficulty when she walked sideways and kept her arms up. A twinge of claustrophobia haunted the edges of her mind in cold strokes. She remembered far too well the incident in the faun burrow, and her heart stopped. The beast of panic was rearing its dreadful head inside of her. All of her muscles froze solid. Here, there would be no helpful wood fauns to guide her out of small spaces. She was on her own.

Keavy closed her eyes and concentrated; found her calm. She fondly remembered the wise advice of the departed Senga and her soul ached with sorrow. Nessa, Tulley, Alder, they all had been orphaned in a sense. Nessa's family had fallen into the jaws of the blachunds, Tulley's to disease and storm, and Alder's had disappeared without a trace. Keavy herself was an orphan, her mother and father dead, and her adoptive sire gone from her life. Her ruby eyes began to well, and Keavy wiped away these thoughts with a sweep of her hand. The feeling of claustrophobia now subdued, Keavy continued to follow the sloda.

She squeezed through tight openings, scraped herself on protruding rocks, tripped over uneven ground, but somehow managed to make it through at last into an open area. There were not many glowing insects here, so the light was scarce, but Keavy's eyes had become accustomed to the dark. She was slowly starting to gain back feeling in her limbs, and could once again feel the warmth of God's Breath at her side. That in itself was comforting.

The sloda were resting in blubbery heaps, some next to piles of smooth round stones lumped with plucked water weeds. Large gray eggs sat among these stones, looking a lot like stones themselves. Their mothers rested around them, peering with brown eyes at the human watchfully but without fear as she shambled into their grounds.

A nest close by began to stir. The three eggs within it twitched and clicked together. Their attentive mother took notice to this and hovered over them while they hatched. Keavy observed in fascination. Tiny little sloda replicas broke out of the eggshells using horny protrusions on their noses. They cheeped much like baby birds and rolled out of their shells quickly, looking to their mother with open mouths and tiny waving lures that did not light up yet. The mother sloda dipped her head down and retched. Goopy white paste dribbled out of her mouth like drool, but the babies lapped it from her jowls eagerly. Keavy was disgusted and yet engrossed. All around her, this was happening very rapidly. The silent cave filled

160

with the sounds of breaking eggs, cheeping young, and retching adults in just a few seconds. The clearing soon filled with the pungent smell of vomit as well. Keavy gagged and pinched her nose shut. This roosting behavior went on for several minutes, during which she tried to breathe through her mouth.

The adult sloda began to waddle away from their nests, forming a single file line again, and their newly hatched young latched onto their parents' flippers and climbed onto their backs. Keavy had been sitting down with her head in her hands, almost unable to keep from dozing off. She was very weak and still cold, and she knew that she had to get out of there as soon as possible. Keavy woozily pulled herself to her feet just as the last big sloda lumbered away, hooting to its herd.

She was about to follow when a squeaking youngster peeked its head out of the nest nearest to her and cocked its head, blinking curiously at the non-sloda looking down at it. Keavy daintily plucked up the straggler and followed the adults out of the nesting grounds. It cheeped in her hands, but didn't seem afraid. In fact, it gaped at her, asking for food. She was surprised at how light it felt, and how slippery and greasy its fur was. This was probably an aid of sorts to get the creature through the tight cracks in the walls.

The sloda lead her through the dully illuminated caverns into a realm of misty tunnels. Keavy slipped in the thick oil they left on the ground and fell on her behind a number of times, being careful to not to drop the newborn when she pulled herself up again. The animal ahead of her made a leap and landed into its own leavings then propelled itself along on its belly until it was sliding smoothly down the trail. Keavy gave up in her fight to stay on her feet and sat down. Placing the newborn into her lap, she used the palms of her hands as makeshift flippers and slid after the sloda down the trail of oil.

Faster and faster she glided, following closely behind the animals, through the misty tunnel where no insects glowed. Her hips and shoulder scraped past jaggy rocks and she almost became stuck a few times, but she was covered in the oil now, and nearly as pliable as the sloda. Groaning at the feel of it, Keavy finally lay on her back to allow herself to skid down the trail more easily. The baby chattered and dove from her lap into the oil slick, rocketing off like a shooting star much more easily, and disappearing along with the rest of the sloda. Keavy closed her eyes and held her breath. She prayed that the trail did not end at a wall.

At the bottom of the tunnel, she shot out from a mouth-like opening and landed face first in something as gloppy and slick as mud. It was thick as molasses and stank like dung and sloda oil. Keavy moaned, gagging at the stench and yakking out the foul stuff. It was also difficult to stand up in, and tried to suck her down when she rose to her feet. All around her, the sloda rolled around happily in the muck, coating their bodies in it. Keavy couldn't tell if they were producing the junk or if it just stuck to them. She wasn't really keen on finding out.

It was now that Keavy realized that the lights were back, the insects on the ceiling of the cave. She cried out in despair. Had she made a circle somehow? Ended up inside another cavern? But on second look, and after much squinting and adjusting, Keavy saw that the lights were no longer coming from insects but from the moon and stars. The cavern had released her. Perhaps the god of protection was watching after all.

***

Tulley was not going to survive this. The beating the rocks had given his fragile old body had shattered ribs and ruptured organs, and the long grueling swim to the shore had sucked him dry of his energy. Now, the old oxman lay shivering on the bank, his lungs filled with broken glass and his muscles stringy and useless. He'd lost his glasses, his clothes were torn, and he was soaked to his broken bones.

In the cold of the cave, it would be only a matter of time before the frost sickness would send Tulley to a chaotic, godless Erayon. Without the Painter of Life to care for them, Tulley's soul and the souls of countless others would collect at the gates and wait for the witches to absorb them, rendering their amulets futile and their power immeasurable.

His whiskers already felt heavy with forming ice crystals. Tulley drew in a ragged breath and tried to let it out smoothly; the effort caused enormous weighted pain in his chest and him convulsed with dry coughing. His eyes could not stay open. dying. He was dying before his purpose could be complete.

were not meant to happen this way. It was not right by the prophecy. He had to do something drastic, unnatural. He had to commit the ultimate sin against the Law of Idris.

A raspy phrase huffed slowly out of the wheezing catman, a phrase spoken so quietly that Tulley could not even hear it coming from his own mouth.

"Vervi een mor sholi'k."

God of Life heals me.

"Inu dah sal'ka."

Pain leaves my body.

When he called upon the Language of the Blade to save himself, he was well aware of the blackness he would invite into his soul. It was forbidden by Idris Rotonzael, the original Knight of Siavon, to call upon the power of the sacred language for self preservation. Mortals were considered wicked if they were to seek these words out at all. In the afterlife, Tulley would suffer greatly for this sin, but he didn't care. He had been bound by the shackles of duty to see to it that Keavy fulfilled the prophecy. One old creature's soul was worthless compared to the fate of creation.

"Vervi een mor sholi'k."

An eternity in darkness was a venom leaching away at the fibers of his being, but at the moment, he felt life returning. Tulley began to sit up, his veins flowing hot blood throughout his small orange body, delivering health and healing inch by inch. He rolled onto his hands and knees and rested this way for a very long time, focusing intently on reclaiming his vigor, blocking from his mind the future consequences of his actions.

"Inu dah sal'ka."

The world of death melted away from him, and his senses were flooded with new information. A household scent teased his nostrils. It was a pungent stinging odor, offensive, reminiscent of sloda oil, a substance Tulley sometimes used to lubricate the hinges on his front door. In the air here it was heavy. Tulley followed its rank perfume further up the shoreline. He had to place his steps carefully. Their muck was everywhere, a greasy brown goop that they released from glands on their bellies. The cave floor was covered in it, as were the walls and the crevice where they had slipped through. Tulley could make out the trails their smooth bodies had left behind, marred with several light boot prints. Keavy had been through here.

Feline cleanliness made him reluctant, but the overpowering urge to find his lost youngling rendered that feeling vain. Being small and versatile, Tulley was able to squeeze into tight spaces more easily than even the sloda, and before he knew it he was inelegantly sliding on his belly down a thick oil slick head first. This slide emptied his muck covered body into a basin of sludge where the sloda were happily rolling. They honked and skittered out the way as he landed amongst them with a splatter.

Keavy was slogging through the knee deep mire and heading towards the rocky walls of the basin when he spotted her. The sloda were playing nearby, unbothered by her presence. A few of the youngsters were even chirping at her with open mouths and raised lures, interested instead of afraid.

"Stop, Keavy!"

She turned around. The poor girl was a horrid sight. Her normally wavy auburn hair was a heap of greasy worms pasted to her face by oil. Those eyes, though, they shone with the unspoiled clarity of the stone they were so named for. Tulley clumsily ran to her. He kept his bent tail up out of the oil and his arms spread out for balance. Terrible feeling it was, dragging through that mess!

Keavy's eyes fluttered rapidly, making sure what they were seeing was real and not a result of dehydration and fatigue. Tulley was not only alive, he didn't have a scratch on him. Except for rips in his clothes and dirt clumping in his fur, the old catman who could barely walk on some occasions was completely unharmed by his expedition over a waterfall in a pitch dark cavern full of predators. As little sense as it made, Keavy didn't mull over it. She was too incredibly happy to see him. He reached her and grabbed hold of her

164

shirt for balance in the slippery mire, then got a good look at the blood on her sleeve.

"Bloody hellfire, child! Your arm!"

Keavy looked at it, just now remembering that she had been bitten. Seeing it made her feel the pain again. Stinging sensations coursed in between each throb of her ragged heartbeat.

The catman muddled around her as if she were his kitten. He grabbed her left arm and scrunched up the sleeve to examine her. The wound itself didn't look too bad underneath the caked mud and blood once Tulley started to clean it away. The rat had not pierced with its tusks, just its back molars. It was deep, down to the bone, but no veins had been severed. She would get away from this one with a wee scar at the most.

Muttering worries, Tulley wiped out the goop as best as he could without clothes and clean water. Keavy allowed it, though mere days earlier she would have been mortified at having her scrapes and bruises scrutinized by one of her elders.

"Have you ingested any oil?" Tulley rambled on, "If so try to vomit immediately. The stuff builds up nasties in the bowels. Most likely will not kill you, but we've little time for rest stops."

Preachy speeches came naturally to Tulley. Others around him had grown accustomed to hearing the old windbag talk himself into a puddle on a daily basis. It came with his background. Having had as much experience in life as Tulley earned one the right to be a bit bigheaded. Being of the catfolk race, as well as a master of potions, only accentuated this right. He should have viewed Keavy's interruption as terribly rude, but Tulley merely stood rigidly as the youngling kneeled down in the filthy brown soup and pulled him close, cuddling him like a doll instead of bowing to him with the correct level of courtesy deserved of a revered master of science. She burrowed her face in the exposed fur fluffing out the neck of his tunic, shuddering, trying not to cry. Tulley permitted it for a moment, then gently but firmly lifted her head with one hand and combed into her wet hair with his fingers.

"I am pleased to see you unharmed, dear," he said in a soft simple way that showed warmth through his poise.

"I thought you were dead," she sputtered over her rising emotions "How did you ever survive the falls?"

Tulley looked away painfully. "Touched by luck, I suppose."

165

His discomfort caused Keavy to release the catman in a hurry and stand. She felt foolish, but didn't want Tulley to know it. She believed he acted so because of the way she had shown affection for him so blatantly, but Tulley had been touched by the gesture. Sometimes all an old cat needed was to be petted once and a while, even though he would never ask to be.

The two of them simultaneously headed for the basin wall. Tulley scaled it a few feet above Keavy so he could alert her to good footholds. Thankfully, the basin was not deep. First to the top, he peered against darkness and distance without the aid of his glasses and spotted the blemish on the face of the world. Crocotta's lair loomed ahead, an ominous toothy maw surrounded by spurting fire craters. In front of it, two figures stood against the smoke, one human, the other canine. Crocotta in her human form and an army of drooling mongrels enclosed them, blocking chance of escape, yet Alder and Avalo looked eager for the fight.

The blachunds closed in on them gleefully, and it was now that Tulley took Keavy's hand. She looked down at him, anticipating his next words. The urgency in his green eyes foretold a vision from old, possibly seen by a younger Tulley sitting cross-legged in front of a crackling fire, bag of vision dust at his side.

"The time is now," he whispered. "Let your ancestor's blood pump through your veins. Let the sword of Idris guide your hand. Let the gods sanction your spirit."

Her hand fell to the magnificent white hilt of God's breath tucked safely into her belt. The sword pulsed against her like a heartbeat and its stone twinkled against the night sky. She drew the heavy weapon forth and held it firmly in sweating trembling hands. Her memory from then on went blank.

***

Nessa searched frantically for a father that could not be found. She couldn't even smell him in the very spot he had been standing and coaching her on how to expel the horrid poison she had ingested. The night sky was littered with bright stars, the moon entering the waning crescent phase, cradling the blue world of Siavon above it as a bassinet for a newborn. The wood faun was forced to give up her search and reside by the safety of the horses.

Her vision had returned to normal, as had her sense of smell, so she had no trouble finding them this time. It seemed that Gnal had been right. The plants growing close to End of the Path were enveloped by Crocotta's influence and as such were poisoned by her. It was not safe in the forest anymore.

The horses slept under cover of tall bushes. Nessa curled between Annick's front legs, gaining warmth from his body heat. She trembled not from cold, but sorrow. She missed the company of other fauns. Normally, she would be snuggled up with her siblings for the night, in the safety of the Mool burrow. Now, she was all alone, her and Gnal the only wood fauns left in Nodens. But her father had disappeared into the air like a breeze. He had never abandoned her like that before. Nessa wondered if she had even really seen him at all. She drifted into an unhappy sleep, but not for long. The air had begun to hum a note so low it thundered inside her thin ears. The vibration made her skin itch and her teeth chatter. The horses bucked about, whinnying in their displeasure.

Nessa crouched in cover of the poisonous bushes, keeping her mouth tightly shut to avoid any accidental ingestion, and plugged her ears with her stubby fingers. Something was happening, and Nessa wasn't sure if it was good or bad. She only knew that hiding was her best option. It was the only thing she knew to do. She wished the other fauns were there with her, snug up inside a burrow and safe. Most of all, she wished her father hadn't gone away, if he had even been there at all.

***

Keavy pulled forth God's Breath, heavy with oil, her aching muscles so weak she had to muster forth the last of her energy to lift it. As the hilt rose before her encased by two white fists, the stone glowed hotly in its bed of white gold. Its warmth spread to Keavy's arms, soothing them, revitalizing them. The ruby child became empowered. It traveled into her eyes, causing them to buzz in her head. They grew itchy and hot like an unbelievably terrible allergy, yet her vision was as clear as it had ever been. She was unaware that their deep ruby color had begun to spread from her irises to the whites, enveloping them completely in fire as ominously red as the stone embedded in the majestic weapon she held.

Tulley allowed himself a great distance from the ruby child. He had seen her this way in his visions just after Vorian Tranore rescued her as an infant, but he never imagined her to radiate so much energy. The air was vibrating with it. Every inch of his body itched as if a swarm of tiny insects were burrowing into his flesh. His teeth ached in his gums and the roots of the claws in his fingers and toes throbbed. Tulley took cover as far away from Keavy as he could and covered his ears. He hunkered behind a boulder and peeked out from behind it, watching with a combination of scientific curiosity and religious wonder.

She was deathly still. Every muscle in her body had gone rock solid. Her hair and clothing swayed in a gale that had come from a thought. Her eyes visibly pulsed in their sockets, scorching hellish crimson, too bright to look into. The expression on her face was vacant, bare. Her eyes were wide, but her cheeks sank and her mouth gaped open like a rusty gate. She no longer looked like Keavy of Nodens, but of the true descendent of Idris, the child of prophecy who would deliver Aryth from the grips of evil. God's Breath, the sword handed down from Siavon, crafted from Garric the Elder's very own hand, was a beacon of pure light. The white hilt sparkled, its ruby stone as richly red as the child's eyes. The blade spoke in a deep resonating hum, and the sound of which alerted Crocotta and her minions.

The blachunds pricked their white ears in the direction of the humming a hundred feet away. Whines of uneasiness issued from their throats, and they began to disperse, breaking up the circle around Alder and Avalo. Alder paled at the frightening sight of his childhood friend with her hair and clothing dancing wildly in the wind and her eyes appearing as gateways to the sinister bedlam of Hell's gorge. Though the sound was nearly deafening for his highly developed ears, Avalo did not cringe as Crocotta's pack did. He did not appear frightened as Alder did either. He simply stood and looked on with calm curiosity, tail curled over his back, blue eyes waiting and watching.

Crocotta clasped her hands over her ears and shrieked a cry of ghastly, brutal torture that was mutant mix of human and animal voice. The blachunds were crashing into each other, yowling and barking in their terror. Their mistress's influence over them had been shattered, and now they were free to be simple scared animals. In

168

little time they fled the scene, leaving just the naked, bleeding, screaming witch.

"*I will destroy you!*" Crocotta's roar was barely detectable over the deafening drone of God's Breath's mysterious song. "*I will tear you apart!*"

The child did not react. She did not blink her brilliant red eyes. She held God's Breath in vibrating fists whitened from bloodlessness. White light glimmered around her body in all directions. The humming increased, now so deafening that Crocotta's threats were completely drowned out.

Crocotta staggered, making her changes in strange order. Her svelte human legs bent into the backward jointed shape of a dog's and she lost her balance and fell face first to the ground. She rolled onto her back, kicking her canine feet skyward, reaching with grotesque twisting claws. Her body stretched and then contracted, and her spine broke in two and reformed. Her head melted on her shoulders, exposing her ugly breaking skull, then at once the toothy muzzle and large hate filled eyes washed over it, snapping and blinking in an erratic fit.

The beast turned over onto its stomach and rose to all fours. The sword's song swelled to an unholy bellowing that was unbearable. Crocotta's neck stretched out and her jaws parted to free a roar that could only be seen. Blood trickled from her curled devil's ears. The hair down her back stood straight up, her eyes blazed, and bubbles spurted from between long fangs and drawn back lips. Crocotta charged across the wicked grounds of End of the Path alone, her minions gone. The charm round her neck gleamed.

Tulley stood suddenly from behind the boulder and pulled an item from his sleeve. It was the red sphere he had shone Keavy and Alder earlier, something called a Sunspot, that was essentially encapsulated pepper sage and other ingredients ground into a grainy powder that exploded on impact and temporarily blinded adversaries. By miracle of Siavon, it had endured alongside Tulley his ordeal in the caverns. Tulley did not question for a moment that its survival was a gift of the gods.

"*Lao sen ra'palo spekta!*" the catman screamed at the top of his lungs in the Language of the Blade, then repeated it in the Common language louder yet. "Travel true to the eyes of evil!"

Tulley pulled back and winged the Sunspot towards the charging beast as hard as he could. Spinning wildly in midair, the Sunspot flew until it died in a burst between the manic red eyes of the beast closing in on Keavy. A spark broke over her face and at once her eyes clouded over white. Crocotta wailed, veered off course, stopped and pawed at her face, sneezing, growling, and shaking her head in an effort to cut the fog that hung over her eyes loose. The effects would give Keavy time, but not a lot of it. Tulley cupped his hands around his mouth and screamed for all he was worth, hoping his hoarse words would reach Alder through the deafening drone of God's Breath.

"Now, Alder! Remove her chain!"

Alder didn't hear what Tulley was screaming, but he understood nonetheless. He and Avalo ran as fast as they could towards Crocotta, who was now dragging her drippy snout in the dirt and bellowing her anger. Her eyes were already beginning to clear, and she would regain her sight quickly. This was the only chance they had to complete his task. He only hoped that this time, the result would be far different.

"SOHA!"

Alder nimbly jumped onto her prickly back and scrambled for the chain holding the amulet around her neck, gritting against the expected shock. She stood and one toss of her head was plenty enough to throw him. Alder landed on the rough ground and rolled, the amulet clutched tightly to his breast. This time, his fingers were unharmed, feeling nothing but the coldness of the amulet against them. Crocotta turned her snarling head and made a step towards him, but Avalo lunged forth and latched onto her muzzle with an iron grip. She rose to her haunches and seized the blachund with her horrendous claws, ripping him and a large flap of flesh from her face and smashing him into the ground beneath her. She dove into him, taking his throat in her jaws and shaking his limp body wildly.

The witch was so incensed, so disoriented, that she did not realize that she had begun to transform until her strength failed her and Avalo became too heavy to hold in her jaws. Her muzzle sucked into her face and grew lips, her ears slid down the side of her head and reformed, her entire body shrank rapidly, twisting and writhing once again into a woman's shape. Crocotta hunched over Avalo in a crouch, growling with human vocal chords.

The drone from the ruby child's sword grew louder still. The world seemed to pulsate with its own heartbeat. The landscape shifted and turned, rippling the way a reflection in a pond does when a stone is tossed into it. Tulley was thrown from his feet. Alder could not even stand on his. Only the child remained still and clear. Crocotta stood before her, furious, the amulet gone from her person, the power gone from her body. She tried to throw the child with her mental abilities, tried to change to beast and tear her to shreds, but Crocotta's desires went unfulfilled. She was for the first time in her long life, mortal.

The ruby child gained incredible speed when she attacked. She pierced the woman's body with ease, punching through until the hilt thumped against her breastbone. God's Breath shivered in the witch's heart. Crocotta quaked as if lightning had hit her, while the ruby child remained firm and locked onto evil's hopeless eyes.

The two of them stared at each other, one's face the epitome of serenity, fiery eyes narrowed, mouth drawn into a smile, the other filled with utter fright, mouth gaping in surprise, dark eyes watering in pain. They remained this way for quite a time, and at once God's Breath became still, and Keavy's eyes dulled. The ruby child then spoke for the first and last time to the witch who had killed her family.

"Idris sends his regards."

Crocotta screeched as Keavy pulled the bloody sword from her body and sheathed it, smiling at her as she watched the once immortal being breathe her last breaths. Crocotta's body charred from the wound out. The blackness overcame her body, searing her hair from her head, curling her lips back from her teeth. Her eyes sunk into her skull until nothing but empty sockets remained. Her fingertips and toes began to disintegrate first, and then the rest of her followed. Her smoldering skull, agape with a horrific screaming grin, lay cradled in a pile of cinders, and then it too turned to lifeless ash swirling in a conscious breeze.

Silence.

The humming stopped, leaving not but an annoying ringing in the ear. The rippling effect had ceased, and now at last, Alder and Tulley could see what had been happening around them. The gray clouds hanging in the sky above them had disappeared, replaced with a red and yellow horizon and a friendly rising sun. Where the gray rocks and obsidian shards had been scattered over perilous land, grew green healthy grass from rich soil. The cave where Crocotta had hidden was gone, in its place just a patch of brown deadness. Large fat flowers poked up from the hills instead of snake shrubs, with arrow shaped golden petals streaked with blue, permeating the air with weedy perfume. The boulders had grown over with thick green moss, and the fire craters that had once belched up smoke and flame had now become bubbling hot springs filled with clear fresh water. Behind them, the muck pit had become a small swamp occupied by ordinary fauna, ducks, minnows, and other creatures of the norm. The sloda were gone.

Alder groaned and opened his eyes. His body ached with every effort, but he managed to pick the amulet from his chest and sit up to examine it in the new sunlight. Three golden moons rose from a stone made from silver. The two moons on each end were in opposing crescent phases, and the middle one was full. It was a pretty trinket, but that was all it was now. Alder cradled it in his hands like a baby sparrow as he stood and cautiously approached his friend. He bowed his head as he held it out for her to take.

"This is yours now," he managed to croak. His throat was thick. He could hardly speak to or look at her.

Keavy looked at the charm, numbly, and her magnificent ruby eyes rolled over to the whites. Alder interrupted her fall with a quick arm, and Tulley came forwards and helped him ease her slack body to the ground.

"What will become of her?" Alder asked softly, a tremble to his voice. He cradled the unconscious lass in his aching arms. His tears dropped onto her forehead.

"She will sleep," Tulley said somberly. "And we will watch over her until she wakes again."

The catman silently gestured to the lad for the amulet, and Alder gave it to him. Tulley placed it carefully on Keavy's rising and falling chest, even as it began to crumble in his hands. Once it touched her, the amulet and its chain collapsed like their mistress into dead ash. Keavy took in a deep breath. The ashes swirled and floated aimlessly in the air above her and allowed her to inhale them in her sleep. Alder looked at Tulley for an explanation, his grip tightening on Keavy's shoulders.

Tulley hovered over his youngling. A caring hand reached out and wiped away the dirt caked on her face. Alder's tears left brown smears over her forehead.

"Crocotta's power is yours," he murmured to the resting youth. "Once a curse of Garric's kin, now a gift of yours. Use it wisely and benevolently as Garric so intended his own. The gods hold you in their favor, darling. Do them proud. Do *us* proud, Keavy."

Avalo gave a whimper where he had fallen, and they looked over to see the creature lying on the blood drenched ground. Alder gently laid Keavy down and went to his companion, aghast by the sight of his injuries. His throat had been practically ripped out, and his spine was broken, but he was miraculously still alive.

Alder touched the hound on the flank, and even in his poor condition, Avalo conjured up the strength to wag his tail. The lad hung his head in sorrow. Tulley crouched down beside him and put a hand on his knee, and he looked up with both bright green eye and cloudy blind one full of regret.

"I was wrong about him, Alder." Tulley admitted sadly. He glanced down at the fatally wounded animal and gently stroked him on the side with as much kindness as he could possibly show a simple cur. "Forgive me, Avalo."

Avalo muttered a drawn out stony note of dying. His time on Aryth was drawing to a close. The friendly beast stretched out his neck and licked Tulley's hand. His last breath came out in a sigh, and the wagging tail stilled.

Alder stood, quivering with sadness. Tulley tugged on the lad's pants leg, urging him to leave the body at peace and return to Keavy.

They took it as a sign when the blachund's body began to move that he was still trapped in his painful existence. The respectful thing to do then would be to render the poor creature's suffering silent. But this was not the case, they realized looking on longer. Whilst the bones inside of their friend's body began to make that horrible crackling noise, they knew what was really happening. Avalo's body was shifting.

Alder balled his fists. Tulley crouched and extended his claws, his fur puffing out around his face, making him look bigger. All at once, their sorrow was replaced by defensiveness. Could it be that Crocotta's evil had not been vanquished?

The dead blachund's broken spine snapped back into place and elongated. His paws stretched and grew into fingers which shed their fur and claws to become human hands. Legs bent backwards, knees moved upward, feet stretched and grew toes. Avalo's rendered throat shrank back and thickened, the torn flesh regenerated and healed over.

The head changed last. Avalo's muzzle shriveled into a stubbly jaw overshadowed by a large nose. The black fur on top of his head grew longer and softer, but shrank away around the face. The eyes burst open, cerulean and seasoned with knowledge. In the spot that the mysterious blue eyed blachund had died, a naked man lay on his side. He sat up slowly, and blinked hard through his changing vision at the bewildered pair in front of him.

"Tulley, my old friend," Vorian heedlessly grunted in a strained voice. "It's good to see you without a mace in your hands."

***

Fourteen years ago, while trying to protect Keavy's siblings, Vorian Tranore had been bitten by a blachund. The bite had granted him the ability to become a blachund at will, strange, considering that blachunds possessed no magical abilities. Vorian believed it was due to his own powers, which meshed with Crocotta's influence on the beast and gave him some of her powers as well. Over the years, he had avoided using his newfound shape-shifting ability, fearing it would possess him, but when he began having dreams about

174

Keavy's fate, he started following her as a blachund to keep a watch on her. Vorian knew Alder was a vital part of her fight against the Danaan, so he protected him as well, became his constant companion, adopting the personality of a tame dog. When Avalo died from his wounds, Vorian's shape-shifting power vanished along with Crocotta's influence. He was able to repair himself, for his spirit had not left the body yet. All through the morning, the ruby child slept off her ordeal, and Vorian explained himself to the catman and the Devnet lad.

"I believe fate, as we have come to know it, is changing," the Knight told them. "I can feel it, as there are gaps in my visions."

"Fate cannot change," Tulley argued tersely. "That is why it is fate."

"You have been bent on the old ways of thinking for too long, my friend," Vorian said with a chuckle. "Do not forget that we are always making new discoveries in science. Perhaps fate is a science in itself. You see it as well as I do, Tulley."

Tulley closed his eyes and nodded. "I have noticed gaps in my visions over the years as well; places where things are jumbled and unrecognizable. I always believed it was my age that disallowed me from seeing it all, but you are right, Vorian. There is a cloud over the horizon."

"Yes."

Vorian grunted softly. He placed a hand to his heart and sighed against something deep inside.

"Are you okay, my lord?" It was a tentative question from Alder, still recovering from witnessing his companion fall and rise as the legendary Man of the Blade.

"My soul aches to return to Siavon."

"Does that mean you...you are dying?" the lad asked. "Again?"

Vorian inclined his head. "Not again, Alder. I died as you watched over me, and I thank you for your compassion." Vorian stood, naked from the waist up, Alder's cloak tied around his middle.

"You have a good soul, but it is unripe and can easily be manipulated."

Vorian placed his heavy hands on Alder's shoulders. His touch was calming, but intimidating nonetheless, and Alder bowed his head under the warrior's gaze.

175

"Don't let that happen, Alder," the Knight told him. "You are a very important part of Keavy's future."

Alder sniffed back his emotions, and sharply nodded, not able to look him in the eyes. Vorian turned from him to his old friend. The catman was knotted and dirty, but he had done his best in combing out his fur with his claws.

"Why did you not reveal yourself to me sooner?" Tulley asked with the playful breeze at his back, "I would not have treated you like such a...*dog.*"

Vorian threw his head back and laughed.

Keavy stirred in her sleep and moaned unintelligible junk. She would soon be waking up and would probably not remember what had happened.

"She cannot know of this," Vorian warned them. "I must depart before she rises."

"Can we do anything for you?" Alder asked.

"You have done it," was the response. "And, I am grateful."

Vorian touched his chest again and winced. The color of life was fading from his body and his knees buckled beneath him. He was forced to sit down again. Tulley and Alder sat with the warrior all through the morning. He grew weaker and weaker, but the air of calm was upon him. His purpose had been completed at last.

Vorian died by early afternoon. Alder and Tulley buried him where he had fallen, in the circle where he bravely fought against Crocotta. They shared a silent prayer over him, and went back to greet Keavy as she awoke. She remembered nothing after touching God's Breath, and was badly shaken, so the details of her victory were spared. While honoring Vorian's last request, they told her that the loyal beast Avalo had been killed and showed her the grave where her sire now slept, allowing her to pay her respects to he who had died for her.

After finding where the supplies had been left, at the mouth of a gorge that was filled in now, the trio began the long hike back to retrieve Nessa and the horses. It didn't take as long without the perils of End of the Path to hold them up, so they found their way back by the time night had settled over a newly liberated Nodens.

Nessa was happy to see them, and eager to tell them what had happened to her and how Gnal had appeared and disappeared suddenly. She begged Tulley for clarification, but the old catman could only guess that her father was a spirit that had not yet passed to Siavon. He believed Gnal had stayed so he could help his last child, for it was her fate to accompany the ruby child as it was the fate of Alder and Tulley. He told the younglings that many spirits would remain bound to Aryth until the witches released their hold on Siavon and Garric could return to the throne. With the death of Crocotta, Tulley was positive that Nessa would not see her father again until she too made the journey to Siavon. She accepted this with a broken heart and spent the rest of the evening alone with her grief in the woods. Tulley did not ask her to take his mace with her this time.

They slept soundly through the night with no fear of what it might bring. The forest had been released of Crocotta's evil, and the blachunds would stay away from them now. The survivors of Nodens could begin to rebuild. The horror was over for them at the moment, but three lands still cried out for their *hrotage* to free them. Living blood remained coursing through the chambers of three black hearts.

The Danaan's poison poured heavy over Aryth, thick with vengeful hate for those who slaughtered their kin. They would not fall as easy as their unwary sister. They would be ready for the ruby-eyed youth to venture into their lands, concentrating their influence on the elements around them, claws clutching their sacred amulets. Many moons would die in the dawn before all of Aryth would be safe again. Many suns would warm the path to salvation. Now, Siavon burned low in the sky, awaiting the return of Garric, order, and the balance of life.

But the ruby child did not dream of her destiny that night. That night, her subconscious thoughts hugged tightly to the memories of home and family, friends and good times. In her dreams, she imagined a world that was without the barriers that evil placed in front of her. A perfect world.

Tomorrow, they would be bound for the sea.